Robin Vicary is aged 73 years and lives in North London. He started writing two years ago and has written 16 short stories (self-published as A Dangerous Affair.)

His first novel, The Pendant Sapphire, a story of the disappearance of a Faberge egg, is set in 19th century Russia and was self-published in 2019.

In a former life he was a gastro-enterologist at the Whittington Hospital, London

Robin

Dedicated to the memory of two men, who filled their lives and our world with beauty.
Alessandro di Mariano di Vanni Filipepi, artist, known as Sandro Botticelli, creator of Beauty with his hands.
AND
David Livingstone, explorer, missionary, and campaigner for the end of slavery, creator of Beauty with his ideals.

Robin Vicary

AN ADORATION OF BEAUTY

AUSTIN MACAULEY PUBLISHERS™

LONDON ★ CAMBRIDGE ★ NEW YORK ★ SHARJAH

A CIP catalogue record for this title is available from the British Library.

ISBN 9781528971591 (Paperback)
ISBN 9781528971713 (ePub e-book)

www.austinmacauley.com

First Published 2021
Austin Macauley Publishers Ltd®
1 Canada Square
Canary Wharf
London
E14 5AA

Table of Contents

The Adoration of the Magi

Now when Jesus was born in Bethlehem of Judaea in the days of Herod the King, behold, there came wise men from the east to Jerusalem, saying, 'Where is he that is born King of the Jews? For we have seen his star in the east and are come to worship him.'

Then Herod, when he had privily called the wise men, inquired of them what time the star appeared.

And he sent them to Bethlehem, and said, 'Go and search diligently for the young child: and when ye have found him, bring me word again that I may come and worship him also.'

When they had heard the king, they departed; and lo, the star, which they saw in the east, went before them, till it came and stood over where the young child was.

When they saw the star, they rejoiced with exceeding great joy.

And when they were come into the house, they saw the young child with Mary, his mother, and fell down, and worshipped him: and when they had opened their treasures, they presented unto him gifts; gold, and frankincense and myrrh.

And being warned of God in a dream that they should not return to Herod, they departed into their own country another way.

The Gospel according to St Matthew Chapter 2 vs 1–12
In the King James version of the Bible, 1611

A brief Introduction to the Greek Myths

And the production of beauty (or Aphrodite as she was called.)

In the wondrous world of Greek mythology, from the origin that was Chaos, two entities emerged – Gaia, the God of the Earth, and Tartarus, the God of the Underworld. Gaia then had two children without any of the nasty coupling otherwise thought necessary (she was a god, after all) – Pontus, the sea, and Ouranos, the sky. At that time at the beginning of everything, it would be fair to say that attitudes of what we might believe nowadays to be 'proper behaviour' were not strictly thought through. It was, after all, early in the evolution of the world; the gods hadn't got morality and ethics completely under their belts. There were more pressing matters (such as the introduction of death, war, etc.).

Gaia, then, not needing to worry about ethics, had children with her son Ouranos. As Stephen Fry puts it, the union was 'gratifyingly productive' – if that is how you might wish to describe a conjoining that at first created six boys and six girls, and after that two sets of triplets, the Cyclops and the Hecatonchires.

The youngest of the six boys was named Kronos. For various reasons which we need not go into here, Gaia inveigled him into cutting off the genitals of his father Ouranos with an enormous scythe, requiring an accuracy probably only possessed by a god. Kronos picked up Ouranos' genitals, covered in blood and semen, and proceeded to hurl them far out into the Mediterranean Sea, into which they fell in a hissing stream. A furious frothing of the sea then occurred and out of it emerges…the most beautiful thing ever seen so far. She is called Aphrodite in Greek, which is a (very) approximate translation of 'from the foam'. Her Latin name is

Venus. The west wind blows her gently ashore on the beach of the island of Cyprus, at the site of the present-day town of Paphos.

Characters in Order of Appearance

(Those with *names in italics* existed in real life.
The remainder are of my creating.)

1. THE MAJOR CHARACTERS (In order of appearance)

Lady Judith St John James; direct descendant of Charles St John
James, Viscount Dearly; and our heroine.
Darius Ivanovich Bukhari; art historian; and our hero.
Alessandro di Mariano di Vanni Filipepi, known as *Sandro Botticelli;*
1445–1510; Artist; Florence, Italy.
Dr Thomas Fielding; medical practitioner, Wimpole Street, London.
Charles St John James, Viscount Dearly; poet and friend of Fielding.
Mme Amelie Deschambres; assistant curator, National Gallery.
Dr David Livingstone; 1814-1874; explorer and missionary.

2. THE MINOR CHARACTERS

Casper Bukhari; Iranian-born economist and father of our hero.
Elena Dmietriova Agapova; Russian-born mathematician, violinist,
and mother of our hero.
Fra Filippo Lippi; 1406–1469; artist. Teacher of Sandro Botticelli.
Filippino Lippi; 1457–1504; son of Botticelli's teacher. Apprentice to
Botticelli, and later a fine Florentine artist in his own right.
Giorgio Bianchi, Master of Botticelli's workshop in Florence
Domenico Ghirlandaio 1449–1494; Florentine artist and friend of
Sandro.
Justin Crampton; Head Curator of the National Gallery, London.

Professor Sir James Marcus; Director of the Courtauld Gallery.

Sir Roger Court; Director of the National Gallery.

Sir William St John James; father of Judith, Director of the School of Oriental and African Studies.

Heather Greenbanks; Lecturer in Southern African Languages at the school of Oriental and African Studies, University of London.

Edith Wharton; Emeritus Professor of Social Anthropology, University of Southern California.

Paul de Vries; Medical superintendent, Chikankata Hospital, Zambia.

Charlie Chikankata; Chief of the BaTonga, Monze District, Zambia.

Umberto Rossi; Director of the Galleria Uffizi, Florence.

Chapter One

London, May 2007

Darius Ivanovich Bukhari sat motionless in the corner of his room, watching the vernal rain hissing against the glass. A whiff of sweet soft tobacco smoke drifted through a small crack in the window frame. He watched the huddle of smokers outside shifting in their guilty postures by the entrance, dragging swiftly and desperately, cigarettes clutched in furtive fingers. Inside the room, the air was still – the only sound a fly, buzzing endlessly.

She had just left, the oh-so-pretty Lady Judy St John James. In the future, he would understand that at this instant of time, this moment of her departure, a chance of understanding and discovery had been presented to him and was destined to be his moment of opportunity. His life was to be changed in a way that he could not have ever imagined but changed it would be.

Long, long ago, before Daniel's birth, his father, Casper Bukhari, had been on a scholarship from Iran as a postgraduate student at the London School of Economics, studying an obscure aspect of exchange rates, when, hurrying along one of the ground floor corridors one morning, he had first seen Elena Dmietriova Agapova. Casper had been so shocked that he had tripped, almost falling, dropping the three books that he was carrying. Elena Dmietriova had not been able to stop herself from laughing at the sight, realising, in the way that beautiful women do, that she had been the cause of his misadventure.

She had known that she was good looking, when, in secondary school in Petersburg, where she had been pursued by many of her fellow students and even by two of her younger teachers, one of whom was female. Elena's mother had helped her through those years and kept the girl's eyes focussed on her mathematics, in which Elena had excelled. She had been offered and had accepted a place in the mathematics department of St Petersburg State University, where she took advantage of the first-rate teaching and the excellent social and cultural life.

Her love of the derivations of mathematical theorems and her understanding of the violin sonatas of Johan Sebastian Bach had come together to enhance each other in her sophisticated neural networks. One evening, Sophie-Ann Mutter had come to the Marinsky theatre and played the concerto in A minor by Bach. Elena Dmietriova had hurried home and played the same soaring melodies until 2am. Her father had been furious.

Her days had been spent immersed in mathematics and classical music. Her thesis, *On the mathematics of the harmonies in Bach's Preludes and Fugues within the piano playing of Glenn Gould*, had won her the Gold Star of the State University. She had also won a scholarship from the university to study abroad and chose the LSE because of the known strength of its mathematics department, and the reputation for excellence of the London classical music scene.

She was in the summer term of her first year, when Casper Bukhari knelt at her feet, collecting his books. She couldn't help noticing two things; firstly, he was dark and handsome, secondly, that he was wearing odd socks. Afterwards, there was something about those socks – she was hard put to explain it. She waited while he gathered up his load, all economics, she noted, and stood. His slightly mournful dark brown eyes looked into hers. She was lost.

"Forgive my foolishness," he had said. "Maybe I could get you a coffee to apologise for interrupting your journey."

Suddenly, coffee seemed to her as the finest nectar that Zeus might ever have consumed. In the great cafeteria of the LSE, he had spilled out the story of his birth in Amol, close to the Caspian Sea in Northern Iran. Of his teacher of mathematics at his secondary school, of his degree in economics from Teheran University, and his subsequent travel to London.

He had confessed to her that her long flowing Russian blonde hair was unknown in Iran, where women, in any case, covered their invariably dark locks. And marvel of marvels for her, his hobby appeared to be the playing of the piano. After an hour of neglecting their classes, he had asked a question – the following week he had two tickets to a concert at the Royal Festival Hall where the world-renowned Russian violinist David Oistrakh would be playing the Sibelius concerto. Would she come with him? She had said 'Da' before he could start on a description of the remaining contents of the programme.

A few days later, sitting beside him in the magnificent hall, she had resonated to the wonder of Sibelius' magic description of cold, the shimmering of the snow, and his pride in his Finnish nation. The brilliant display of Oistrakh's violin gymnastics had left her reeling in an ecstasy that only an experienced musician could feel, as her eyes were opened to the beauty of Sibelius' construction. In the last movement, she had been overwhelmed by the sensitivity of his phrasing of the 'Polonaise for Polar Bears', as the great British musicologist Donald Tovey had described it. And sitting next to her was this handsome man who had opened her eyes to all of this beauty.

Later, it had seemed to both of them that the progression of their relationship had been inevitable. They went to concerts, played Bach's sonatas, discussed mathematics, and were married before the year was out.

Her father Ivan was furious at her marriage to a Muslim but was mollified when Elena included the patronymic of Ivanovich in their rapidly arriving son's name. By the time that Ivan was invited to London for the christening in the Russian Orthodox Cathedral of the Dormition of the Mother of God and All Saints, his annoyance had vanished. Ivan was overwhelmed by the beauty of the small cathedral, hidden away in the back streets of Kensington, and by the wondrously vibrant bass tones of the celebrant.

In contrast, Casper's father was not at all upset by the Russian Orthodox setting of the christening, despite being of little faith himself. For him, the occasion was a delight, as he was able to beat Ivan using the

Smyslov Gambit in a game of chess at the celebration after the service. Their game was only mildly ruffled by interruptions from the watching deep-voiced celebrant's insistence that Russian chess players were the best in the world and that the game had started in India and not Iran. International warfare was only prevented by Elena bringing the baby between the combatants.

Darius Bukhari grew rapidly, and to the dismay of his parents, showed little interest in mathematics or music. His father, by then more British than the British themselves, had insisted that an English boarding school would make a man of him, and had duly carried out his educational experiment, sending Darius to a school in the Dorsetshire countryside, which was noted for its prowess in teaching mathematics. Its music school also had a fine reputation, with at least two famous British conductors in its alumni.

But Darius was having none of that. For himself, he had loved the beauty of the school's setting, the parkland, the lake, and river, and all the aspects of nature that gave him such a feast of colour. He was able to draw, paint, and imagine a landscape of long ago. His teachers were mostly hopeless, stuffy, old men, who smoked pipes and talked to themselves. But his art teacher, John Arbutson, saw the promise and talent in the boy, and spent hours talking through techniques of paint and colour, showing the lad the skills to translate the views of design from Darius' brain via the palette and onto the canvas. Another master, Arthur Clark-Willams, ostensibly taught history, but his true passion was art history. Darius started with the world of Gombrich and graduated to Vasari, and beyond.

By the time the boy was doing his A Levels, he knew that he wanted to live, not only in the world of art, but in Italy itself. In the first summer holidays of his sixth form years, he mentioned this to his father. In response, his father acerbically pointed out that there was a minor flaw in the boy's plan. He had never been to Italy, so how could he possibly have come to that decision?

Casper Bukhari, by then a successful economist working for the Bank of England, did not know that Arthur Clark-Williams was at that very moment preparing to undermine his paternal stance with a plan for a school visit to Rome and Florence for his sixth form students the following November. The letter arrived on Casper's desk three days after the conversation with the boy. Also, regrettably for Casper's case, Darius' mother was very much in favour of Darius being allowed to make the trip. The beleaguered father appreciated that forces had gathered to prevent him winning any forthcoming battle, and gave in.

Darius thrived in Italy. He worked hard on speaking the language, based on his excellent knowledge of Latin, and made some good Italian friends along the way. He adored the Palazzo Vecchio and the Duomo in Florence and would have spent the whole day studying Ghiberti's bronze gates if he had had his way. The highlight of the trip for him was the visit to the Uffizi gallery.

On his return to England and based on his newly acquired knowledge of Florentine Renaissance art, he wrote a masterly application to London University to study Art History – and was successful.

And now here he was five years later, apparently working on his masters, but in reality, knowing that his diligence had led him into a mystery that not only would provide the basis for a doctorate, but could also make him rich and famous – as long as he could unravel the mystery of what she had brought to him that morning.

Chapter Two
Florence, May 1484

Figure One. Botticelli S. Detail from *The Adoration of the Magi* (1480) Tempera on Panel. The Uffizi Gallery, Florence

Self-portrait of Sandro Botticelli aged 35 (or so it is believed)

It is a fine late spring morning. The sun is shining brightly into the upper floor of the workshop of Maestro Sandro Botticelli. The great man himself is looking bedraggled, as if he had imbibed more than his fair share of Florentine wine at dinner the previous evening. His clothing is all awry, his beard stubbly. His long mid-brown hair sits uncombed, flowing down to the nape of his neck. His eyes, although retaining their light green hue, have none of the sparkle that they would be emanating on a better morning. In truth, however, his wrecked appearance is more due to insomnia than to alcohol.

The master often has vivid dreams. In the middle of last night, he is awakened from a dream about the origins of the Goddess of love, whom the Greeks call Aphrodite, but the Florentines know as Venus. In his dream, he sees her naked and being blown to the shore of Cyprus by the wind.

At this moment, he is standing beside a panel in the workshop. He has drawn a sketch onto the panel and is standing back to think about the composition to be transferred to the piece of canvas pinned up next to it. His thoughts are interrupted by his apprentice, young Filippino Lippi, who has bounced into the studio, late as ever. Filippino is a handsome youth with clear blue eyes and dark brown curly hair, spilling down to his collar. This morning's waistcoat is a rather luridly bright red and Sandro's tired eyes are repelled by its brilliance. Bizarrely, the young man's tights are dark blue, but Sandro has come to accept the latest Florentine fashion of mismatching colours for hose and waistcoat. However, the artist in him remains appalled.

"Buon Giorno, maestro," the voice of exuberant youth is vaguely unwelcome.

"Good morning to you, young Lippi. I have not slept well, and I require that you be a touch gentle this day. Try, for instance, to pretend that you are 24 years of age, and not a noisy bambino."

"Yes, master." The boy is chastened for all of ten seconds. "But what is this?" He points to the panel.

"This, as you charmingly put it, is the cause of my haggard appearance and the fact that every syllable of your speech jangles in my ears, like the bells of the Duomo."

Filippino looks again at the panel. He sees a sketch of a woman apparently standing on a small boat. "I cannot understand, master, the nature of your picture. Is it right that the woman is naked? And what is the boat that she stands on?"

Sandro looks at the boy with apparent disgust, but Sandro is essentially a warm and affectionate man, and is unable to be bad tempered for long. He looks at Filippino's face and is immediately reminded of the boy's father and his own teacher, Filippo. A warm smile suffuses Sandro's face.

"It is not a boat, o foolish youth, it is a conch; an enormous shell to you."

"I think master that I am missing something here. Is there a story that I am not aware of?"

Figure Two. Botticelli S. *The Birth of Venus.* (1477) Tempera on canvas, The Uffizi Gallery, Florence.

"A story, a story. Oh my, the boy asks. 'Is there a story?'" and Sandro rocks from side to side. "What did you learn at that expensive school that cost your father gold coins every year? Not to mention the tutor for your younger years, when your father was earning little. Did they teach you of the myths, the stories of the Gods and the Titans? Of the Greek tales of fun and war at the start of the world?"

"Of course, sir," Filippino replies politely. "But I fail to see…" and then he stops and there is a silence.

"Aha!" he interrupts the silence momentarily. "But…" and another pause.

"But?" Sandro asks, amused at the boy's struggles.

"It's Venus." Sandro dances a small jig and claps the boy on his back.

"And so, son of my illustrious friend, where shall we go now?"

"Cyprus?" asks Filippino.

"Yes, yes. Well done. I shall call on my friend, Piero della Francesca, this evening, share an amphora or two of excellent wine from the slopes of Vesuvius, and tell him that the youth of today is not as ghastly as we both believe."

Filippino grins. He has of course heard all this old man's nonsense about 'the youth of today' before from his teacher's mouth.

"And there is a conch in the story? I don't remember Ovid talking of a shell." Filippino stares at the lines on the panel.

"Hmm. Filippino, we are artists. We have to deal with matters that are solid, geometric, linear. We cannot portray a happening without some structure. You are, of course, correct about Ovid. But Hesiod in his Theogony mentions a shell, and I thought that a large shell would underline the young woman and provide a nice structure for the base of a painting. And now here in Florence, I myself, my colleagues, Domenico Ghirlandaio, your blessed father who left us not so long ago, and our other friends have discovered, or perhaps I should say, rediscovered the art of linear perspective so that we can paint distance onto our panels."

"So, what is this material next to the panel that you are drawing upon?"

"Well, I am experimenting. This is called canvas and is made of linen, which is then coated with glue. I was given a piece by my friend Andrea del Verrocchio, who brought some back from Venice, a wet city in the sea, where wood corrupts in the dampness. So, our colleagues there have always looked around for something else to paint upon. Apparently, some merchants from Afghanistan arrived with this canvas material, which the painters there have used for some years for their oil-based paints. So, I thought that I would try it out. Of course, if it works, it will be a great boon. Think – we will be able to fold up our works and put them under our arm! This, my boy, is what progress looks like!"

Sandro is interrupted by another young assistant, laden with cleaned paintbrushes, which he hangs up on racks to dry. Following behind him comes Georgio Bianchi, master of the workshop. Giorgio is a middle-aged man, large of both height and girth. His hair is just greying at the temples and he has a strikingly large Roman nose. He stops dead in the doorway on seeing the canvas. His eyes wide, he walks around it in awe. His fingers caress the back of the canvas.

"And you can paint on it with tempera?" he asks.

"Indeed, I believe so. A venetian friend tells me so," Sandro informs him.

"I shall find more as soon as you tell me to search it out, master," he replies, excitement radiating from his whole body.

"First, I shall finish my sketch and then I will paint everything onto the canvas myself."

"Everything, master?" asks Georgio.

"Yes, yes, everything. It's not going to be one of those works when I swan in and paint the hands and face after you have done all the easy work. Because if anything goes wrong on the canvas, I do not wish to have anyone to blame except myself. I need to be certain that our paints will adhere to the surface in the same way as they would on a wooden panel. I need to be assured that the paint will dry satisfactorily and evenly."

"And then will you require me to travel to Venice for more?" Georgio asks the question a mite too eagerly and Sandro studies his face with a little care.

"My friend," he starts and pauses, searching for the correct words, "I have a very small suspicion in my mind that wonders whether your desire is to seek my materials in your role as ruler of my workshop, or whether the desire is a touch less pure?" Sandro's careful words and amused look are the undoing of Georgio, who is gracious enough to blush.

"And if the latter, less pure desire, would her name be Graciella, daughter of my colleague Giovanni Bellini?" By this stage, young Filippino is smirking at Giorgio's unmasking.

"Your needs, of course, are more important to me than anything else, master." Giorgio tries to squirm his way out, but Sandro is having none of it and laughs uncontrollably at the sight of his slightly arrogant workshop controller being discomforted. The three turn back to the canvas.

"Come, Filippino, let me try to explain what I am trying to achieve here." Sandro moves towards the panel and canvas and points to the figures on the left. "As you know, at night, I am a great dreamer, and last night was no exception. I dreamt that God was directing me to paint a subject that I had never considered suitable for my art before."

"And as you have deduced, eventually with my prompting, this is to be a depiction of the creation of absolute beauty by the gods in the bodily form of Venus, and her arrival in the world of the humans; in fact, the story of the creation of Beauty, way back from when the world began. You might imagine that Beauty was there at the start, but apparently, it had to be created, and naturally enough, there were other priorities for those men on Mount Olympus. For example, it does seem reasonable that the creation of day, night, us humans and other matters should have come first."

"So, the gods got on with creating Helios and Hades and all the other things. Are you listening, lad?" This last because Filippino's attention is distracted by the entrance of yet another assistant, loaded down with recently ground paint.

"Sorry, master."

"Just because young Alessandro over there has a beauteous face, that is no reason for a failure of concentration."

Filippino blushes.

"It will not happen again, master."

"Good. Now, where was I? Oh yes, those gods sitting around creating. You will know that Venus was created in an unusual way, from the reaction of the testicles of Ouranus with the water of our sea. According to the Theogony, the poem by Hesiod, Venus was then blown ashore on the island of Cyprus, although I have no idea why that should be. Frankly, most of the people that I have met from that island seem no more beauteous than we Florentines."

Georgio has been listening to the master's lecture and gives a snort of derision. Sandro turns and observes Georgio with a small grin.

"Aha, a lover of the beauty of women wishes to contribute to my erudite lecture. And my colleague Giovanni's daughter, Graciella, she is blessed by Venus?"

"Undoubtedly, sir. Perhaps she has Cypriot blood?"

Giorgio grins.

"Oh, stuff and nonsense, I am allowing myself to be distracted by detail. So the model for the concept of Beauty, whether it be on the face of my apprentice Alessandro, or in the body of Graciella, or even on a flower of the fields, is brought to us across the waves by the gods. How dull our lives would be without this concept of Beauty! And in my dream, I created a celebration of its formation. I am intending here to create this picture of Beauty within the general principles handed down to us in our Platonic tradition, within our learning, but to add a few modern updates."

"Modern updates…?" queried Giorgio.

"Well, even I, with my careless attitude to money, must bow to the needs of reality. Those gods had everything they desired and had no need for gold coins, but I must pay for my workshop and my food, although mercifully, I am not weighed down by the needs of a wife and children…yet."

Sniggering laughter can be heard, but Sandro continues, "So, I need to think about where this painting is to go. You, my very excellent manager, will need to sell it. Tell us the names of our greatest patrons."

"The Medici family," Giorgio replies simply.

"Precisely. So, let's have a few laurel bushes on the shores of Cyprus so that we can appear to bow homage to them." Giorgio grins, but Filippino is nonplussed.

"Son of my friend, you are troubled." The master puts his arm around the boy's shoulders. "Share your thoughts with me."

"I am sorry, master. I fail to see the connection between our ruling Medici family and the placing of laurel bushes on the shore of a picture."

"So much to learn," sighs Sandro, clearly enjoying his moment of homage to the God of Allegory.

"So, the botanical name of the Laurel is 'Alloro'. The head of the family is of course 'Lorenzo'. The family will understand the homage. It will help one of the Medici young men, who owes allegiance to the head of the family, to cope with the vast sum that Giorgio will be able to extract from him for the purchase of the wonderful new creation from the Botticelli studios."

Giorgio nods his agreement.

"Now for the rest of the content of the picture – here we have the importance of the decorative use of line, which we combine with the outlines of the west wind Zephyr, who is having just a little entanglement as he goes with a nymph. She is going to wrap her supple little female body around him to provide him with the comfort that every busy god needs as he goes about his onerous daily work." Sandro pauses and smiles as he realises that he has the complete attention of his apprentice. "Yes, I knew that this bit would appeal to your mind, full of continual thoughts of the young female bodies, as it clearly is. We were like that, Georgio, were we not?"

"Maybe still are, master?" Sandro plays at being shocked by Georgio's teasing reply and holds his hand to his heart.

"My thoughts, of course, are entirely for my work, o my scurrilous manager." The conversation is broken by another assistant arriving with pots filled with colour for the manager's inspection. The new assistant glances at the painting and is transfixed.

"What ho, Julius. Seen a ghost?" Giorgio chastises the boy.

"Sorry, sir. At my home, my father would not allow any symbol of a woman without her clothes." The lad explains and looks for comfort to Sandro.

"Well, in that case, your father deserves a little explanation, my boy, or else he will believe that I am corrupting your tender soul. This is the goddess of Beauty, and I must portray the appearance of the divine nature of her, unrobed."

"Now the god propelling her towards the coast must be Zephyr, the God of Wind from the antiquity."

In the slight pause as Sandro gathered his breath to continue his monologue, the lad, seeing an opportunity to display learning, asks, "And is the nymph Aura, master?"

Sandro throws his hands to the ceiling. "Aura, Aura, how does Aura come into the thinking?"

"Well," said Julius, "I was taught that Aura was the morning breeze."

Sandro looks at him with a glance that somehow manages to convey incredulity, sadness, and love all at the same moment.

"Well, that's true. But remember that after she was deflowered by that wretched Dionysus in a nasty trick, which I won't go into because you are much too young and sensitive."

He pauses for the round of mirth and mocking, which follows, "And because of that, she became a bitter woman hating men. So, she is most unlikely to wrap herself around any man, let alone a real god like Zephyr. Personally, I have not decided who this is yet, but I expect that it's one of those happy young nymphs who appear in ancient tales, and even sometimes in my pictures, without any genuine place in the story."

"Nice try, Julio," whispers Filippino. Sandro is looking at the pots carried by Julius.

"Show me that green paint, please. Who ground it?"

"I did, master."

"Tell me what you put in, please, Julius."

"Well there is terra verde, and then ochre, but of only half the amount. Then I added the bone dust that Marco had made yesterday, and a bean of vermillion and ground them all together with the well water," explained the lad.

"Hmm. It doesn't look quite right to me. Giorgio, what do you think?"

Giorgio holds the pot suspiciously up to the light.

"I agree. I think the problem is that you have not ground the mixture for long enough, Julius."

"But I ground it for a long time, Giorgio."

"Not long enough, son. You cannot grind the mixture for the colour green too much. The more you grind, the more perfect is the tint."

Julius groans and slopes away.

"Now master, who is greeting Venus as she arrives on the shore of Cyprus?" asked Giorgio.

"Yes, that has to be an important question. The person will give balance to the picture on its right side, but must of course, be relevant to the content of the painting. I cannot possibly have someone just dropping in to say hello. Frankly, Giorgio, it is not totally formed in my mind, but I am minded that Venus is on arrival unclothed, and like Julio's father, the good citizens of Cyprus will not appreciate her gambolling around the hillsides without a stitch. So, my first thoughts here are that the welcomer should bring a beautiful gown at the very least, and I suppose she should really be another god. I don't think we can have a mere mortal greeting such an important persona in the rich life of our world. And it certainly cannot possibly be a Cypriot – they are all so provincial."

"Well, my money would be on Pomona," says Georgio.

"Now there's a thought." Sandro pushes his long light brown hair from his forehead. "There's a thought," he repeats contemplatively. And his many years of gratitude to his beloved manager float into his mind. Over time, Giorgio has become indispensable to him in his work. When he was truly a young man just starting on his life after being an apprentice, Giorgio had suddenly appeared in his life. Giorgio seemed simply to arrive as a rock at the moment of his adult beginnings and the start of his time of loneliness.

"Now lads, help me. Why is Georgio's suggestion rather astute?"

There is a long silence, filled by street sounds filtering in gently on the breeze. The midday sun shines brightly through the studio, casting shadows only in the corners. Eventually, the silence is broken by Filippino.

"I remember that in my Ovid, she was the goddess of trees and orchards and was tricked into marriage by another God whose name I can't remember," said Alessandro.

"That's very good," said Sandro, giving Alessandro's shoulder a warm squeeze of affection. "And if I have an orchard over on the right side, it might well be that Pomona emerging from it would be appropriate."

"And where did Ovid get this idea of Pomona?"

"I am uncertain, master. I believe that it came somewhere in the Metamorphoses, but I can't remember what the Greeks said."

"Unsurprising that you 'can't remember,' because no one knows where the wise old man got the idea. He seems to have created a god simply at a whim! Certainly, no one else mentions her in their stories. But an old poet must be allowed a bit of creativity, and most people think that he wanted to tell another story of seduction, so he just made her up. Anyway, we are surely all happy to have a goddess for the orchards and fruitfulness. And especially nowadays for all those maidens of the temples dedicated to Pomona, who make a good living from the farmers, offering gifts to her so that their harvests will be big."

"Master, your cynicism knows no bounds. Please don't corrupt our sensitive young people," laughs Georgio.

"Yes, you are right. But I do like your idea of Pomona. She can be standing greeting Venus on the shore with a grove of Laurel trees behind her. Now, no more discussion – please allow me to get on with my painting."

But the thoughts keep coming even when the others leave him to his area of silence and tranquillity. His studio can be like a mad place of noise and activity and chatter or, as now, it can be as a sea of calm with small waves of inspiration lapping at his gown.

He remembers the start when he left his teacher's studio for the last time and the floors here were empty of paint and canvasses. There was little but the light of his hometown moving across the floor and around the walls. The light had magic for him as he had sat. It had coloured the boards of the floor, and he had watched it shimmering over the surfaces. He had sat that first day, engrossed in thoughts of the magic that the colours could perform in his mind. He knew, had known since he was a small boy, that there was a special magic in the rays of the light; that the magic came to him, but not to most others; that he held tight to the magic, in case it slipped away into its fragility, dissolving into the ether and leaving him alone. It was his special other self that was given to him and just a few others, like his friend Domenico Ghirlandaio. Domenico saw his light and his colours and his glimmers and glows, and he, Sandro, was happy that he could share these things. His teacher Fillippo had taught him that there were others who could understand these things. And when he knew all of that, one day, his face was suddenly lifted to the light in a truly ecstatic moment, knowing that he was not alone in his world of art and colour. And that moment was wondrous to him, and for him the words at the start of St John's gospel had true meaning and he knew that John was talking to him. He mouthed them now to himself,

"In the beginning was the Word, and the Word was with God, and the Word was God.

The same was in the beginning with God.

All things were made by him; and without him was not anything made that was made.

In him was the life; and the life was the light of men.

And the light shineth in darkness; and the darkness comprehended it not."

As a boy, he had looked at these words and simply seen the letters. And then on this special day, the words of John had slipped into his mind through a new door, and it seemed to him that the light had come around the open door and comprehension had flooded in.

And from then the great light had been there and everywhere in his whole body, touching his work, his being, and his inspiration. The light, his light, was his guide, his friend, his own.

Chapter Three
Florence, Three Weeks Later

Sandro is excited beyond measure. Not only is his painting nearly finished but the paint has dried perfectly well on the new medium. The canvas seems to be entirely dry and not one part of the tempera has merged, run, or suffered any apparent degradation. Indeed, he can see that the glue mix as coating to the canvas stabilises the colour faster than painting on wooden panelling. He is in the studio with Domenico Ghirlandaio. Domenico is just older than Sandro, and the two men have been friends since boyhood. They are standing before the canvas. The day has started with a cool wind blowing down clouds from the north, but the light in the studio is bright. The greyness of the sky brings out the brilliance of the colours on the canvas.

"For myself, although the medium is wonderful, Sandro, I love the utter beauty of Venus. I adore the balance that you have brought to the picture; the way that Zephyr and Pomona lean in towards her. I expect that not everyone will love the fact that Venus is naked, but why should she not be – she is, after all, showing that she herself is the bringer of beauty. What could be more natural than that she should have the most beautiful body in the world."

Domenico is a tall man with a full head of dark hair, worn like Sandro over his ears and curling down the back on his neck to just above his cloak. He has a grey cloak with a green lining, which he keeps wrapped tightly around himself as the weather has cooled, and the streets had been brushed with a little early morning rain.

Sandro laughs. "Yes, I have already been warned about that. ₁ apprentice has told me that his father would not approve. But we will ignore these petty scruples of the common man and their priests."

Giorgio arrives bringing wine and olives for the two men. The olives are Florentine, but the wine is from the slopes of Mount Vesuvius, as Sandro has a dislike of the local grapes.

"Well, Giorgio, have you sold this wondrous work yet?" Domenico stops, seeing the looks between the two other men. "I have said something amiss?"

"Not at all," Sandro reassures him, "but we had a chance visit yesterday from another Giorgio; he of the Esposito family by name."

"The master of the household of Lorenzo, the Great and Wonderful?" Domenico interjects.

"My friend you have a loose tongue. People have lost their heads around here for mockery such as that." The three men laugh.

"But yes, for it was he. And by chance he sees my little canvas work. And, says he, 'My master will want that'. So, my good Giorgio takes him aside and they start to agree a price. But then apparently, this Esposito man comes up with, 'But he's not going to like this canvas material!' Is it believable? So, Giorgio summons me down to this meeting, where the Esposito is all flattery and subservience to me at first. 'Such a wondrous work, master. Such a striking idea. Such lines.' And on and on he goes. And then he comes up with, 'And it's a bit small!'"

"By this stage, I am seething, but what can I do? This man represents total control of our city, and moreover, total control of my income."

Sandro scowls but Domenico laughs out loud.

"This is a great story, Sandro. I am desperate to know the ending," Sandro manages to smile.

"Well, there are three endings! The first ending is that I capitulate totally to Esposito, needless to say. He has the purse strings. I agree to paint a new larger version, on panel. Meanwhile, Giorgio, to his undying credit, has extracted an enormous price from the man – twelve gold ducats."

co whistles.

cond ending is that, as he is leaving Esposito says – 'Of course have much in the way of laurel bushes in Cyprus!' Now, , I have never been to Cyprus, so I have nothing to say. But Giorgio here, much travelled as he is, comes up with 'He's right, master'."

"Personally, I feel like crowning Giorgio on the spot as he could have saved me all that work by raising the subject when we first discussed it. But he failed to do so, and I have wasted at least a day of those few remaining days of my life due to his silence."

"My humblest apologies, master."

Giorgio is crestfallen. Sandro pretends to cuff him, but with a grin on his face.

"So, I turn to the representative of Florentine power, and say, 'What does grow on Cyprus, then?'"

"'Oranges and lemons', says he, after a moment's thought. Well, when I was thinking about this, I realised that the damn man had had an inspiration in his suggestion of oranges for two reasons. Firstly, orange trees would fit marvellously with Pomona, the goddess of fruitfulness, being there in the foreground."

Sandro's eyes un-focus as he is clearly thinking of the orange grove that he will create.

"And secondly?" Domenico brings Sandro back to earth.

"Secondly, what? Oh yes. And wonderfully, the proper name for an orange tree is mala medica. So, we have the perfect reference to our beloved Medici family."

Silence envelopes the trio as Domenico thinks this through. Gradually, his eyes sparkle.

"Genius – sheer genius, Sandro. You win this year's Florentine Allegory Prize that I will create tomorrow. And you also win the prize for Flattery of a Powerful Man – a second award to be held for a year at the Florentine Academy of Creative Arts."

"The Florentine Academy of Creative Arts – and that is where?" asks Sandro, looking serious.

"Try not to be naïve, Sandro. I just created it!" The men laugh and drink a toast to the new academy.

"And, Sandro, the third ending?" remembers Domenico.

"Ah yes. Well, we say our goodbyes and the door is just closing, and I am about to crow to Giorgio about the money when it reopens and his face pops round. 'Oh, and one final thing. Of course, my master will only want one version of this painting in town so please destroy that small canvas one'. The man has the cheek of a monkey, but all I can think to say is 'Of course' in an obsequious tone."

Domenico looks out of the window at the river Arno slipping below the bridges on its normally tranquil way to the sea.

"And you are really going to destroy this wonderful thing?"

"Certainly not. Giorgio and I have been talking and we have come up with a solution. This is the only canvas that I have. I am not having any of this business of destroying my first painting on canvas, and I am certainly not going to destroy this particular canvas. Giorgio would dearly love for me to send him to Venice to buy more canvasses as he has his eyes on a young wench there." Giorgio blushes as demurely as a maiden in love. "So, the solution to this conundrum is that I am going to paint over the top of this painting, as soon as I have finished a larger version. And having thought it through, I am not going to paint this larger version on panel, but on canvas. We are here to make advances in our paintings, not be held back by old fashioned ideas."

"My apprentice and Giorgio and the assistants can start to copy parts of this canvas version as soon as Giorgio brings me more canvas. Filippino is becoming a fine artist, and he can substitute a grove of orange trees for laurels. And I will paint all of Venus, and maybe the hands and face of Zephyr and Pomona."

Domenico approves. "A good solution, and what's more, it will enable you to be certain that a second layer of paint will adhere well to this new medium."

"Good point, Domenico. And on that good point, my hunger for my painting is at the moment superseded by my hunger for food. Let us take a short trip to the Taverna of young Andrea Baptista for lunch and conversation?"

"Excellent – I was told yesterday that his Menestra de Carne knows no superior in all the taverna of Florence. And when we are there, I want to pick your brain on the subject of my new commission."

As the men are preparing to leave, Giorgio walks in.

"Farewell, Giorgio, we are going for refreshments to the house of Baptista. Doubtless when I return, I will need a siesta, so you may not see any creativity for many hours."

"I expect we will cope, master."

Sandro and Domenico smile wryly and walk out into the street, the cool wind making them wrap their cloaks tightly around themselves. They wander through the streets and down to the Lungarno. A barge with stone inside is passing up through the city to the docks at the upper end. They cross the river, surprisingly full for the time of year, at the Ponte Alla Carraia.

"I suppose that there is so much water because of those winter rains," says Domenico.

"Indeed, I had thought that we would all be needing Noah and his ark," opines Sandro, and the two men pause to watch the barge, which is being navigated with a reckless lack of skill.

"That barge will end up under the river!" Sandro exclaims. Both men stop and watch as the bargee is clearly having problems with the heaviness of his load of stone and marble, the strength of the current and the wind. The boat has both sails and oarsmen, and two of the members of the crew are hurrying to take the sails down so that the wind does not blow them into the banks of the Arno. At this point, as the river passes through the city, it has been artificially narrowed by stone embankments to prevent winter flooding. Suddenly, the barge turns sideways on to the current and it appears as if it may crash into the Ponte Alla Carraia. Both men hurry to get across the bridge to the far bank, but just as there appears no hope of avoiding a damaging collision, the boat is turned so that it passes safely under the bridge and travels on its way to the docks.

"A narrow escape. That barge was so heavy, it could have brought the whole bridge down, if it had hit it at speed." Domenico looks truly relieved.

"We are here," and indeed they ate under the sign of the paintbrush and easel, the tavern sign of Baptista's house. They enter the house and are pleased at the relative peace. By evening, the noise and the smell of spilt beer will be overwhelming, but the cold of the day and the hour has ensured that the tables are mainly unoccupied.

Andrea Baptista had aspirations to be an artist himself but has never quite fulfilled some early promise and now runs this taverna. He is delighted to see them and seats them at a quiet table.

"What can I get you, my friends?" he asks.

"We will both have your *Menestra de Carne*, as it is cold outside, and a good meat soup will warm us. For me, I will have the *agnello in aglio* to follow, as your lamb is also excellent. What I cannot understand is where it comes from, as I never see sheep around Florence," asks Sandro.

"My friend Giacomo keeps sheep near Firenzuola, about ten kilometres north of here in the hills, and he brings me three of his finest lambs every week. And for you, Domenico?"

"For me, the *capretto arrosta in sapore*, as I love to eat your succulent goat. And for us both, your best red wine from the foothills of Mount Vesuvius, none of your Florentine rubbish, thank you."

Philippo pretends to look shocked, but he knows from long since that the men do not rate his local wine. He returns with a bottle and two glasses and the men drink.

"Now, my colleague, Domenico, I have a desire to talk with you about a technical matter."

"Ask on, Sandro." Domenico chews on some bread.

"Leonardo has shown me how to use green under-modelling for the flesh, and I want to know your view of it. For me, the green avoids the muddiness caused by the admixture of grey or brown for the tones of the flesh in shadow. Green is, after all, the complementary colour of the flesh paint. I use the green earth admixed with white. When dry, I use the thinnest brown applied in verdaccio as a mixture of ochre and black, itself thinned with much paining medium. So, I find that, for me, the green gives clarity and maintains the flesh hues. Tell me your views."

"I love it also, but I know that several of our colleagues refuse to use it. Frankly, all that tells me is that they understand little of our craft."

Their food has arrived in front of them and they abandon technical conversation for much jollity over the Medicis and a few scurrilous details of their domestic life. Eventually, at the end of the meal, they saunter back across the bridge to the workshop, where Giorgio awaits them with another glass each, 'just to round off their meal', as he rather unsubtly puts it.

"So, we will now finish this excellent wine, and because I have drunk so much and talked so much, I will take a brief siesta when you have left me." Domenico drains his glass, takes the unsubtle hint, rises, and leaves.

And when he has gone, Giorgio asks, "And what will you create over the top, master?"

"I have had an idea for a new version of the *Adoration of the Magi*. I had a dream last night," he begins, but Giorgio has already left, knowing that he may be detained a while if he allows Sandro to elaborate on the details of his dreaming.

Figure Three. Botticelli S. *The Adoration of the Magi* (1500) Tempera on panel Uffizi Gallery, Florence. Another of the seven known paintings of the Adoration by Sandro.

In fact, Sandro's 'idea' had not come to him at all in a dream. The day before, it being a fine early June day, he had decided to walk over to Piazza Santissima Annunziata, where his friend Leonardo's studio stands. Sandro knew that Leonardo was in Milan, but the day before, had heard a rumour that Leonardo had been commissioned to paint an altarpiece. The commission had come from the Sistine monks for the High Altar at a new cathedral to be dedicated to San Donato. This was being built for the monks in the small town of Scopeto, ten miles south of Florence and current home of the Lippi family.

Arriving at the workshop, the master of the workshop welcomed him in. Sandro enquired as to Leonardo's whereabouts, and had confirmed for himself the truth of the rumour of a new cathedral at Scopeto. After some talk, Sandro was allowed to see all of Leonardo's unfinished work and some of the preliminary work for San Donato. And there was an *Adoration of the Magi* with unusual features. Sandro was fascinated and returned to his own studio, determined to start work. When the Venus had eventually to be abandoned, he knew exactly what would replace it. But his new picture would be in his own more poetic style, rather than that of his friend's severe realism.

Chapter Four

Florence, Late July 1484

Sandro

The heat has descended on Florence. The heat is visible; waves of it rise from the pavements in overwhelming streams, sucking the breath from the lungs of passers-by. The smells are worse than ever, a rancid decomposition of human sweat and excretion. By midday, it is so hot that a siesta is the only reasonable option. By midnight, sleep is possible only on days when there is a breeze, but these are few and far between.

Like most citizens, Sandro is irritable from his sleeplessness. He still manages a few of his little jokes, but they are somehow less amusing than normal. The whole workshop is however sustained by the progress on the new, so far unnamed, painting.

Despite Sandro's original decision to paint on wooden panelling, he has stuck to his decision to use the new medium and has obtained more canvas. Giorgio was despatched to Venice to collect six canvasses and rewarded with a night of passion with Graciella Bellini ("Just one night, Giorgio, and then you are to return immediately," Sandro had told him). The two finest canvases that Giorgio brought back are carefully stitched together by Giovanna Mencola, the studio's regular seamstress, a middle-aged woman adept at her needlework, and who, by chance, lives next door to the workshop. She is acknowledged by all as Florence's finest seamstress. Giorgio only uses her for work requiring the finest touch, as she is expensive, but he has engaged her as he understands that something of great importance is afoot.

The canvasses sewn together are enormous, but the painted area will be somewhat smaller. Still, it is a large area, and Giorgio has done the administrative work to ensure that the frame on which the canvas is mounted is made of the finest well-seasoned hardwood from their forester. He has personally worked with Giacomo, the workshop's carpentry assistant, to ensure that the joinery for the frame's dovetail joints is accurate and will consequently ensure a tight and lasting fit for the overall integrity of the frame.

As for the artist himself, Sandro has plunged his whole soul into this creation. He has sat and considered how he will use the colours to create skin tones of enormous beauty. He has lived himself into the depths of the picture and has become as one with it. He can think of nothing else during his days and, at night if he sleeps in the heat, he is overwhelmed by the concept of beauty. He dreams continually as only Sandro can. She is there for him, her long hair caressing him, her eyes boring into his own with an intensity of passion. He feels her longing for him personally and he reciprocates this. He has never fallen in love with the subject of a painting before.

In the studio, he allows his brain to work on the problem of how best to reveal that intimacy of their shared feelings. He knows that the intensity of his feelings will be an integral part of this creation of beauty and wants her flesh to be an especial constituent. He abandons his normal practice of setting a green first layer under the flesh-coloured areas on her body, as he insists that she must have a rosier tint so that her skin appears to glow with colour. He also knows that his mastery of shape and line must be absolute, and that one tiny error of linear perspective will ruin the importance of the expression of feeling.

The assistants bring him the powdered paints and brushes but no one else is allowed near now, except for Filippino, who has started work on the orange grove behind Pomona. Sandro himself is currently working on Venus' beauteous hands, one placed carefully to guide a strand of her long hair to hide her modesty, while the other covers one breast but reveals the other. Moreover, he is creating a spread between the third and fourth fingers of the right hand, as a particular sign between her and him, interpretable to no one else. It is a sign of mutual devotion, understanding, and intimacy. He smiles as he constructs this bond between them, dreaming that many years later, long after he is dead, that another will notice the unusual spread of the fingers. He knows that this other, a person of similar sensitivity to himself, will instantly recognise and share that magical bond.

Giorgio knows that something spiritual is occurring. He watches the progress of the painting with awe and wonder. He too can feel the depth of understanding between man and creation and realises that these are important moments in his studio. He ensures that the assistants are bound to secrecy on the project, threatening any who speak outside the workshop with instant dismissal. At night, he has employed two guards to patrol the entrance of the building to ensure the security of the workshop. He is the last to leave the studio and checks the painting each night, seeing that the blankets are covering it carefully to prevent any possible damage.

Sandro has changed some aspects of the painting, as a result of discussions with Domenico, Filippino, and Giorgio. The original gesso background on the canvas has been tinted with a small amount of a pallid blue to improve contrasts between the colouring of the skin and the sea. Originally, he had put winged sandals on Pomona, but later on removed them, as Domenico felt that they detracted from the balance of the lines of her dress, so Pomona's feet are naked on the sand; a little touch that gives Sandro pleasure. He can feel the sand under his own toes. Domenico, a goldsmith by training, has suggested that he should add gold leaf to the hair colour of both Venus and Zephyr.

In the end, he had decided that the beauty of the central figure would be enhanced by a slight curvature of the body lines, and achieved that by having her standing only on her left leg, with the face tilted to the right and the curve of the left arm leading gracefully into the right leg. Also, to increase the focus of the picture as a whole, the bodies of Pomona and Zephyr must lean in to focus the line of the viewer's eyes towards the central beauty.

Now, early in the morning to avoid the heat of the day, Domenico makes one of his regular visits. Giorgio sends one of the assistants with wine and olives and is so busy that he hardly has time to wish Domenico well at the start of the day.

"My suggestion would be for a very light egg yolk varnish to complete your creation. It would permit the stunning colour to resound through without obscuring any detail," Domenico is chatting to Sandro while gently sipping his wine.

"Yes, I too had wanted the varnish to be as light as possible and your idea of egg yolk is sound, my colleague."

"And another thing, Sandro. I want to inquire as to the state of our relationship."

Sandro looks with amazement at the older man.

"Our relationship is as sound as a ship made of oak, as close as a man to his finest picture, as close as I am to my Venus."

"Good. I am going to make a request which might test it." Sandro puts his arm around his friend in a gesture of physical intimacy.

"Ask – it is yours if I have the power to grant it to you."

"I want to buy your wondrous creation."

There is a long silence, broken only by the sound of horses' feet on the cobbles outside the house. Both men stand, looking into each other's eyes.

"That is not possible. The Medicis have a deposit on it. I have shaken hands. It is not within my gift."

"I understand all of that, but I have a suggestion to help with your promises."

Another silence broken eventually by Sandro, "I am waiting."

"I will hold the picture within my own house for the duration of my lifetime and will bequeath it to one of the Medicis – their choice – and will pay them a reasonable annual sum for the privilege. They will have nothing to lose and will have a regular income. And I will have your painting to look at for my life. We will all win."

Domenico smiles at the anticipated pleasure. More silence as both men think through the plan. Eventually, Sandro calls out to his assistant, "Filippino, please fetch me Giorgio."

Giorgio is not pleased, "Master, I cannot tell you how busy I am with contracts for you. And the lapis lazuli for the sea colour has deteriorated before my eyes. Our new supplier is unsatisfactory. And he blames the owner of the mine. It is a complicated problem to unravel."

"Giorgio, listen," Sandro is uncharacteristically stern faced. "Domenico has a suggestion. Please hear him out to the end in silence."

Domenico unravels his proposal, finishing with, "So, Giorgio – is it possible?"

Giorgio's eyes are almost popping out of his head. He is clearly flabbergasted but is giving the matter thought.

"We will need a first-class lawyer if this is to work. That means money, even if we use our man, Luciano di Salis. We will need the compliance of one of the Medicis. And finally, it will require negotiation as to the exact sum. Frankly, it sounds like an expensive non-starter to me."

"Well I like the idea," Sandro is smiling all around. "For my soul, the picture will be loved and honoured and, for my bank account, ever dear to me, I will receive not a ducat less than in the original intent. Go for it, Giorgio – and you will have a bonus payment on the day that my Venus can be seen in my friend's house."

And so, it came to be. The painting stayed in the house of Domenico Ghirlandio until 1494, when it was moved after his death to the Villa di Costello, home of the Medici family, just outside the walls of Florence.

Meanwhile, as Sandro and Filippino are completing the vast new work, the old single canvas has been painted over in a clear wash. A new *Adoration of the Magi*, has been drawn first by Sandro on panelling, and then the assistants start to work on top of the clear wash, and on top of the old painting and has incorporated the 'dreamed ideas' of Sandro (really, of course, those of Leonardo). Some of the faces in the painting have been given the faces of members of the Medici family, as a form of homage/flattery, as you will, and the Adoration will soon be ready for framing. This new Adoration has also been bought by the Medici family, and it will eventually be placed at the top of the staircase of the public entrance to the Palazzo Vecchio.

Chapter Five
Florence and Rome, 1536

Fifty years have passed, and Giorgio Vasari has been asked to redesign the public entrance to the Palazzo Vecchio. To be honest, the public entrance and staircase had always been a totally messed-up design. The famed architect, Michelozzo Michelozzi redesigned most of the entrance in around 1450. The entrance itself was a part of the original fabric of the palace and we must be fair to him that he did his best, replacing the steep wooden stairs with stone, opening the space out, and creating the Catena, a door attended by a *tavolaccino*, a servant only permitted to admit approved entrants.

Nevertheless, it remained unsatisfactory, and Giorgio Vasari himself has been brought in to improve matters. Before the new works began, all the paintings on canvas or panel on the staircase were removed by servants, an inventory made, and they were placed in a cellar room, locked by a single key. The key was placed in the guarded key cupboard in the palazzo. The fresco paintings on the walls themselves, were naturally lost in the rebuilding and plastering of the newly made structure.

One of the servants who removed the canvas paintings from the staircase, Marco Columbo, was also one of the servants entrusted with guarding of the key cupboard. One night, when he was alone in the Palazzo on guard duty, and being a man of loose ethics and a mind ever open to opportunity, he determined to steal one of the great *Adoration of the Magi* paintings, created by the late Sandro Botticelli.

On a dark, wet Florentine January evening, he collects a small torch from the dying embers of the fire in the hallway, and descends the steps to the Room of Keys, in truth a small cave in the basement. He opens the key cupboard, selects the key for the picture cavern, and walks carefully and quietly towards the cellar room. Suddenly, he hears a sound and stands absolutely still. The sound is coming from further up the corridor, and hardly sounds human. He creeps slowly forward. A large rat slinks away into the darkness.

The door to the cellar room opens with ease and he enters. The paintings and furniture are all piled up around the room, and it takes him a while to discover the Botticelli painting. He stands awhile, admiring the beauty of the figures with their brightly coloured robes, and expressions of devotion on the faces of the baby's parents. Looking at the other figures, he can tell from the faces of some of the camp-followers of individual *Magi* that they are arguing about some matter. He carefully removes the canvas from its frame, as he knows that he will not be able to walk with a large framed picture through the streets of Florence without being noticed. With great care, he rolls up the canvas, leaves the cellar and instead of going back up the stairs, turns left out of the door and walks down a stretch of corridor, which terminates in a small gate, which he knows opens into the street. He leans the canvas against a wall of the corridor by the gate and returns to the cellar. There, he has a last look at the other paintings and makes sure that nothing appears disturbed. He is just preparing to leave when, to his horror, he hears voices on the stairs and the sound of steps approaching.

He quickly extinguishes his own torch, but immediately sees another flickering light approaching. He sinks back into the depths of the cellar, hiding behind a pile of panels and canvasses. The voices became more distinct and he hears the easily recognisable basso profundo voice of Master Vasari himself. He appears to be talking to a fellow artist, but the tone of that other voice is unknown to Marco.

"And so, dear Bartholomeo, only the most radical reconstruction will solve the problem. Fortunately, my masters have given me a skilled workforce and plenty of gold ducats to finance the operation. Those beloved masters appear to have unending resources."

They both chuckle. Marco hears the footsteps halt.

"The door is open, and the key is in the lock," says Vasari. "That should not be."

"Maybe there is someone inside," says the unknown voice. "Let us investigate."

"But supposing there is a robber, and he is armed?" asks Vasari.

"I have this dagger," replies the voice.

There is silence. Marco sees the light from the torch begin to illuminate the cave and sinks back further into the shadows. Footsteps appear to be all around him. He is sweating with fear. Eventually, he hears the voice of Vasari again, "There is no one here. Let us leave and lock the door. I will return in the morning with the guards and we will conduct a full search."

Marco hears the door close, and the key turn in the lock. Muffled footsteps can be heard retreating up the stairs. He is in a state of despair. He searches desperately in the utter blackness for some other exit but can find nothing. Eventually, in the dark he trips over some protrusion, hits his head, and falls to the floor, where he remains.

He awakes to the sound of a key in the door, and groggily tries to remember what has happened. It comes to him and he is aware that his life may soon be ending if the Medicis choose to have him executed for his outrageous crime against them. Maybe they will want to make a public example of him and hang him slowly in the marketplace. He has seen one of those hangings last year. A man had been attempting to steal from their kitchens. He was strung up and the executioner raised the noose enough for the man's toes just to touch the boards and then just not to touch the boards. It took half an hour for the man to die, clearly in a great terminal agony.

A face is looking down at him, with the light of his torch illuminating his astonished face.

"Marco, what is this?" the voice asks. Marco looks at the face, and to his amazement, he is staring into the eyes of his friend and fellow servant and guard, Roberto.

"Thank God, it is you. I was locked in here last night by accident."

"But why were you here?"

"I was just checking on the paintings, which I love with my heart. I missed having them on the walls of the staircase, so I came to gaze at them. I know that I shouldn't have but could not resist the opportunity. Then I heard voices approaching and hid because I knew that I should not be here. And the strangers locked the door behind them, so I could not escape."

And then while composing this story, Marco has an idea.

"But I saw them take away a canvas, I know not which," and his plan matures in his mind. "But now I think of it, I do believe that one of the men was Giorgio Vasari."

Roberto is aghast.

"But why would he take a canvas?" demands Roberto.

"No idea – but I am certain that we should keep quiet about it, or he might get us strung up. He is in absolute charge here. We could be in much danger."

"That's true. Let's leave quickly. I will return this key to the key cupboard immediately, so that there is no sign that either you or I have been here."

They both leave and after locking the door, Marco touches Roberto's arm.

"I'm going home now, as I am totally exhausted after my night alone in the cellar. Good night, my friend." And he leaves down the corridor to the left while Roberto climbs up the stairs to return the key.

Marco is relieved to see that the painting is still propped up against the wall, where he left it some hours earlier. He opens the gate and looks out. The rain has ceased. There is a little light in the streets, and it is clearly very early in the morning. The street outside is completely deserted, so he simply picks up the canvas and walks the short distance home. A few people are up and about nearer his home, but he recognises no one, and they pay him no attention. When he gets home, his wife is still asleep and he takes the canvas upstairs and hides it in a corner of the attic room, behind some old rugs that are used as bedcoverings against the cold Florentine winter nights. He descends and sits alone at his table, wondering at his good fortune. Later that week, he will take the painting to the house of his parents and hide it behind the wines in his father's cellar.

Meanwhile at the Palazzo, at about the time when Marco is leaving by the side gate, Giorgio Vasari is arriving at the main entrance. Roberto has just had time to replace the key in the key cupboard and close its door, when, to his horror, he sees the great maestro approaching him with two armed guards. They stride past him, ignoring him as they go, and Giorgio opens the key cupboard. He takes the recently replaced key and the three men disappear downstairs. Roberto thankfully returns to his duties around the Palazzo.

One year later, when the hullaballoo of the stolen painting has died down and been forgotten, Marco's parents, by chance, take a visit to see relatives in Pistoia. Marco takes the opportunity to remove the painting from their cellar and places it proudly on the walls of his own dining room. His wife however, being Algerian and a Muslim woman by birth, is not amused to find a painting glorifying another religion in her dining room. He is outraged. She has failed to attend mosque for prayers for months and now has the audacity to complain about a painting.

"'I don't want icons in my house' she says." He is furious but speechless. "She doesn't want icons," he mutters to himself, "So what shall I do with it?" He realises that he has no option but to get rid of it, so, taking a risk, he simply puts it under his arm and carries it to the weekly Thursday market in the Piazza della Signoria.

Stefano Ricci is a strong man, born near Pisa, who, by dint of careful study and hard work, has created an important business. By his mid-forties, he has built this business up so that he can take it to Rome, which he has done, and is currently making a great success. But earlier this week, he has received a long and disturbing letter from his father concerning his mother's health, and as a consequence of its contents, has immediately left the city and made the long journey home. When he arrives, he is shocked by her appearance. She is gaunt and wasted and has a sallow yellow hue to her skin. The whites of her eyes have an orange tint to them. His father is in despair.

"I have asked the Dottore and he just shakes his head. He says that there is nothing he can do for this illness. She does not want food, even though I prepare her favourite zuppa di zuppa, made with zucchinis from my garden. My son, I fear she will die soon." And his father weeps large tortured tears. He stays a few days, talking with his father and sitting holding his mother's hand for long periods.

Yesterday, he left as there was little, he could do – and his business would not remain unless he returned to Rome. He had just stopped in Florence for a short period for refreshment, before continuing his journey home to Rome via Arezzo.

By chance, he arrives in the Piazza della Signoria, shortly after the arrival of Marco with his painting. It is Marco's great misfortune that Stefano Ricci's excellent thriving business is that he is one of Rome's main art dealers. Stefano is wandering around the market in a desultory fashion, thinking of his anxiety about his mother when he comes across this man holding…and Stefano stops in his tracks, totally amazed. He looks more carefully.

This cannot be, I must be deluded, he thinks. He rubs his eyes and walks slowly forwards, keeping the painting transfixed in his eyes. This man appears to be holding…a painting by the great maestro Sandro Botticelli. And it seems to be at first glance an *Adoration of the Magi.*

For Stefano, the style is instantly recognisable; those vertical pleats on the robes of the *Magi* are unmistakeable; the beauty and purity of the colour. Only Botticelli or maybe Filippino Lippi and their workshop could produce that purity of the greens and the reds. The line is perfect, the disappearing point exact.

He stands still and watches the seller for a few minutes and realises that this man is no art expert but is evidently just an ordinary citizen. Not only that, but the man has no other pictures for sale. He must have come across this painting by chance and clearly has no idea what he is holding.

"Good morning to you, sir," Stefano intones. The man looks straight at him, but with a dazed and weary look in his eyes.

"You have a fine painting here. May I ask how you acquired it?" he continues.

The eyes look away. Stefano understands the significance immediately.

"It was my father's. I have no idea where he got it. He's dead now." The lying is so obvious that Stefano wants to laugh but manages to restrain himself.

"Well, perhaps one of your other relatives remembers when he acquired the picture?"

The man is sulky, "All I know is that I found it in the house after my parents' death. Now I need the money. I want ten gold ducats for it."

Stefano looks at those eyes again. He knows what to look for, and he sees the flicker, just a momentary one, but it is there. So, he haggles, just a little. And for eight gold ducats, he is holding a Botticelli in his hands. He leaves Florence immediately and rides quickly to Arezzo with the canvas carefully protected in a small cart being dragged behind by his horse. From there, having rested over night, he travels on the stagecoach to Rome, where he hides the picture in his house.

The following day, before he opens his shop, he spends some time alone examining his find. This is an extraordinary painting. Not only is it undoubtedly by the great Florentine master, but there are several truly unusual features. The picture is painted so that the camp-followers of the three *Magi* are each separated by three roads approaching the baby's manger, in such a way that the attendants of the great men are clearly delineated. Remarkably, some of the soldiers in the retinues appear to be arguing. He is unable to recall ever having seen that feature of an *Adoration* before. *What is the significance of it?* he wonders. He has no idea but will mull it over.

One of the *Magi* has a truly recognisable face. Cosimo di Medici is looking back at him. Stefano knows that both Sandro Botticelli and his pupil Filippino Lippi had painted a number of paintings of the *Adoration of the Magi* in a similar vein, but none is at all like this one. Clearly, this is a truly unique painting, but where was it before he acquired it? He has no provenance at all. He contemplates his best action.

He realises that he could sell this painting for a large sum but his finances at the moment are excellent. He could display it in his gallery, but it would arouse comment, and he does not want trouble over how he has acquired it. After a day of thought, he determines that his best action is to put it away, and so he places it in one of his upper rooms, wrapped in cloth.

It is to lay there for a long time.

Chapter Six
London, April 1853

Thomas Augustus Fielding contemplates his twenty-eight-year-old face in the mirror. He is gratified by the general appearance, although marginally disturbed by the smallness of the pupils of his eyes. He is unhappy with his moustaches and, although he is slightly behind schedule for the morning's work, he comes to the unexciting decision that his moustaches could do with a small trim, and proceeds apace with the accomplishment of this minor improvement. Overall, though, his black-as-tar hair and general demeanour give him pleasure.

He shivers and, having recognised the significance of the shiver, knows therefore what he must do. He takes out his pipe and detaches the bowl. He takes a small knife, scrapes the bowl clean of ash and fills it with a small plug, and re-connects it to its bamboo stem. He takes the special lamp, lights it, and holds the pipe over it, until he can see the plug starting to vaporise. He then lies back on his couch and takes a deep suck on the stem and holds his breath. He can feel the effects almost immediately, as the tension leaves his muscles. He enters the state and very soon starts to see his habitual angels dancing on the ceiling of his garret. After a short while longer, he feels that he can bear to face the day ahead.

Now, really late for his work, he dresses in his frock coat and hurries downstairs, where his receptionist greets him with a frown of disapproval and an unsubtle stare at the clock opposite her desk.

"Mrs Smythe-Aubrey has already asked twice when you will be here. Only with difficulty have I been able to persuade her to stay. You will have no practice left if you are always late like this." He regards his receptionist with animosity.

"You sound like my mother. Desist from your viper-like tones or you will be on the streets, Georgiana."

"You know that I will not be on the streets. The other medical staff, and particularly Dr Greerson, think highly of me."

"Dr Greerson is well past the date that he should have retired to the countryside to keep chickens, or whatever the very old do before they die."

She looks at him and cannot really believe that a man clever enough to pass his medical exams can be so offensive. Her only consolation is that she knows that he is unpleasant to everyone, even on occasions, to his patients. He stumps off to his consulting room, eventually putting his head around the door to say,

"Well, where is she?" He cannot believe that he is going to spend another whole day listening to the moans and complaints of rich garrulous old ladies. He sits waiting for her to gather up her skirts and for the timid knock on the door. He knows that he will shout 'Enter' as loud as he possibly can, purely to frighten her.

The scenario plays itself out. She sits in the chair opposite him.

"Well?" he says, glaring at her.

"My arthritis is no better, doctor," she simpers, trying to smile at him.

"And you have taken the medicine?"

"Oh yes, doctor. But it tasted so terrible."

"Of course, it tastes terrible. It is the bark of Salix, the willow tree, ground with water and a little alcohol. You may wish to know that its use was discovered by a country priest from close by the town of Warwick. He saw many of his parishioners from that swampy low-lying area of land who suffered from the rheumatism and the ague. Being a devout Christian, he knew that where the Lord had placed a disease, he would place a cure. Looking around him, he saw many willow trees thriving, so he took the bark of the willow, ground it in a pestle and mortar and made it into a medicine and his fortunate neighbours got relief from their pains."

"So, madam," he continues, "shall I presume that because it 'tasted so terrible', you failed to take it in the dose that I prescribed? Or are we to assume that my esteemed colleague, Dr William Allen, and his nephews by marriage, the brothers Hanbury, who have joined him in his apothecaries' business in Plough Court Pharmacy, are charlatans?"

"I did indeed go to Allen and Hanbury's pharmacy, sir, and they mixed me the medicine while I waited in their front room. And I have taken my medicine regularly. But still, to my sadness, my joints are no better. Please look upon them again, sir."

He reluctantly looks at her joints, and to his horror, sees not the deformity of rheumatoid disease but that of...the gout. There are chalky deposits under the skin – the so-called tophi, and not only that but the distribution of the deformity is all wrong for the rheumatism. In this patient, the joints are affected irregularly and there is no fluid around the joints. He touches her hands with the back of his right hand. None of the joints is at all warm – indeed, she has rather cold hands for the time of year. How could he have got the diagnosis so wrong when he last saw her six months ago? He considers carefully how to change the medicine without having her believe the truth of his mistake.

"Well, if that medicine is not working, we will have to try something that I only reserve for my patients with the most intractable of the disease – some Colchicine. This is a medicine, extracted from the bulb of the autumn crocus flower, *Colchicum autumnale*, and often brought to us directly from the slopes of Mount Arafat itself. In this site close to the land of the Armenian peoples grows this particular crocus. So, I have an important medicine for you in particular, Mrs Smythe-Aubrey," he remarks pompously.

"But I have autumn crocuses in my garden in Hampshire," she complains. He retreats somewhat.

"Yes, I believe they are found in this country, but only those from the east have these particular properties. It's the summer heat in these climes; it gives them the potency," he wriggles. "Here is my prescription. Pay my girl on the way out. Try not to come back to see me." And he sweeps her away to the door.

Immediately, it seems, there is a cry from outside, and a loud knocking at his door.

"You cannot enter. The doctor is engaged," he hears from the mouth of the ghastly Georgiana.

And then, "Well, he won't be when I barge in, will he?" in unmistakeable tones, and his door bursts open. The vast bulk of Charles St John James, Viscount Dearly, oozes through his doorway.

"Morning, Tom," says the aforementioned, thrusting out a large bear-like hand towards him. "I was passing and wanted to put an idea into your small but fertile brain."

"You are most welcome, my artistic friend." Tom rises carefully to his feet in order that the effects of the opium should not cause him to tumble. "If I never had intrusions from the likes of yourself, then how could I cope with the minor illnesses of the very rich?"

The bear, dressed smartly in morning attire, slumps into the chair opposite, and surveys the doctor with interest.

"Did it ever occur to you that you were in the wrong profession, my friend?" He flicks a wisp of brown hair, worn rather unnecessarily long, from his forehead. "It seems to me that in medicine, compassion for your fellow mortal should be an essential feature. It seems to be essentially lacking in your personality."

"Aha, you spot the defect. I admit these days to a certain lack of interest in my patients. I have had no holiday for months and am at a stage of utter weariness, if the truth were known," confesses the expert in conditions of the very rich.

"Then I am here at a perfect moment. I have a proposition for you." And he pauses to make sure that he has the absolute attention of the physician to the upper crust, "You will know that I am a poet of some renown and that my poetry circulates even as far as royal circles. Our noble queen, Victoria…" They simultaneously rise to their feet, both raising a pretend glass to their lips in salute, and after a moment for merriment, sit down again. "Our noble queen has even been gracious enough to suggest that should Alfred Tennyson pass away, that I might be in the consideration for the next Poet Laureate."

Tom looks at him with total incredulity.

"But he has only just been appointed after Wordsworth's unfortunate demise. Also, surely, he can only be in his early 40s and is in rude good health, or so I hear."

"Yes, sadly you are right." Charles, the bear poet, starts to become contemplative, "He was, of course, an amazing choice really in my view. Frankly, I thought that his *Ode on the Death of the Duke of Wellington* was a disgrace, and as for that *In Memoriam* – vast and miserable, is all I can say. I fear that there must have been political skulduggery – personally, I blame that Peel chap."

"I assume that you refer to Sir Robert Peel, destroyer of Corn Laws, lately beloved Prime Minister and founder of our Conservative Party."

"Indeed, the same." Charles was mournful.

"Well if you believe that he is far too soft and liberal, I would agree with you. But I expect that you are simply full of emotional poet's views."

"Oh, I suppose that you are right." He pauses to look at the ceiling of Tom's consulting room, beautifully decorated with an Italianate theme with red plaster roses around the edge. "And your ceiling brings me back to my reason for being here. Italy."

"Italy," repeats Tom, "what about Italy?"

"I need to go to Rome to pay homage to Shelley and Keats,"

Tom is amazed. "You need to pay homage..." He leaves the words hanging in the air and stares at his friend wondering whether he has lost his mind.

"What has induced this state of mind, my muse dreamer?"

The vast viscount stares at the ceiling again, entranced by the scenes of nymphs, shepherds, and numerous putti. "I just must go and seek inspiration from their graves."

"Well what about the noble Byron then, hadn't you better include him?"

"Hmm. I have thought of that, but it's a whole journey again to Greece, where his heart is buried. And I didn't think that you would want to come that far."

The very not-noble doctor is on his feet. "I am coming too?"

"I hoped that you would." The doctor looks at the poet carefully to ensure that this is not one enormous joke and decides that his friend is serious. "Well, I must give it some thought. But remarkably, as I have already mentioned, I was thinking just this morning that I had not taken a holiday for too long and that I must get away from all these complainers."

"Don't hesitate for too long, my friend, as I have two cabins booked for the night train to Calais for Friday."

And the great bulk pulls himself to his feet, crushes his friend's hand in his, and leaves. The doctor spends the rest of the day continually late for his appointments and feeling completely exhausted. By evening, he knows that he will go with Charles. Besides, he has another reason for leaving the country for a while.

"Georgiana, I am going away on Thursday for three months. Please cancel all my appointments."

And he is gone.

Chapter Seven
To the Eternal City, April 1853

Dr David

Rome is spread out before his eyes. It is an azure blue day and the hills all around seem peppered with a lapis hue. He has slept well and is refreshed after the long and often tedious journey through France and Switzerland.

It was midmorning on April 20th, 1853, when the steamer had safely delivered them to Calais from Dover after a rather choppy overnight journey and they had taken the newly opened train service from Calais to Paris. He had hoped that they would be whisked into the city by an exciting express train but not a bit of it. French trains had clearly not reached the advanced state of those in England and there were continual halts, for no obvious reason. In addition, the route that the train had taken to get to Paris was to him totally bizarre. The train had wandered first to Lille, then Amiens, and finally, they had a prolonged stop at Pontoise. Unless his geographical senses had left him, he had no idea why they should travel from Amiens to Paris via Pontoise, a small insignificant village well to the west of Paris.

There had been no refreshment car on the train, but they had occasionally stopped at stations en route, where they had been able to buy bread, cheese and wine, often rather poor quality and acidic. In Paris, they had slept well in attic rooms in a small pension close to the Gare du Nord, and the following morning, he recalled the sun beaming in to their rooms while he had watched the citizens of Paris going about their business far below.

After an appallingly tasteless breakfast, they travelled another excruciatingly slow journey to Troyes, with much starting and stopping in the middle of nowhere. There had been little for him to do except watch the French peasants tending their fields. The line had ended at Troyes, and they had then travelled by coach to Mulhouse and Basel in Switzerland. The travel across Switzerland was increasingly exhilarating as they started to climb the Alps. Charles had read Mary Shelley's *Rambles in Germany and Italy*, published in London a few years previously, and had insisted that, as part of the pilgrimage, they should travel over the Simplon Pass. They had dismounted at the top of the pass and, lodging there at the inn, had spent a few days attempting to follow the routes of the Shelleys' climbs through the high Alps. Charles, despite the enormity of his stomach, had proved to be well fit for mountain walks, and they had also been blessed with stunning early summer weather.

So, they put on layers of their warmest clothes, laced up their walking boots, and attempt to follow her routes, often to no avail. Sometimes, the routes are not signed well enough or her descriptions are not precise enough. Occasionally, the routes are overly steep or dangerous looking. But one morning, they discover a simple, relatively well-demarcated path, well-suited to their relative lack of athletic prowess. On that day, not a cloud obscures the cerulean sky. The surface of the snow has been warmed by day and frozen at night, so the mix of ice and snow crystals shines in the reflection of the sunlight, nearly blinding them at places. Individual tiny sheets of ice glisten at them. Occasionally, a mound or two of grass shows isolated green colour contrasts through the glory of the crystal whiteness of the snow. Above them, the precipitous peaks, and slopes of the mountains hang threateningly down on them. Once across a small valley, Tom sees the white of a mountain goat, crossing the side of a grey slate cliff. Large dark-hued birds, maybe buzzards, wheel above them from time to time. The silence and peace of the mountains envelop them. They are alone in the vast grey and white stillness. The beauty of nature in the high mountains has, for the moment, banished any anxious thoughts from Tom's mind.

And he has seen no one on the way. He has, of course, looked everywhere as soon as they stopped at each inn on their travels. But no one has been following, bending suddenly to tie shoelaces, pretending to stare with fascination into windows, lurking in the bars of the coaching inns.

He has known that he must deal with the fear. What had they said to him about tearing out his finger and toenails? And then they had brought in the leader. He had strolled in when Tom was tied to the chair and had looked him up and down. 'Well, well, they never mentioned that you were so good-looking. Now let me see…' and he had looked carefully at Tom's face. 'Bring me the paintbrush, Mullins, and the jar of acid'. And he had sat down opposite Tom and opened the jar. The liquid inside was hissing and bubbling. 'I usually think that the treatment on a handsome boy like yourself, is best applied to the forehead first, where it will drip into one of the eyes or occasionally regrettably into both if I don't get the tilt of the head quite right. And then afterwards, I normally put a few touches on the lips. No more kissing for you, neither boys nor girls, I fear,' and he had laughed at his own joke. Tom had been nearly hysterical with fear.

'It will be there tomorrow, I guarantee,' he had mouthed.

'You should have said at the start', the leader had said to him. 'We wouldn't have needed this little chat, would we, boys? Untie him'. This to the men standing on either side of him. And they had gone. And next day, he had paid, after his father had loaned him the money.

And now at last, after many days coaching through the northern dukedoms of the Italian peninsula, they have arrived in Rome. For their meal on their first night, they visit Trattoria Keats near the Spanish Steps. The restaurant owner, Guido, personally known to Charles, pays homage to the 'much lamented English poet', as he puts it. The walls are hung with his, Shelley's, and Byron's poems and paintings. Tom notices that on one wall was a painting of a funeral pyre, entitled *The Cremation of Shelley* on a beach apparently near where he was dragged out of the sea. Charles is scornful.

"All staged," he snorts.

"Staged? I don't understand," the doctor doubts.

"The facts are that in reality Shelley drowned at sea off Viareggio with his companion Edward Williams and a boy called Charles Vivian and was washed up on the shore ten days later. A so-called cremation was staged by a fool named Trelawny, aided by none other than his Lordship, George Byron. But it wasn't Percy Shelley's body on the bonfire."

"Whose body was it?"

"It is not quite clear. But Trelawny seems to have acquired a body from somewhere, and he and Byron took it down to the beach on the back of a cart, along with a few branches and set light to everything. They were apparently so moved by the solemnity of the occasion that they went for a swim afterwards – or so Byron said." By this stage, Charles is tucking into his *pomadello con funghi*.

"Rather poor form," comments Tom.

"Indeed. Now let us ignore most of the trivia on the walls, although that copy of Adonais is rather wonderful. Go and read it." And he half-rises and points with his fork to the framed script on the opposite wall. The movement causes the napkin tucked into his enormous neck to loosen and a cascade of pasta is deposited on the floor. It only halts the exposition for a few seconds.

"In fact," he continues, "it is a magnificent elegy to his friend and fellow poet Keats. For myself, the truest lines for his friend come close to the beginning

But now, thy youngest, dearest one, has perish'd,
The nursling of thy widowhood, who grew,
Like a pale flower by some sad maiden cherish'd,
And fed with true-love tears, instead of dew."

"Also, pay particular attention to the last verse, which seems to most of us to be remarkably prescient of his own death at sea."

66

So, Tom rises and reads the long poem, eventually arriving at stanza fifty-five and returns to the table, but after such a long break that his pasta with seafood is a congealed mass of rubber on the plate.

"What a wondrous creation – and you are right; it certainly looks like the last stanza is predicting a death at sea, but surely Keats died in Rome of consumption."

"Good Lord, all that medical education to the fore again." And Charles' jelly-like vastness wobbles merrily against the table, causing a small tidal wave in the excellent Valpolicella. "You are essentially correct, my friend. And talking of the death of Keats, let us plan our trip tomorrow. I think that a day at the Protestant cemetery is called for. It is close to the Tiber, bordering the Porta San Paolo, so we will have a reasonable walk from our accommodation." The waiter brings their deserts and Charles tucks into his enormously rich tiramisu while Tom has opted for the *Bigné di San Giuseppe.*

Charles looks suspiciously at Tom's dessert.

"And what is that?"

"This is a traditional Roman delicacy. They are light deep-fried pastries filled with cream, with powdered sugar baked into the surface. They are often made in the weeks before St Joseph's day on March 19th."

The viscount, "I am impressed. How do you know all that?"

"It was written in English on the back of my menu." Charles laughs so much, temporarily overwhelmed with the short culinary lecture from his colleague, that once again he has to recover his napkin and tuck it back in. They consume the last of their desserts and Charles turns to his friend.

"I am curious. After I approached you that day in your rooms, I was truly amazed at your rapid acceptance of the concept of this trip. I had anticipated that you would be reluctant to up sticks and leave with such little warning. So, tell me what swayed your decision?"

Tom looks at the opposite wall and tries to decide how much he will tell Charles. They have been friends for so long – since school, in fact. There is a long pause while Tom gathers his thoughts.

"Of course, you don't have to talk to me," says Charles, "but there is another reason behind my question. I have noticed that wherever we have stopped for the night, you have had eyes to your left and right, as if looking for someone or something, I know not which."

Tom stares at him unseeingly. In the end, the need to share his fear to this comfortingly large kind human wins out.

"I am being blackmailed by a gang from the city of London." Charles looks at him in horror. "They are powerful, evil men who have me over a barrel. I owe them a large sum of money and cannot pay them. They are charging me interest and the sum mounts every day. They have said repeatedly that if I fail to repay them, they will use violence." Tom holds his head in his hands. Charles regards him with concern.

"But how do you owe them so much money?" Tom looks at him.

"I am a man of many weaknesses."

Charles laughs, "But that is why I like you."

"The first of my weaknesses is my smoking of opium." Tom has said it and feels the better for it. A silence reigns. Charles looks around the restaurant. The tables in the restaurant are far enough apart for them not to be overheard, and anyway, everyone seems uninterested in them. All the other diners appear to be Romans and are gesticulating and talking loudly in the local fashion.

"I see," Charles smiles gently to his friend. "But that is nothing serious."

"But it leads to my second weakness. When I take the opium, I care for nothing in the world – and I gamble on the horses. And I am not so talented in this field."

"And you lose money."

"And I lose money. A lot of money. So, I have had to borrow. And now, I cannot repay the money and I am being chased for it by these appalling men, who threaten me with harm. So, I decided that leaving the country with you would give me a welcome relief – and maybe they would forget about me."

Charles looks at him with incredulity. "They would forget about you? Whatever made you have that ridiculous idea? They will be awaiting you with some anger when you return, I would have thought."

"Oh Lord, do you really think so. I had hoped that they would give up," Tom drains the last of his *Valpolicella* and stares morbidly into his glass.

"I am pleased that you have confided in me. I will think on your predicament," Charles too drains his glass, pays the bill, and they wander back to their lodgings through the warm Roman evening.

Chapter Eight
Rome and Home, June 1853

Charles

"I shall now begin a short lecture for the education of my friend Thomas Fielding of London," begins Charles. The pair are wandering down the *Via Nicola Zabaglia*, having just crossed the Tiber at the *Ponte Testaccio* from their lodgings. "The Protestant, or non-Catholic, cemetery as it was called at first, was initially just a simple paupers' graveyard where bodies of undesirables – tramps, prostitutes, foreigners – were thrown." They both smirk. "It took the arrival of King James of England with a large retinue of followers to embarrass a pope sufficiently to have the area properly designated and staffed with gravediggers and the other accoutrements of a cared-for-place of burial."

They stroll down the street and Charles turns to Tom, and asks, "And do you know the origins of this street?"

"Was it named after one of my favourite desserts, *zabaglione*?" assays Tom. Charles roars the laugh of a large man.

"No, but what a great try, o *dottore*." Charles detours to avoid an old man seated across the pavement. "The dessert was named after a particularly unpleasant 15th century mercenary, who was besieging the city of Reggio Emilia when the mixture was invented, and who does not deserve to have such a delicious dish in his memory." He pauses for thought, and then continues, "In fact, this street was named after an 18th century inventor named..."

"...Nicola Zabaglia," Tom finishes his sentence for him, rather irritating the large man.

"Indeed. He was a clever engineer, who devised various types of scaffolding. Not fascinating, but I was just passing the time of day," he sulks.

"Apologies for my rude intervention. My error," Tom is gracious, and the smile returns to Charles' face as they enter the main gate of the cemetery.

The cemetery is one vast, enormous ocean of peace and tranquillity, leaving behind the noise of an Italian city. The gravestones are dotted through an enormous field of green. There are grassy stretches, interrupted by simple gravel paths. The anarchic gravestones form a mix of styles; large, small, winged, rectangular, sculpted, plain, with few words or short chapters.

"And now we must first find the grave of Keats. Only twenty-five. So sad," mourns Charles.

"What killed him?" asks Tom, ever the doctor.

"Consumption, I believe." They find the grave in a quiet corner of the cemetery.

"This grave," reads Tom," contains all that was mortal of a young English poet who, on his deathbed, in the bitterness of his heart, at the malicious power of his enemies, desired these words to be engraved on his tombstone. Here lies one whose name was writ in water. Feb 24th, 1821."

"What extraordinary statements. What on earth is it all about?"

"We think that there are two themes here. Shelley and Leigh-Hunt have told us that he was exceptionally bitter about any critical review that his poetry received. *Endymion* got a bit of a slating in the Quarterly Review and in Blackwood's. But most of us poets are accustomed to occasional bad reviews. Keats couldn't stand them."

"To be honest, I don't think that any of us quite understand the bit about 'writ in water'. In fact, his friend, Jo Severne, who still lives here, I believe, wanted the whole inscription changed to something less bitter, but no one has got around to it."

"And how come there are all those little flowers strewn across it?"

"Yes well, again that's Keats' fault. He wrote that he pictured his grave 'strewn with daisies and violets,' and he even said that he could already feel them growing over him. So, the locals keep the grave covered in them." And they stand in respectful contemplation.

"Now we will find Shelley. He was also young, of course – only thirty. After his death, his body was stored for several months in the British consul's wine cellar for some extraordinary reason that again is not quite clear. And even more extraordinary was the fact that when Mary died, his heart was found amongst her clothing, wrapped in a page of his poem, *Adonais*."

They walk not far and find his flat ordinary stone. It reads simply:

Percy Bysshe Shelley – Cor Cordium 1792–1822
Nothing of him that doth fade
But doth suffer a sea change
Into something rich and strange

"*Cor cordium*. Heart of hearts," muses Charles. "And the quote is from the *Tempest*, of course. Rather apt, you might think." And they did, of course. Again, they paid homage in silence and in their thoughts for these two men of such talent, struck down so young.

"And now, we are going to wander away," continues Charles. "I would like to walk the streets in this wonderful warming weather, stare into the shops, admire the local architecture, and above, all keep away from the Romans."

And so, they strolled through the *Trastevere*, and were walking down the *Via Carlo Porta* when they both look idly into the windows of a small art shop. In one window, there is a large painting of a boat being lost at sea. They are both struck with its apparent similarity to paintings of the boat in which Shelley had died. They walk through the door and a bell over the door rings a desultory chime. A young man emerges from the gloomy interior.

"You have a painting in the window of a boat and a rough sea. What is it a portrayal of?" asks Charles.

"I have no idea, I fear," says the lad. "I am tending the store for my father, who has been called away this afternoon, as my grandfather is unwell at his home down by the sea in Fiumicino."

"May we just look around then." This is Tom.

"Of course. Please do."

The shop, quite large and extending deeply backwards is, curiously for an art shop, rather poorly lit. There are gloomy recesses and paintings hidden behind others. Most of the picture frames have a fine layer of dust on them. The overall impression is that of a shop riddled with total disorganisation. It is as if the owner had given up on any system and that pictures have been put down in piles and left where they had first been placed, possibly some years before. Tom glimpses a movement on the floor over to his left. It flickers and is gone. He thinks that he saw a tail and assumed that it was, to his horror, a rat.

"This is the strangest store," he whispers to Charles.

"Yes, rather marvellous, methinks."

The pictures on the walls are a mixture of landscapes, portraits, and a large number of cityscapes, many instantly recognisable as Roman, with piazzas filled with statuary. The hanging appears totally random, without theme or thought, having been accorded to their placement. A magnificent view of the *Villa Borghese* is jostling for space with a portrait of an unrecognisable red-robed bishop.

They plunge further into the ever-gloomier depths. Two rolled-up canvasses are propped up in a far corner of the room, covered in a blanket. Tom drops the blanket to the floor, idly inspects one of the pictures and is rather taken. It appears to be a crowded scene, and from the costumes, must be old. He calls Charles over.

"Look at this, Charles. It looks rather splendid to me." Charles hauls his bulk from the far side of the shop through the small alleyways between piles, to look at his friend's findings. He stares at it for a couple of minutes in utter silence. After a while, Tom turns to his friend and is a somewhat surprised at the intensity of Charles' stare. Charles has picked up the canvas with great delicacy for a man of his size, spread it out and is examining it closely on an adjacent table, covering the paperwork underneath. Charles looks carefully around and notes that the man in charge of the shop is attending to another customer at the front of the shop.

"You have found a treasure, Tom," he whispers. "I have no idea what it is, but it is very, very old. We need to try to acquire it. Please don't speak and let me do all the negotiating. What is the other canvas that was with it?" They both look at the unattractive picture of a fat smug prelate.

The shopkeeper, having disposed of his customer, walks back down the shop to them.

"My friend noticed these two leaning here against the wall. Are they for sale?"

"Oh, everything is for sale," the young man smiles wryly. "But I have not had a chance to show them to the owner, as they only arrived this morning. They were brought in by a man I had never seen before, and I gave him a few lire for them as he looked dishevelled and was rather desperate for cash. I hardly inspected them myself, to be honest. Shall we take them to the front of the shop so that we can all view them?"

"Good idea," agrees Charles.

The shopkeeper spreads out the first one, and comments, "This is an *Adoration of the Magi*, I would guess." There is a pause while he inspects the other. "And this painting is a portrait of *il Papa, Pius 7*, Niccolo Chiaramonti, a fine man and a religious expert," he continues. "He was captured by Napoleon and imprisoned but survived and raised up by the power and influence of Catholicism. He was opposed to slavery and inaugurated the building of many important works – see the painting has a depiction in the background of the Obelisk at Monte Pincio."

"But I will have difficulty selling these paintings to you because the owner of the gallery has not inspected or priced them yet."

"How much did you pay for them?" asks Charles.

"Well, I gave him a hundred and twenty lire for the two."

"We will give you two hundred. Then you can boast of your sales prowess to the owner. Maybe he will give you some of the profit." And Charles laughs in a relaxed manner. The young man looks at the floor, then at Charles.

"Two hundred and fifty and they are yours."

"Two hundred and twenty," comes back Charles, clearly unfazed by the process of negotiation.

"Two hundred and forty," counters the man.

"Two hundred and twenty was my final offer," and Charles starts towards the door.

"All right, all right, Two hundred and twenty – but in cash," Charles reaches into his cloak and produces the money. The storeman wraps the two canvasses in a blanket, and they leave.

There is an unusual silence between the two men as they emerge into the warm Roman sunshine and walk back towards the Tiber and their lodgings. By way of contrast, the *Trastevere* is its usual bustle of noise and activity. There are stalls everywhere, selling all manner of foods from the countryside. Some are selling cooked food and wine, and they stop for a slice of pie and a glass of rather rough wine. They get back to their lodgings and spread the pictures out on the bed. The picture of the pope is well drawn and the reds of the papal robe shine brightly. But their real interest is the other bigger canvas.

"This must be from the 15th or 16th centuries, Tom, and to me, it must have been painted by one of the maestros of that time. See the faces and hands. These have been drawn by a true master. Look at the robes of the *Magi* – I believe that this must be the work of Sandro Botticelli or Fillippino Lippi or someone from that Florentine era. Maybe it is a product of their workshops. They worked together; you know. Botticelli was taught by Fra Lippo Lippi, and in turn taught his son, Filippino Lippi. So, it was all one big happy artistic family. And they all worked in turn for the Medicis. Now this is an amazing picture – truly wonderful. And who is that as one of the *Magi*? I believe it must be Lorenzo di Medici."

Charles looks up and sees a look of total blankness on Tom's face and realises that Tom has no idea what he is talking about.

"What did they teach you at our expensive school?"

"Not a lot – I was too busy seducing the young ladies of our 'sister' school down the road, or that is, trying to seduce them."

"Yes, I recall that you were incredibly lazy. My memory was that most of the 'young ladies' rejected your crudely amorous assaults."

"Most…" muses Tom, a far-off grin covering his face.

"Anyway, let me explain. By chance, there grew up in Florence at the end of the 15th century a remarkable collection of talented artists. And although some of it was chance, there must be little doubt that the affluent and peaceful climate created by the wise rule of the Medici family encouraged it. In particular, the family encouraged the development of the arts by commissioning great works both for public areas of the city, and privately by buying individual works of art. And of course, the discovery of linear perspective by Brunelleschi completely revolutionised painting. Suddenly, artists could represent three dimensions on a piece of wood, or later on a canvas." He pauses for breath – but not for long.

"Various popes also encouraged Florentine artists to decorate the Sistine chapel here in Rome. They enlisted Michelangelo for the ceiling, and Botticelli and Ghirlandaio painted Frescos on the walls. All of this was done by Pope Sixtus the Fourth, and Lorenzo di Medici to share a reconciliation between their families. So, if I am right, and this is Lorenzo di Medici who is staring at us, then it is quite possible that your painting was created in the 15th century, and maybe by Botticelli or Fillippino Lippi."

"Maybe?"

"Well it could be a copy…" and Charles roars with laughter. "But it's just that I don't recall seeing this anywhere else. Or indeed, anything similar."

"But I had thought that *The Adoration if the Magi* was a common subject for painters." Charles looks at him in complete astonishment.

"And I had thought you totally ignorant of any of the history of art."

"My father took me to the National Gallery on occasions. And once to the Dulwich Picture gallery in South London, where I did see two stunning pictures by Rafael. Was he Florentine?"

"Well, sort of. Certainly, a part of the brilliant era of Florentine artistic development."

"So, what do we do now?" asks Tom.

"Well, I suggest that we spend the next couple of days viewing the great sites of the city and that we eat and drink as much as possible, and then we return home and visit a friend of mine who by chance is curator at London's National Gallery, and by good fortune, is an expert on the early art of Florence."

And indeed, they spend two gloriously pleasant days doing exactly those things, and then spent three tedious and uncomfortable weeks returning by coach, and towards the end, by train to London.

Chapter Nine
London, September 1853

Charles

Two days after their return, they have arrived at the National Gallery and entered as instructed through a large black door on the left of the main entrance. They have knocked loudly, using the enormous metal knocker, been let in by a servant and walk up the short flight of stairs. They sit on the benches, pew-like and possibly from a church, admiring the tall grandfather clock especially made for the gallery by the esteemed workshops of Vulliamy a few years before. It had been commissioned for the opening of the new building in Trafalgar Square, as it has just been renamed.

After a short wait, the curator himself appears and shakes Charles by the hand. They walk along a corridor, through a tall pair of double doors and enter a room with a ceiling of such height that it is impossible to make out much detail in the closely worked plasterwork on high. The room is almost bare but for a desk strewn with papers, and two hard-backed chairs. The curator takes a seat on the far side of the desk, and promptly clears it of papers by sweeping everything to the floor, much to their amusement. The curator himself is a tall man of middle years with a lugubrious manner, receding grey hair and a slight twitching of the left hand.

"Welcome, I am Justin Crampton, curator of this place."

"Justin, permit me to introduce my friend and old school chum, Doctor Thomas Fielding of Wimpole Street. He has a small prize under his arm for which we would value your professional opinion." Thomas places the canvas on the table in front of himself and shakes the curator's proffered hand.

"Gentlemen, please be seated. You must enlighten me of the provenance of what I am about to look at."

"Well, it's not that clear," says Charles, and proceeds to tell the story of their trip to Rome and their find. Justin clearly finds the whole story disappointing. The curator is by now inspecting the back of the canvas.

"This canvas is very old. Yes, extremely old. Indeed, indeed," and again, he is lost for words. He rings a bell. A female face appears at the door.

"You rang, sir?"

"Miss Featherstone, is Mrs Deschambres in the gallery?"

"Indeed, sir."

"Do not call her at the minute, but I may need her shortly. Simply acquaint yourself of her location so that you may call her if necessary. Now leave."

"Yes, sir."

And just as the door is closing behind her, "Miss Featherstone."

"Sir?"

"Place one of our gallery constables outside my door and tell him that his duty is to ensure that no other visitors enter."

"Yes, sir," and the large door closes gently behind her.

And slowly and infinitely carefully, he inspects the back of the canvas. Tom, sitting and watching, thinks of the nonchalant way he had treated the canvas on the way home, even at one point throwing it into the trunk at the back of the stagecoach. He shudders.

And then Justin Crampton picks up the canvas and gently unrolls it. The painting is before him. Justin Crampton stares at the unrolled painting on the desk. His face sags and a look of wonder passes across it.

There is a great silence – of anticipation on behalf of the two travellers, and of professional interest on behalf of the curator. The silence would never be broken by the travellers.

Eventually, the curator speaks, "I am more excited than I have ever been in my professional life. You have brought me a jewel that has been hidden, been lost for four hundred years. It sparkles like a raw diamond; it talks to me from across the ages. I can feel the breath of Sandro on my neck. I can hear his whisper in my ears. He is speaking of his Christianity, of his desire to tell stories, of his faith, and his love of platonic philosophy. He speaks of the Medicis, of his studio, and of course of *quattrocentino* Florence."

And then he is quiet again. The silence reverberates around the huge room and returns to them. At last he speaks, "You have brought to me what is undoubtedly a painting of Alessandro di Mariano di Vanni Filipepi, the Florentine master known to us as Sandro Botticelli. The painting was almost certainly created in the late 15th century in his workshop in the house of his parents. The depiction is clearly an *Adoration of the Magi*. I intend to call my fellow curator, Madame Amelie Deschambres, an expert on Florence and the Medici family. She has written a marvellous thesis on the family and its connection with the artists of Florence and will guide us in our understanding of your treasure."

He walks to the doors, opens one, notices the large blue-uniformed constable with truncheon at the ready, and calls, "Miss Featherstone!"

She arrives instantly. "Please ask Mrs Deschambres to attend me. And please bring tea for the four of us. We will be here for a while. Finally, absolutely no other disturbances."

"Yes, sir." A short while later, a knock.

"Come." She enters and both gentlemen rise to their feet, partly because they are well-mannered and partly because they wish to express their admiration of her physical loveliness. She has the face that a painter would wish to paint, that a poet would create a sonnet about, that a doctor would want for a patient, and that any ordinary man would die for. It is supplemented by honey-gold long tresses, a fine figure, and a radiant smile.

"Mrs Amelie Deschambres, may I present Viscount Charles Dearly and Doctor Thomas Fielding. They have brought us *un petit bijou Italien.*"

"Gentlemen."

But by then her eyes are upon the desk. She walks slowly around the desk and stands next to Justin Crampton. Her hand goes to her mouth, but despite that, a little supressed cry can be heard. Her fashionably pale skin has gone a little paler. Mr Crampton notices and brings his seat around behind her in a rapid movement, presumably in case she is to faint. She slowly subsides, but her eyes never leave the painting. She turns over a small corner to inspect more closely the canvas.

"The provenance, *the provenance*?" she asks, her English inflected with a charming Parisian accent. Charles tells the story again.

"But that is not a provenance at all." A tense silence. "I can feel the Botticelli touch in the pleats of the robes. Unless of course, it is by Filipino Lippi. It is sometimes hard to be certain, *ne c'est pas*, M Crampton."

"Indeed," he replies, "but for me it has the feel of a Botticelli."

"And this is a detailed and complicated piece of art. Because it is from the 15th century, there will be many grand and small allusions within the art. For instance, I can see Lorenzo di Medici's face there already. Maybe there are other Medicis and maybe other prominent Florentine citizens in the numerous retinues of the three *Magi*. I would wish to have time to study this important work in peace and over many weeks, if possible."

"And of course, if you are in the market, the gallery would wish to make you an offer for your possession," breaks in the curator. This brings Tom back to earth, as up to that moment, he has done nothing but stare with large round eyes at the beautiful woman.

"I regret that it is not possible to leave the painting with you at this moment," Tom speaks, shaking his head slowly and looking at the floor. Charles looks up in surprise but does not speak. "We must now leave you. I thank you for your time and trouble." And he rolls up the canvas and walks to the door, followed by a bewildered Charles. As soon as they are outside the door and walking back through rooms of the gallery, Charles clutches his arm.

"What are you doing? Your peremptory manner will have caused dismay. Why are we leaving?" Tom stops, considers his friend, and sees the distress that he has caused. He slowly subsides onto a bench close to the exit onto Trafalgar square.

"I cannot explain to you in this place. We may be overheard. It is a long conversation. Let us return to Wimpole Street and we will talk."

And at that moment, he sees Amelie Deschambres walking in the distance between rooms of the gallery. He leaps to his feet and pursues her. He catches her in a room full of enormous Italian masterpieces and stares around in wonderment. She stops and waits until he focuses back on her.

"May I be of assistance, Dr Fielding?"

"Um, yes, well," Tom is momentarily tongue tied in her presence but gathers his wits. "There is another picture."

She regards him with increased interest, "Another picture?"

"Yes, we returned with two pictures. I wondered whether you would do me the honour of inspecting the second one for me?"

"If it is anything of the quality of the treasure that you have shown me today, I will be delighted," she smiles at him. He thinks that he will faint.

"Perhaps you could come to my rooms in Wimpole Street?"

"Of course, Dr Fielding, but my work here requires my presence most days."

"Perhaps after your working day – maybe on Friday at 6pm?"

"Yes, that should be possible. And your address is?"

"19, Wimpole Street. My receptionist will let you in and call me."

"And would I be able to spend a little more time with this?" and she points to the canvas. And as she does so, he notices that there are no rings on either hand. *No rings. How can that be? But she is madame, not mademoiselle?* His heart skips a beat.

"Indeed, Mme Deschambres, indeed." Slowly, he leaves her, trying to supress the facile grin that he imagines must seem locked on his face. He feels it deep in his chest and can scarcely breathe. Her image dances across his mind, both in a moving form and still and solid. He recalls the small details – the perfect slimness of her fingers, the intense concentration as she observes the details of their painting, the suspicion that she might faint when she first sees the beauty of the picture, the ivory skin at her neck. He wonders at her reaction to him. She looked – he knows that, and not just the once. Her eyes had fixed his – how many times, maybe thrice, maybe four times?

He does a little jig as he returns through another gallery towards the exit and he and Charles both walk out into the rain shower that has suddenly appeared from nowhere and threatens to drench them. As is customary when it rains, no hansom is to be seen so they decide to walk the short distance back to Wimpole Street, trudging up through St James and then along Bond Street, with Tom protecting the painting under his coat.

They fail to notice the two men who are following them, watching their every move.

"He's still got it under his coat then," says the first, a short and powerfully built individual, well-dressed, and with his face partly hidden by a cloth cap.

"Indeed, he has, Arthur," responds the second, a relatively tall and unsmiling man.

"I will follow them, while you go and tell the master that they have taken it into the gallery and come out with it still. When you have done that, meet me at Wimpole Street, as they are probably going there. If not, I will send a message by a lad as to my whereabouts."

The rain quickly stops, and a warm June sunshine suffuses onto the doctor and the poet, who are quite unaware that they have company. The smell of the passing rain has imbued the streets with a mixture of smells – of leaf, of horse, and of grass in a rural cornucopia of senses. Their skins are warmed by the heat of the early summer sun, and that sudden warmth appears to have brought out some jollity amongst the passers-by. On the streets this afternoon, prosperity is everywhere to be seen. The ladies' gowns are richly coloured; the silks are fine. The gentlemen are well-fed and seem to be thriving in the wealth of the mid-Victorian era. Indeed, as the pair pass an inn, a toast to 'Her Majesty the Queen' bursts loudly through the open doors, followed quickly by a toast to 'Her Majesty's

Government'. They hasten on, overwhelmed by the foul smell of stale beer, oozing through the doors and onto the street. Inwardly, Tom laughs to himself. As a student, the smell of beer could never have seemed foul, no matter how stale or rancid. He smiles at how old he has become, apparently overnight.

"Well, for myself, I am not amused by our government." The Viscount Dearly brings him back from his thoughts. "Reactionary, old fashioned, and that fool Aberdeen is far too old to be Prime Minister. Also, of course, he is an appalling leader and unable to control Palmerston and Lord John Russell. He is not solving the Eastern Question of those expansionist Russians, and we are now in an alliance with France and the ghastly Napoleon, who has overturned democracy in France."

"What is wrong with France?" Tom asks. "It seemed prosperous and well-ruled when we were there a short while back. They may not have the vote, but the common man appeared content there."

Tom is aware of his comparative lack of political awareness and knows that he would be wise to be careful with his views, aware as he is that the viscount does, after all, sit in the House of Lords by right.

"In my view, we need a whole lot more democracy and votes for all both here and in France. Under no circumstances do we want any more of the revolutions that the French appear to enjoy. As for fighting the Russians over who controls the sites in the Holy Land, this is an appalling throwback. Are we crusaders from the 12th century?" The viscount appears to be getting a touch carried away for Tom's taste.

"Steady on, my dear Lord, we are now approaching Wimpole Street. We doctors have a rule preventing the discussion of politics within Wimpole and Harley streets."

"Really?" asks the apparent politician.

"No of course not, you numbskull. I was simply getting you off your high horse," and Tom laughs at the simplicity of his friend.

They arrive at Tom's rooms, knock as Tom appears to have no key on his body, and the dread Georgiana admits them. Her expression turns from the caring receptionist to that of annoyance when she sees who she is admitting. They ignore her until she says, "There is a man following you, sirs."

Charles looks mildly curious, but Tom is clearly alarmed.

"What, are you certain?"

"Well, as I opened the door, I noticed him on the other side of the street. As I let you in, I noticed that he had stopped and was pretending to inspect the flowers arranged at the window of number sixteen."

Tom looks anxiously at her and enters the reception room, where a patient is reading a newspaper, looks up, and returns to his reading. Tom hurries to the window and, concealed by the partly drawn curtain, pulls it aside a little so that he can view the street, and not be seen. Sure enough, a man lurks a few paces down the street and appears to be doing little but idling. At that moment, he is joined by another and they both glance at the door of number nineteen. He waits a short while, and again peeps around the edge of the curtain. They are still there.

Agitatedly, he returns to Charles and Georgiana.

"What is going on, Tom?" asks Charles. Tom does not reply but gathers up the canvas and starts up the stairs. Charles follows, and the perplexed Georgiana returns to her receptionist's desk.

They reach Tom's door, enter, and he places the canvas on his desk, on which also lies the other Roman painting. He sits on the chaise longue with his head in his hands. Charles also sits and waits, knowing that an explanation will eventually come. Eventually, it does.

"It really all began at school. As you know, I was academically rather a failure, and this weighed on me as I did not achieve in other ways such as sport. I had a fairly hefty allowance from Papa, and temptation was put in my way. One of my friends had a hookah and used to smoke opium. I joined him one afternoon in the woods surrounding our school in the Dorset countryside, where he used to go to heat the pipe. We both smoked and I was transported to a place of such peace and tranquillity that I was truly overwhelmed. I could not wait for the next session, which occurred the following Saturday. I lived for my Saturdays, and of course, initially the payments to my friend were no problem, as I was comparatively rich." He pauses, remembering his school days.

"Meanwhile, my father discussed my future with a few of his medical friends and as a result I was accepted into St Thomas' Medical School despite my appalling school record. To my surprise, I loved the place, and even more amazingly, loved the studying of medicine." And he pauses, goes to a cupboard, pulls out a bottle of red wine and two glasses and starts to pour.

"Not for me," says Charles. The second glass disappears into the cupboard. Tom has a large mouthful and regains his seat, clutching his glass fiercely, his knuckles showing white.

"Anatomy fascinated me, I thrived and made friends. But all the while, my love of opium had become an addiction. I could not get enough of the stuff. At the time, my father had fallen on hard times, his business importing sugar using the slaver galleon's return visits was hit by a series of catastrophes. One ship was sunk by the French, another attacked by pirates, and yet a third appears to have vanished after leaving Port-au-Prince. Stupidly, he had insured his boats, but not their cargo. 'I forgot' was all he could say. So, my hefty allowance dried up."

"As well as the costs of the opium, I had run up a series of debts backing the wrong horses at the racing, and then made it all worse by borrowing money to make it all better, so to speak. I continued to make poor judgements based on bad information about which horse had a chance. And so now, I am in debt by a very large sum. And the people that I am in debt to are some of the worst kinds of chaps. They have made the most terrifying threats as to what they will do if I continue to fall behind in my repayments." He pauses and empties the glass in one gulp.

"So, I assume that it is they who are watching us." And then he has a thought, "And maybe they saw us enter the National Gallery with this picture, and maybe they saw us leave with it."

"And maybe they might work out that it may be valuable," adds Charles. "Somehow, you must 'lose' it again or they will break in and steal it. Perhaps I could smuggle it out and keep it for us at my place."

"That's an appallingly dangerous thought," says Tom. "Supposing they torture me, and I tell them where it is. Then you will be involved. These are evil men. They will stop at nothing."

"Well, where will it be safe? Where can they not get at it?" A silence while both men think.

"The National Gallery," says Tom. "We will accept the gallery's offer to have it inspected for a period, which will then give us a breathing space while we consider what to do about it."

"Brilliant, quite uncharacteristically brilliant," laughs Charles. Tom looks hurt but still smiles wanly. "So, I will have the pleasure of taking it back to the gallery and handing it to the lovely Mrs Deschambres."

"Be sure to tell her that she is still due here on Friday," adds Tom.

"She is coming here?" Charles, of course, knows nothing of the little tryst that Tom has arranged. His eyebrows suddenly are close to his hairline and a grin emerges.

"You are a fast worker. How did you fix that?"

Tom explains, and at the end of the tale, Charles laughs.

"Now, as to your scheme, I agree that it is a good one, as long as they don't attack me between here and the gallery, I will give the canvas to the lady curator, and I hope that you will have a good evening on Friday." Tom gets to his feet and looks out of the window and way down below can just see the two men still present.

"They are still there. Go now before they leave – and make sure that you carry the canvas obviously, and that they follow you."

Charles drags himself out of the seat and takes the canvas and wraps it loosely under his arm. As he is leaving, he turns and asks, "And the canvas of the pope, what will you do with that? Surely you can't leave it here in this room?"

"Aha, I have an easy solution for that. My senior partner, Dr Greerson, has the rooms below me. He is away for two weeks and I have the key to his door, as I care for the rooms while he is on his travels. I will just put it in his rooms."

"Brilliant," mutters the viscount. "Brilliant – and what fun."

"It may be fun for you, but I am living in fear for my life. I will need to think of what to do in the longer term. This will only provide us with a brief respite."

Chapter Ten
London, October 1853

Mme Amelie

"A week is a short time in our profession, but I have had the chance to determine some features of your picture," she tells him.

Tom has been summoned by her and Mr Crampton to the gallery. Unexpectedly, however, the Foreign Minister of France, M Guy-Depoivre, is in London for discussions at the Foreign Office about the Russian threat in the Balkans. M Guy-Depoivre has expressed a desire to visit the National Gallery in between the talks, and naturally, Mr Crampton has been delegated by the civil servants at the Foreign Office to accompany the Minister and Mrs Guy-Depoivre. Regrettably, therefore, Mr Crampton has had to delegate the further discussions about the painting to his underling. Tom, needless to say, is not averse to this change of plan.

"Firstly, it is a picture undoubtedly by Alessandro di Mariano di Vanni Filipepi, known as Sandro Botticelli, painted around 1480. It is impossible to be more certain of the date at the moment, but there are features suggesting that it is one of his more mature works, and certainly not his first *Adoration*. It is exceptionally exciting because he has peopled the picture with notable Florentines. It is possible that it may be a truly unique work, as my colleague and I believe that he has painted his own likeness into the picture. We have never seen this before – but I am jumping ahead."

"This is a painting from the early renaissance, the late fifteenth century, of the *Adoration of the Magi*, as depicted in the Gospel in the

Bible, according to St Matthew. We see a grand depiction in tempera paintwork on canvas of the Baby Jesus with the Three Wise Men kneeling at his feet. The parents are depicted here," – and she points – "and the retinues and followers of the Wise Men are here," and she points out three roads peopled with soldiers and followers.

"As for the Three Men, here at the Madonna's feet, is specifically in person the great Cosimo di Medici. The other Wise Men are also of the family, Piero and Giovanni di Medici, Cosimo's sons. And these other two, are his grandsons Giuliano and Lorenzo. The next question we asked ourselves was, 'who is this in the brown gown looking directly and somewhat arrogantly at us?'. It seems to us, based on descriptions from Vasari and others, that it is quite possible that this is the artist himself."

"Botticelli?"

"It is possible. And if it is true, then your painting's value has just increased enormously, because although we have many portraits of the Medici family, we have none of Sandro. We will need to compare this face with other possible pictures of the artist. In those days of the 15th and 16th centuries, artists were starting to be recognised as important people, but it was uncommon to have paintings portraying an artist. Rich people paid for portraits of members of their families, or they might commission a portrait of someone famous, for example a pope, as you yourself have, or a king." She stops and continues to look at the picture.

"We will have another problem with your picture – the provenance." Tom has a little difficulty with the word but decides that he had better be honest and portray his ignorance.

"I fear that this is not a word that I am familiar with."

"Oh, it is my fault." She looks at him with warmth. "This is a word that those of us who study the history of art use daily but people outside our narrow world, use rarely. It means 'the travels of the picture, who commissioned it, when the artist painted it, and where it has been for the rest of its life'. In this case, we have no answers to any of these questions and this both unusual and alarming."

90

"Alarming? What is alarming?" Tom shows his surprise at her use of the word.

"There are people in the world who try to produce fakes. All paintings without anything written about their provenance are suspicious. Paintings where there is no record of the artist painting the picture are highly suspicious in the minds of most of us." She pauses with her eyes still riveted by the picture. "But the quality of the art here really speaks for itself. But I just must determine where it comes from. I have much reading and research to do. Somewhere, there will be something written about this canvas and this painting. In the end, there will be some small thing, maybe a workshop note, maybe an invoice. For instance, there will be an invoice for the payment for powders for the paints. There must be something." She gives a small and slightly weary sigh, looks a little pale, and collapses into the seat. He is naturally alarmed.

"Should we have a cup of tea?" He decides that this might be a strategy for keeping her on course a while. That he is right shows in her immediate agreement.

"Thank you, and my apologies that it is not myself offering you the tea – how impolite of me." She summons the ubiquitous Miss Featherstone, who returns with the tea – Earl Grey on this occasion. They solemnly sip the tea, with the cups distanced from the canvas. She appears somewhat revived and a little touch of pink has returned to her cheeks.

"And the parents of the baby Jesus, would they too have been famous Florentine nobles?" She is shocked.

"Oh no, that would have been considered quite improper in those days. Remember that although the Medicis have promoted a liberal attitude within the city, and especially in the realms of art and expression, nevertheless, in matters such as religion, there is still a conservatism of view within the land. Mostly, the word of the Bible is sacred, even though some men of science are beginning to question some of the specific details. The population, as a whole, regard the thoughts of such men as sacrilegious and far beyond the limits of any reasonable sceptic thought. This is a city, where, although they do not know it yet, the inhabitants are about to come under the influence of a monk named Savonarola, who will cause them all to go a little mad in the head. The townspeople became so inflamed by the puritanical nature of his teachings that they burned books."

"They burned books? Really?"

"Oh yes, it was a reaction to the relative tolerance of the Medicis. They had what is now called the 'Bonfire of the Vanities'. Even Botticelli was sucked into the atmosphere of hysteria that pervaded the city, and apparently threw some of his own paintings onto the bonfire." Tom looks at her in amazement.

"How could you destroy your own paintings? How do we know that that was true?"

"We have a man called Guicciardini to thank for the historical account of it all. Sometimes, it is easy for a community, whether it be a group of friends, a village, or a great city to be dragged into episodes of perverse or deranged thinking. History gives us many such tales." She gets up and walks around the room for a moment, before returning, and looking at him with a serious expression. "And now, Dr Fielding, may I suggest that a little walk might be good for us? Perhaps we could go to Green Park, my favourite space of the country in this our city."

He is charmed at the idea and they go out into a fine late autumnal day, the leaves changing to an auburn hue, backed by a clear azure sky. They walk amongst others along the small recently redesigned lake, enjoying the tranquillity.

He desperately wants to touch her, to hold her small gloved hand, to receive some recognition from her, but dares not, fearing rejection. He experiences the lightness of her step beside his, felt the movement of her body as they walk. The birdsong seems heightened in its intensity in his ears – never before has he been so aware of his surroundings, and yet so unaware of other passers-by. This is quite a good thing, as he really would not have wanted to be aware of the two men trailing behind him. Recognising them would have somewhat spoiled his idyll. She is talking to him. His attention is dragged back to the words.

"I love your great city for precisely this reason," she is saying.

Oh, what is she talking about? I have missed the start.

"I am sorry. I was dreaming. Forgive me." She looks at him with a smile. "I was talking of the comparison between Paris and London, and the better arrangement of your parks. Here, you could walk for miles from this park, into Green Park, thence to Hyde Park, and from there to Kensington Gardens without hesitation of greenery." He hears the words '…hesitation of greenery' and wonders at her command of his language. Could he have spun that phrase? He fears not. This woman is a small treasure in many differing ways.

They pass the pelicans and herons on the little island in the centre of the lake.

"One of those pelicans can fly, you know," he tells her, stopping, and pointing to the island. "They clip the wings of most of them but leave one so that we have the spectacle of the flight of an enormous unwieldy bird for our pleasure."

She is standing very close to him. He feels the lightest of touches on his arm. Her gloved hand is resting imperceptibly on his arm. They both stand very still, not looking at each other. After a few seconds, he rests his hand on hers and moves on as they walk comfortably side by side along the south side of the lake. Suddenly, she stops and pointed

"I have never seen those towers and roofs before. Where are they?"

He glances up, "Oh yes, they look well from here. They are the bizarre turrets of Richmond House. No one quite knows why the architect added them, but they add a certain mystique, I think."

They continue on around and pass the little warden's cottage. Two herons sit on the roof, contemplating them. Eventually, they emerge onto the mall, where they part; she to the gallery; he to his patients.

A week later, a further summons appears, and she spends some more time discussing the picture's merits. He tells her that he would like to have the picture returned to his and Justin's care, and she arranges for one to the gallery's porters to have it returned to his rooms. Later, he takes her to Rules restaurant in Maiden Lane, and she enjoys the Englishness and the history. He talks to her of his life and upbringing and watches the sparkle of her eyes. In her own way, she begins to understand that the courtesy of the Victorian English man is somehow more genuine than the French equivalent. She feels the sincerity of the politeness and wonders at the manners. This man has started to fascinate her and sometimes at work, she will stop looking at a picture and allow her mind to wander into his rooms and consider the atmosphere of a consultation with him.

And now, she reminds herself of his eyelashes, his long beautiful, slightly upturned lashes. She would like to be his patient and allow his eyes to look at her. More than anything, she wants him to look at her body. She wants to take her clothes off so that he could imbibe the beauty of her body.

At that point, she will drag her eyes back to the painting before her, embarrassed that she has roamed so far. She knows that she has only known him for a few weeks, and yet she also understands that all of her, mind, and body, lights up in his presence. She has begun to want to be with him each day, even for a short while. She sends notes regularly to Wimpole Street to request his presence or to arrange for a walk in a park at lunch time.

One day in early October, with the sun still unseasonably warm and a shallow southerly breeze blowing gently, he has arranged to meet her at London Bridge Railway station. He would not tell her why, but she has to meet him under the station clock at 9am on a Saturday morning. She is early. Eventually, he appears, carrying a large picnic hamper, and holding out two tickets. She thinks that she will swoon from the excitement.

"Are we going for a ride? How exciting. Tell me where, do." But he will only put his finger to his lips. They walk towards the third platform, where a train with four carriages is standing. Porters are loading cases and people are standing at doors, saying farewells. They hardly have time to enter the First-Class carriage when the whistle blows, and the train has started with an enormous clanking of couplings. A sign on the window says, 'Brighton – spend a day at the seaside'.

How could he not tell me? she wonders. *Are my shoes strong enough to cope with the pebbles on the beach? Is my dress suitable? Can I calm myself or will I faint with the excitement?* And a thousand other questions crowd her mind. And then they were travelling past houses blackened with coal dust, their backyards filled with urchins, making rude gestures to the passing train, and wearing dirty, torn clothing. And he is sitting there, smiling at her in his lovely way. And the happiness washes over her, and tears come to her eyes. And she sees the alarm gather in his kind face, so she sooths his concern by stroking his large male hands. She comes and sits next to him. She kisses his cheek. To her, he feels exquisite. He smells of brilliantine and man. She is overwhelmed with desire and can feel her cheeks burn a little. Suddenly, she understands that she loves her English doctor with all of herself.

They stop at Croydon, and after that they are in complete countryside, thundering through fields of green with the harvest all in. Occasionally, they see a horse, pulling a plough or children lining the trackside to wave at the train and its passengers.

"Did you have breakfast?" He is talking to her.

"Not really," she replies. He produces two apples, apparently one for each of them. The apples have a glistening red appearance and taste of nectar.

"Russets," he informs her. She has no idea what that is but assumes that he is talking of the apples. She nods wisely, she hopes. It is nearly midday when they pull into the modern station at Brighton and wonder of wonders, the station is not too far from the sea. Despite the sun, the sea looks rather grey and muddy and uninviting, but she is enchanted by the beach, even if there is no sand but only pebbles.

She looks out to sea and, although she can see no land, she realises that somewhere out there is her France. She cannot stop the shudder that ripples over her shoulders. She remembers the unhappy days with her parents, her feelings of intense loneliness in the family home, where she grew up in her tiny village in the Aveyron valley. That her parents were devout Catholics was not really the problem. That they believed that all the other households in the valley were devil-worshippers was. She remembers that she was allowed no contact with other children when not at school. No friends to play with at home, nor any brothers or sisters, alone in her world. Of course, at school, there were friends. The teachers were sympathetic to her plight but appeared powerless to help her. At last, she had won a place at the Sorbonne to study art and the day of the arrival of the letter is still clear in her mind.

When there, she had married the first man who had shown an interest in her – a lecturer, fifteen years older – and, as it transpired, a brute. He drank absinthe heavily, and every evening, would scream and shout at her. On Friday and Saturday nights, he would beat her with a leather strap. Just as she was beginning to think that she could bear no more, the typhus had taken him. She immediately left Paris and travelled north simply to escape. She reached Dunkirk, where she obtained a place on a coal steamer bound for England. She was given a mattress in the hold and, after an uncomfortable night, had arrived at Folkestone. The train had taken her to London, where she quickly gained employment on the strength of her first-class Sorbonne degree in a gallery newly opened in Mayfair. About a year later, sitting in the sunshine on a bench in Trafalgar Square, she had fallen into conversation with a charming middle-aged gentleman. After a few pleasantries on the weather, the man had discovered that her favourite subject was the history of art. They had talked of Giotto. He had been simply amazed to discover that she knew more about the famed artist, and in particular of the fresco cycle of *the Life of Christ* in the Scrovegni Chapel in Padua than he himself did. The man she was talking to was Justin Crampton. Within a few days, she had been appointed Assistant Curator for Italian art at the National Gallery.

She had come a long way from the ghastly start to her life, but the fact of the few miles separating her from her early appalling conditions still hung over her. Beside her, he has been talking of many things, and holding her hand. She feels the warmth, the reassurance, the caring in his fingers. She drags herself back into the happy world of Thomas Fielding, medical practitioner, and charmer of people. She knows, of course, that he is a 'charmer', but purely rationally, prefers his comfortable easy charm, even if a tiny worm in the back of her mind is telling her to beware.

In fact, the great charmer is himself being charmed by the sweet thing struggling slightly to keep up over the pebbles which skid and slip under her sandals. He is feeling a great peace descending onto his shoulders and a feeling that he can tell her everything; well, maybe not everything yet. But they talk of Botticelli and the National Gallery; of medicine and Wimpole Street; of the Russians and the Crimea; of English weather and the people of Paris. Eventually, he says to her, "Let us sit and have a picnic."

So, at last, she can rest her chaffed feet and hopefully stop the burning sensation from the rubbed skin. He produces a rug and opens the hamper. She peeks and is delighted. Even a bottle of Sauvignon Blanc from the Loire valley. Proper glass wine glasses. Large china plates. Ham. Brie. Even a long baguette to remind her of home. He has even remembered some linen napkins. She sits as straight backed as she can, considering the shifty pebbles under her buttocks, and watches the people, mostly young, enjoying the salty sea breezes wafting off the English Channel, as the arrogant English call this stretch of grey gull-filled ocean. At that moment, a large gull is indeed watching them. It has its head on one side and is clearly contemplating their picnic with its tasty morsels. She decides to throw a little piece of baguette, but as she raises her arm, feels a strong male hand around her wrist.

"Don't," says the owner of the hand. "The gull's friends will be all around us once you accede to his blackmail."

She lowers her hand and notices something curious and warming; the strong male hand is still on her wrist, but now with added gentleness. She feels the warmth from the fingertips and the slight male roughness of the skin of the palm, as if he had once been a manual labourer. Her eyes seek his and observes that they are already smiling into hers. She watches his lips with a trivial tremor and understands immediately that this is an important moment. She wonders for an instant of time whether she should extract her fingers, now held in a feather-like grasp, but somehow paralysis has gripped the muscles of her forearm. He moves his face slowly towards her. She does not move and slowly closed her eyes. The kiss, when it eventually comes, is the most delicate of brushes on her lips. They tingle. Her whole body burns with desire. After, they sit simply, hands touching, looking out across the terraced pebbles towards the sea with the southerly sun causing sparklets of light twinkling on its surface.

Gently, he breaks the magic by withdrawing the soft hand and asking her if she is hungry for lunch yet. She could have stayed immobile for a week but forces herself back into the reality of nutrition by acknowledging that although her mind has been on matters other than food, she was indeed happy to eat.

He balances the glasses precariously on a small piece of bleached driftwood lying close by on the stones. Her mind speculates on the wood and its travels across the oceans to end here, beside them on the beach. He pours the wine. It has a deep, nearly orange colour, befitting its Loire appellation and tinkles as he pours it carefully into each glass. He raises his glass, as does she, momentarily fearful as to what he would drink to, but he carefully lightens the atmosphere.

"To the colleagues of our seagull, may they go elsewhere." She laughs and feels a surge of warmth at the lightness of his phrasing. They clink glasses and drink, and she feels the sting of acid on her tongue and palate.

He quickly unwraps the ham and brie and, slicing the baguette with a rather vicious-looking knife, he makes her a sandwich and gives it to her without, she noted with some amusement, asking her as to whether she wants both foods in her bread. He notes her looking at it, and instantly wondered.

"Was that what you wanted?" he asks, with anxiety.

"Perfect," she reassures, trying her best to eat her rather overfilled bread with the decorum befitting of a lady. They sit, happy with their food, their wine and each other. The gulls circle, crying plaintively, but do not interfere. They talk of small unimportant matters and watch children playing on the edge of the waves, which gently lap the shore in the light whispers of the breeze.

Eventually, they pack the hamper, leave it under an arch, and walk westwards, at first along the beach, and then along a promenade being constructed on the outskirts of the new town of Worthing. Everywhere were glittering seaside houses, addressing the front, built in the latest modern Victorian styles, with porticos and columns, ornate doors and stained-glass windows set into them.

At some point during their walk, their hands have met again and seem to stay together in a comfortable, shared warmth. They turn around and walk back to the station, and thence to London, arriving back around ten o'clock. They share a hansom first to her place and then to Wimpole Street, where he collapses into his bed and is asleep with a small smile on his lips within minutes.

Chapter Eleven
London, Three Days Later

Tom

His excitement at the approaching hour of Mrs Deschambres' visit is marginally tempered by the continuing presence of Giorgiana, who seems to have decided to stay late this afternoon, although normally she leaves early on a Friday. Irritatingly, she seems to have much paperwork to accomplish this afternoon, just when he wants her out of the way. At last, she puts on her coat and leaves with a cheery, "Farewell." He responds with relief.

Within five minutes of her departure, he hears a hesitant knock from the front doors. He springs out of his seat and almost runs to the door. He welcomes her in, and having closed the door behind her, rapidly reopens it, and looks out into the street. His position at the top of the small flight of stairs, leading up to the door, gives him a long vista up and down the street. He sees smartly dressed men and women entering and leaving consulting rooms in other houses, he sees hansom and larger cabs in the street, but he can see no one suspicious, and certainly no one resembling the two men who were watching previously. He returns inside to find her eyes watching him in some alarm.

"You are looking for someone, Monsieur? Was I being followed?"

He is momentarily lost for words but recovers his poise.

"I was concerned, of course, for your safety. We have had a number of purses snatched in the street by footpads and I needed to be assured that no one was lurking." She looks at him with eyes that show a measure of disbelief, but clearly decides not to pursue the matter.

"Please come in," and he ushers her into his consulting room. He admires her olive-green silk dress, tightly cinched at the waist, with long sleeves and a large matching green bow at the neck. Her hair tumbles down with tight curls around her long slim neck. He was mistaken – she is even more exquisite than in his memory. He offers her a cup of tea, but mercifully, she declines as, in reality, he has no idea whether there is any tea in the small kitchen that he never ventures in; this is Georgiana's world. He understands that he is staring overly at her and with difficulty averts his eyes.

In preparation for her visit, he has taken the picture of the pope downstairs and spread it across his consulting desk. She notices it, and instantly her eyes focus on the pope.

"Of course, this is not of the same quality as the other picture," she has started to analyse the picture and he drags his mind to the matter in hand. She is treating him with some seriousness, and he tries to respond to her mood by looking with care at the picture unfurled in front of them.

"Essentially, this is a poorly crafted picture, but an important story," she begins in an assured manner. "The man that you can see here is an important pope. Pius VII, Niccolo Chiaramonti, was a man who brought strength to the Papal See by having an excellent concept of strategy, and despite his problems with the Emperor Napoleon, managed to achieve much in his long reign, and also despite his years of imprisonment. Sadly, however, your painting is not of similar importance. It is painted by one who has little talent. Also, it is not that old, and was probably painted within the last hundred years." She pauses, and he is aware of her attention on him, looking for his reaction. Frankly, he does not care at all that she is unimpressed by this picture.

"So, you are saying that it is of no importance in the world of art?"

"Yes, I fear so, but the obelisk at Monte Pichio does catch the eye." He wonders how she can possibly know all this.

She continues, "But there are other paintings of this pope with this obelisk, so it is by no means unique." She has finished.

"So, I shall frame the picture and hang it here in my rooms and pretend that this is an ancestor," he lightens the atmosphere and she shares in the little joke.

"Indeed, I was thinking that there was a slight resemblance." He is mortified. Her antennae pick this up, and she adds, "But you are, of course, more handsome." He has forgotten the first sentence instantly. They smile at each other and he watches her blue eyes.

"And now, I fear that we may not go to see the *Magi*, as you will know that my friend has returned it to the gallery. In recompense, I will make you some tea in my rooms. Please follow me," and he leads her up the narrow staircase to his rooms at the top of the house. She sits on the chaise longue and he returns with a tray with his best china."

"I am impressed," she tells him, "Sevres porcelain. Should I be flattered, or do you use this for everyone?" There is a twinkle in her eye.

"Of course," he laughs, and carefully places the cup and saucer in her hands. He notes again the slim beauty of her fingers. *And how much better they appear unadorned by rings.* He decides to be brave and ask.

"So, forgive me if I am impolite, but I cannot help but notice that there are no rings on your fingers, and yet you are called Madame Deschambres at the gallery." He looks anxiously at her, hoping that he has not made a personal comment too early in their relationship.

"Indeed, Monsieur, I was married." There is a pause, and he knows that he has overstepped the mark. "Sadly, my husband died of the typhus four years ago. At the time, I was devastated, but I seem to have recovered now." His relief knows no bounds as she is still smiling at him.

"My condolences," is all he can say.

"In fact, it is little problem. To be frank, he was a brute and behaved appallingly to me. I was only seventeen when we married. In my youth, I thought him to be exciting – he was fifteen years older than me. What I did not know, as he concealed it from me until our wedding day, was that he drank large quantities of absinthe every day. He had descended into a pathetic state before the typhus took him. It was a relief that suddenly the Good Lord took the burden from me. I had prayed for relief to Him every night for the four years, until his death. My prayers were answered. In the meantime, I had my degree in the History of Art from the Sorbonne, and I was working in a small gallery near the Pantheon. I decided that I must start afresh, and I came to London seeking work. I was lucky enough to meet M Crampton by chance. For M Crampton, I appeared at a fortunate moment as he had just lost his assistant curator to the misfortune of pregnancy." She giggled at him, and he smiled in return.

"And so, I am employed at the wonderful National Gallery of London, where I work with kind people and spend my days with beautiful art. I am a lucky woman."

"Madame, I am happy to hear your story, but I have just realised that it is seven o'clock, and I wonder whether you have a dinner engagement. If not, perhaps I could entertain you at a local restaurant?"

"That would be wonderful. Foolishly, I missed lunch today as I had so much work to finish for the weekend, and I too am hungry."

"Excellent. We will catch a hansom, and travel around finding somewhere that will have us. We will start at my favourite, Simpson's Grand Divan Tavern." And they travel to the Strand, where there is indeed a vacant table for them at the dining room of the newly renovated club. They leave their cloaks, enter the high-ceilinged dining room and are given a table for two along the wall.

"This eatery started its life as a chess-playing coffee shop and is now England's foremost chess centre. But a few years ago, they started serving food and have acquired a remarkable chef, who insists that the place serves only the finest English food. If you order meat, the whole joint is wheeled to you on a silver trolley."

In fact, they both order the roast beef and an enormous joint duly arrives before them, accompanied by a fierce-looking moustachioed chef wielding a large and dangerous-looking carving knife, which he sharpens ostentatiously at their table. He promptly slices four thin pieces of beef, giving Tom the slightly bigger pieces, clearly much to her relief. The vegetables, Yorkshire pudding, and roasted potatoes are piled high on their plates, and he leaves with his trolley before him. She is clearly amazed and impressed. Tom orders a bottle of Crozes Hermitage, and they eat and drank contentedly.

She tells him about the turmoil on the streets of Paris in her last year of studying at the Sorbonne, about the outrage at the actions of the king, and his eventual overthrow, to be replaced by the Second Republic. But then how everything that they had fought for had been wiped out, and how in the summer, there had been a terrible massacre with bodies everywhere on the streets, and how a nephew of Napoleon Bonaparte had been elected President, and then made himself King. She explains that she is pleased not to be a part of her native land at this moment.

And in turn, he tells her about being a medical student and his journey to and from Rome by way of France. He tells her of travelling by train and coach, of his newfound admiration for the romantic poets, of Shelley and Byron and Keats. He manages to leave out stories of his debts, and without too much difficulty to keep the word 'opium' out of the conversation.

Before leaving, at Tom's insistence, they walk up the ornate staircase on their right to the upper rooms, where, in total silence, games of chess are taking place. Six tables have been set up in the centre of the room, each with a chess board set up on them. At each table, a person is seated on one side, with the other seat opposite, unoccupied.

"A match is taking place against the Reform Club."

"But where are the opponents?" she asks.

"Aha," he says, "watch for a moment." She sees nothing except men sitting deep in thought. Suddenly, one of the men moves a chess piece and then writes on a piece of paper. He then hands it to a young man, wearing a top hat and the uniform of the club, who is one of six similarly dressed, standing on the periphery of the room. The young man speeds off, clutching the paper and taking the stairs two at a time. She has no idea what is going on and looks at Tom.

"At the Reform, a similar scene is occurring at this moment. The club servant that you saw has just taken the move from our player on Board Three and will deliver it to their player on their Board Three." She looks at him in bewilderment.

"But why not just go to their club, or they come here."

"We feel more comfortable in our own clubs," comes the response.

"But couldn't they or we cheat?"

"Cheat, cheat. This is England. We don't cheat at games," he pauses and adds, "or indeed war." Immediately, he regrets his unwarranted remark. He has always held the view that Napoleon Bonaparte used appallingly unfair tactics in some of his battles. Mercifully, she does not understand his remark at all, and the comment disappears into the air.

After watching for a while, he realises that she is bored with chess, and suggests that it is time to leave. Their coats are retrieved, and the doorman hails a hansom for them. He has to ask her where she lives, and the driver takes them to Tottenham Court Road. Afterwards, alone in the cab on the short distance to Wimpole Street, he is lost in his thoughts. Her image dances before him as real as she could be. He sees the haze of his cloak against the glass of the window. He feels the touch of her gloved hand and he knows that the touch is real and perfectly light. He wants to feel the touch of her lips and knows that it will be exquisite. Somehow, he feels an aura, a sense of lightness in her soul that he is unable to define truly. It is as a waft of perfume, a shimmer of a pearl in the ear, and a glitter from an exquisite jewel necklace all intertwined.

Chapter Twelve

London, November 1853

Tom

The next few weeks pass with the moments of true delight (mostly) and deep despair (just occasionally) that occur to all lovers. They meet as often as possible. He rearranges his patients so that his lunch breaks mean that he can arrive at Trafalgar Square at the start of her lunch breaks, leave her at the doors at the end of her time, and get back to his rooms so as not to be too late for the first patient and incur Georgiana's wrath. He even manages to be repeatedly charming to his disliked receptionist so that eventually, even if he is sometimes still a little late for his patients, she starts to warm to him.

In the evenings, they see each other on Thursdays and Fridays. He shows her some of the new restaurants that are springing up, or they stay home together. He discovers that she enjoys playing draughts and they often have chats about improving their skills and laughing over their mistakes. Each look for an excuse to touch each other and they acknowledge their physicality with long and passionate kisses of farewell. After he leaves her, he is always bereft and will often walk home so that he can cope with his sadness at being separate.

Winter continues and is unusually mild that year with frosts, snow, and even rain hardly troubling the capital city. The leaves fall but remained crisp and brown and golden until the streetsweepers remove them. He invites her home for the Christmas break, with some fear and trepidation as his father can often be irascible, but she charms him, and there are even moments when Tom manages to be jealous of the old man's ability to discuss so many different subjects with ease and knowledge. His mother is delighted and makes a few unsubtle hints about the future of their relationship.

Through the following January of 1854, the relationship blossoms in the many little imperceptible ways of these things. They continue to see each other regularly, and Tom starts to be invited as her partner to events at the National Gallery. At the beginning of January, there is an evening reception for the visiting tsar of all the Russians, Alexander Romanov, and his tsarina, who were visiting their relative, Queen Victoria. The visit is also important for the politicians, still worried about Russian ambitions in the Crimea, so the planned visit to the National Gallery, personally requested by the tsar, assumes much significance.

She tells him later of the charm and culture of Alexander, and his great knowledge of the world of art, and in particular, of Italian art, acquired apparently through the great and famed collection of Catherine the Great at the Hermitage museum in St Petersburg.

"The best in the world," she has told Tom. Tom is taken aback when she has told him that for every painting of the Renaissance in the National Gallery, Catherine has acquired ten in the Hermitage.

The tsar has brought a gift for the gallery of an ornate delicate brooch, covered in diamonds and rubies, made by their famous jeweller, M Faberge. She has described its great beauty and the intricate gold engraving of the Russian goldsmiths.

"How could that be?" he asks, bewildered that Russia could be seemingly as rich and powerful as England.

Later in February, Tom receives a letter that causes him great turmoil. It reads:

To - Dr Thomas Fielding of 19, Wimpole Street
Sir,
*   You are now in our debt to the tune of five thousand three hundred pounds.*

This sum must be deposited at our house in Shoreditch in cash by the last day of March 1854.

Failure to do so will result in your own slow and sadly painful death.

We have every confidence that you will take the necessary steps to preserve your own future.

Yours sincerely,
Arthur Stokes

When his friend Charles visits that evening, Tom is so distressed that he blurts it all out to him and even shows him the letter.

"And is it all true?" Charles asks.

Tom confirms the sum and Charles has shared in the horror of the occasion. They drank a bottle of wine, trying to find a solution but to little avail. The sum is so enormous that borrowing the money is out of the question. Tom feels that his parents are unlikely to be sympathetic, nor even would be able to find that sum of money without selling the family home. Involving the police seems impossible, as there is no doubt of the sums involved, and the police will be unlikely to act, in any case, unless a crime has actually been committed.

When Charles has eventually left, Doctor Thomas Fielding, late of St Thomas' Hospital, spends an hour deep in thought on trying to find a possible solution to the danger that he appears to be in. Then, unable to find a workable solution, and for want of anything better to do, he picks up a copy of that day's Times of London. When he gets to page four, he reads an advertisement which stops him in his tracks. He carefully cuts the advertisement out, reads it though with great care, and places it on his desk. Suddenly, a glimmer of hope for his future has opened up. Eventually, he comes to a conclusion that this copy of the Times has an option for his own safety that no other solution would provide.

The next day, he cancels all his booked patients, to Giorgiana's fury, and sets off towards the centre of the city, deep in thought. Every now and then, he thinks that he sees one of the two men who had previously followed him, but they miraculously disappear whenever he looks about himself with care. He is so preoccupied with the advertisement that he does not take in his surroundings, let alone whether he is or is not being followed. *And what would he do about Amelie and his love for her?* He has no ready answer. After wandering unseeing for a long while, he suddenly wakes to the fact that he has crossed the Thames and has arrived in the slums of Lambeth. Mercifully at that moment, a hansom passes without passengers. He hails it and travels uneventfully back over Westminster Bridge and thence to Wimpole Street.

At the door of Number Nineteen, he pays, thanks the driver and is just about to ascend the steps to the front door with his key at the ready, when two men appeared, as if from nowhere. They grab his arms and wrestle the key from him. He fights back, but he is finally subdued by a sharp punch in the face from one of his assailants. He is being dragged through his front door when he hears a familiar booming sound.

"Put him down or you both will surely die," says the voice. Tom lifts his head to see a large cloaked figure holding a revolver. The two men drop Tom unceremoniously on the ground and raise their hands.

"No need for any of that, guv," says the taller of the two. "We were just helping him into his house."

"Get out, and if I see you again, you won't live for long."

The two men take off down the poorly lit street. Charles fires after them to hasten them on their way and then goes to tend his dishevelled friend. He gets him inside and sits him in the reception area.

"Where did you appear from?" asks Tom, nursing his head.

"I walked past on my way home an hour ago and spied those two lurking in the street near your door and recognised them from before. So, I dismounted from my cab around the corner in Harley Street, walked back behind them, and awaited your return."

"Well, I owe you a debt of enormous gratitude. You have probably saved my life," he says, looking with distress from under his battered brow. "And I can see that I will need to consider my future with even more care. I am unsafe in this city. And the solution that I have thought about will have to be enacted – and with rapidity."

"Tell me about this solution of yours, then."

Tom looks at him. "We must go upstairs." They ascend the stairs with its wooden banister posts and dado rail. Tom unlocks the door and they go into Tom's study. He picks up the piece of the Times and hands it to Charles without speaking. The whale of a man collapses noisily onto the chaise longue while reading the advertisement.

He reads:

Doctor Livingstone needs
A qualified Medical Practitioner
To spend a minimum of a year with him in Africa.
Interested persons should get in touch with
The Most Reverend Roderick Farquhar at The London Missionary
Society

Charles closes his eyes. He can smell the stale smell of male sweat, mixed with red wine. He can hear the street sounds from below, drifting in through the window. He tries to blot everything out so that he can order his thoughts. His friend has clearly lost his senses, and at the same time, needs good advice.

"So why would a trip to Africa solve your problem?"

"It would get me away from these people. You saw what they started to do. Who knows what they had in mind for me."

"But they will look for you when you return."

"Well that is possible, but I don't have any other ideas. I will be going to see Mr Roderick Farquhar in the morning."

Chapter Thirteen
London, March 1854

Roderick Farquhar turns out to be a middle-aged Scot with a broad Highland accent and a dog collar.

"Welcome, welcome. If you are here about David Livingstone, you are doubly welcome," and he ushers him into a fine room, looking over Piccadilly and Green Park. He wonders whether he would drink tea, but he declines.

"Shall I tell you a wee bit about Doctor David and what this is all about?" he asks him once they are comfortably seated. He, of course, agreed.

"Well, the great doctor is having a hard time in Africa. He is crossing Southern Africa at the moment and is looking for a way to set up a trading route between the Atlantic Ocean to the west and the Indian Ocean to the east, converting the heathen as he goes. So, he set out a year ago from a village called Linyanti on the Zambezi river, right in the middle of Africa, and is voyaging towards the west coast, aiming for a town called Loanda where the Portuguese have a trading station. They started off going north up the Zambezi river and are now travelling westwards through unexplored territory. They were expecting to be at Loanda by March but have had a series of problems. We have just had word from the doctor that he now expects to be in Loanda towards the end of May. I will show you the latest letter which arrived three days ago from him. As soon as I saw it, I went to see the editor of the Times and got the advertisement inserted the following day. Here, read it yourself." And with that, he is given some sheets of paper, somewhat dirtied but written in a neat hand.

Shinte, Central Africa January 1854
To: The Reverend Dr Roderick Farquhar
The London Missionary Society, 126, Piccadilly, London.

This letter will be taken by native runner across the continent to the port of Loanda. The runner will then deliver it to the captain of one of Her Majesty's ships. He, in his turn, will bring it to yourself hopefully in time for you to fulfil my need.

Dear Revd. Farquhar,

Greetings in the name of God from the continent of Africa.

Having spent a while in the land of the Bichuanas to the north of the Colony, I determined that more work was needed further to the north. To that end, I set out with determination, accompanied by many helpers from amongst the Bakalahari and accompanied by my wife and children. I have also taken along with me a trader by the name of Oswell, as I am convinced that along with the message of salvation through Jesus, the heathen needs to be dragged from his poverty by both wealth and education in order that his Christianity might grow on a solid base. So often conversions will take place, but unless the tribe sees an improvement in material standards, the message of Christianity will slip away. I am determined that this will not be and that my conversions will prove of a lasting nature.

So, my message to you and my converts is that a sound base for the work of the missionary consists of three parts:

- *the telling of the salvation of the Lord,*
- *education, such as numeracy and literacy*
- *trade and physical enrichment.*

I am therefore progressing by attempting to create a trade route from the West Coast of the continent to the East. Initially, I had thought that I should aim for the port of Walvisch Bay, where there is already an old, established trading post. But on reflection, I could see little advantage to it, and am aiming in truth to decide whether it would be possible to use the mighty Zambesi River as the main trade route. The great advantage is that there has been to my knowledge, no exploration by the white man of the Zambesi, and the native tribes have consequently had no exposure to the word of the Lord.

And so, I and my retinue have travelled north encountering the Zambesi, where it joins the great River Chobe in the lands of Sesheke, a great native leader and a man who has helped me in my work both of exploration and of missionary work. From the chief's village of Sesheke, we have travelled north again up the river in our convoy of canoes and everywhere that we travel have been greeted with love, kindness, and most importantly, food. We are now in the upper reaches of the Zambesi and surrounded by enormous herds of game, both large, e.g. lions, hippopotamuses, eland, many types of deer and zebras, and small. We are turning west now and heading hopefully towards the port of Loanda. The going is much harder, as the great river has disappeared, and we travel in wagons pulled by oxen.

I myself have been remarkably well until recently when an attack of African fever has wreaked havoc with my strength. I am also prone to dizziness on looking up and a few other more minor complaints. And here we come to my request to you.

I need a colleague.

If I had a young man to accompany me, my work would be strengthened. And most importantly that man should be a medical practitioner. I am woefully ignorant now, having been in Africa for so long, of modern advances in treatment. It is ten years since I have had a colleague to share ideas with, not to mention discuss modern medicines. So, in short, I would value a young medical man, needless to say in the best of health as the travelling is arduous. If he had strong Christian values, that would be of benefit but not essential, as I am still myself strong in the Lord and capable of preaching the message of Christ with power in my soul. Perhaps he needs to be warned that it will be likely that the *passage from one side of the continent to the other will take us at least a year.*

So, my dear friend and minister, if you could find a healthy strong medical lion, send him to me to meet me in Loanda, where, at this rate of progress, we will arrive around the time of May in the year of our Lord 1854. And if this man could bring with him quantities of up-to-date medicines and treatments, we could together bring some healing to the natives and consequently improve their faith both in us and in the strength of the message that we preach.

My blessings to you and all my friends in the London Missionary Society,

David Livingstone

He reads the extraordinary letter with incredulity and excitement. He, of course, knows of the great missionary doctor – who in the breadth of their Isles does not? But to see his words before him from so far away, brings a gasp of astonishment to his lungs. He reads the letter for a second time to ensure that he has the content accurately before his eyes. And then he sits in silence while he considers the nature of the required commitment. It is clear to him that he fits Dr Livingstone's requirements rather well. He is young, medically qualified, and fit of limb and mind. He is unencumbered, and up to date with new medical progress. And he will have no difficulty bringing medicines with him, although being unfamiliar with many tropical diseases, might not be certain as to what treatments might best be required.

And of course, he will be able to leave this country and the evil gang who is chasing him behind. Hopefully, after more than a year, he might be forgotten. On the negative side, he will, of course, miss his country and his friends greatly. But in his young heart, a chance for this great adventure with the famous missionary will be an opportunity of a lifetime.

And then of course there is his darling Mme Deschambres, entwined in his heart. This would be the hardest part of all.

"When would I have to leave?" he asks. He regards me with care.

"The timing is tight for you to get to Loanda in time. The letter has taken longer to get here than Dr Livingstone would have estimated. I have made enquiries. You may wish to know that there is a British ship, the Aurora, headed for Loanda by way of Lisbon and leaving Bristol on Thursday, March 27th. You may also need to know that it is just possible that she might be a slaver, who could be taking up slaves at Loanda."

He is distressed. He had thought that slavery had been abolished some twenty years before, and he mentions this.

"Yes, in theory, but apparently the practice still continues illegally. I have heard yesterday from Lord Dudley, with whom I was lunching at his club, that the recently reinforced West Africa squadron has all but abolished the trafficking of the slaves from the African continent. Also, the owners have assured me that the Aurora now carries out peaceful trade with no slaves on board, and I must trust them."

He considers the matter. It is now the 10th of March. It will take him maybe just the one day to travel by train to Bristol, now that the gauge wars are over, and Temple Meads station is served regularly from Paddington. He will need a few days discussion prior to that with Dr Allen at Allen and Hanburys to establish the medicines that he will take with him.

His thoughts are interrupted by Mr Farquhar.

"Perhaps you might tell me something of yourself?" And indeed, it is remiss of him to be considering options before he ascertains Tom's suitability. He sets out for him the achievements of his life to date, omitting a few minor details, such as his appalling achievements at school, his opium habit, and a few other insignificant details. He must confess also that he did marginally embellish he achievements at medical school, and the size and fame of his practice in Harley Street. He manages to look impressed but, as with most Scots, displays some caution as Tom nears the end of the history of his professional life by inquiring as to whether he could produce three persons of good standing to act as assurers as to his probity.

"One should be a medical practitioner, one a layperson, and of course, the clergyman belonging to your regular place of worship."

"Of course," he mutters, doing his utmost to suppress a growing feeling of anxiety spreading over him. Tom can see the medical practitioner, his senior colleague at the rooms, Dr Greerson. He can rely on his friend, the viscount, as a layperson to lie sufficiently about his personal qualities, and of course to have a viscount as a person of good standing will count well. But for the moment, he cannot see his way around the clergyman. Perhaps a little imagination is required.

"Well, that will be all. As soon as you get the letters of commendation to me, I will speak with my colleagues. In the meantime, I will send word to Captain Emmanuel of the Aurora to have a berth provisionally reserved for you. And on the matter of supplies for the good doctor, my society will of course pay for everything – it would be the least that we could do to support our missionary." And with that he stands and stretches out his hand.

"God bless you, my son," he smiles at Tom. "Be assured that you will be in our prayers each Sunday when we pray for the good doctor Livingstone." Tom puts on his cloak and passes out into the cold, rainy day.

He has little doubt that he must leave the country. This is an unusual opportunity to 'disappear', and it certainly will provide a means for him to vanish into mid-air. Clearly, one important principle will be to ensure that as few people as possible knew of his strategy. Charles, of course, will have to know. His main worry is what to do about Amelie. She will be safer not knowing where he is, but to leave without saying goodbye will devastate her. And of course, his pain will be great as well. For the time being, he determines to shelve the problem. He has many pressing matters, not least of which is Dr Livingstone's need for 'up-to-date medicines and treatments'.

The following morning, he is awake early and distresses Georgiana by telling her to cancel his patients for the rest of the week. Needless to say, she is full of complaints. He shrugs his shoulders and departs. He walks down to Welbeck Street and enters Allen and Hanbury's marvellous chemist's parlour. He explains to Dr Allen that he is journeying to Africa to be a medical practitioner at a mission hospital.

"Just like Dr Livingstone!" he exclaims rather too loudly for Tom's taste. After that, Dr Allen treats him rather like a long-lost friend. To be truthful, Tom did not know him well, and suspects that the prospect of rather a large order may have coloured his rosy view of him. They sit over a cup of tea and discuss appropriate medicines, quantities and, rather importantly, the means of transporting these to Africa. He feels that I will need to have a large wooden crate and offers to have it made up, crate and medicines, by his company. This seems an excellent idea. He will choose the medicines and quantities, and then manufacture a crate to contain it all. By the end of our talk, Tom is feeling much at ease about many of the practicalities.

On his way home, he deviates to Chandos Street, where he enters the house of the Medical Society of London. He became a Fellow as soon as he qualified, in order mainly to use their excellent library. Frankly, the lectures have not excited him as, for himself, he always learns from reading rather than listening, and he is never facile at medical small talk, so the dinners bore him. So, seated in a large comfortable library, he spends the rest of the day reading as many up-to-date journals as he can, including an excellent article in the Transactions of the Society on the treatment of African fever by one Dr Malcusant, recently returned from the Belgian Congo. He returns home to find a familiar form sprawled across two seats of his reception room.

"Aha, there you are. I have been looking all over for you. Where have you been all day? Even Giorgiana had no idea."

"Come into my room, I have much to tell you." And Tom told him of his interview with the Scottish Farquhar and his day at the chemists and then in the library.

"So, you are determined to go," he observes somewhat mournfully.

"I feel that I have little choice. There is no possibility that I can raise the money, so my life is under serious threat."

"Yes, I do understand that. But what shall we do with our most valuable asset?"

"I know. It is a terrible conundrum. But I cannot tell her, or they might try to find out where I am from her." He looks at him quizzically.

"I did not mean the lovely Mrs Deschambres. I was referring to the painting."

He laughs, "That, my friend, is a good question. They clearly know that we have something of value. If we leave it in my rooms, they will break in and steal it. If we leave it with you, they will break into your house."

They think in silence. Then Tom says, "Supposing I took it with me?"

"To Africa?"

"It would be safer there than anywhere in this country. My debtors would have no idea where it was. I would have to conceal it, of course."

"How would you do that?" Another long pause for thought.

"I told you that the chemist was making a packing case for the medicines. Perhaps a carpenter would be able to make a false floor and chamber in the bottom of the crate, and I could conceal it in there. No one would see it, and it would always be with me, totally invisible."

"I, myself, could do that with ease. I have some experience in the art of carpentry." The viscount amazes me. Yet another skill.

"But that still leaves me with my dreadful dilemma of Amelie, Charles. I love her dearly and separation would be a dreadful trial. Can we discuss what I should do?"

"So, are you sure that you have asked the right question? Do you want to know what you should do, or what you could do?" asks Charles.

"Both. I am troubled with both questions."

"So, there must be a number of dimensions. Is this a selfish matter – a concern for your personal feelings towards the woman? Or is it concern for her emotional wellbeing? Is it a concern for her personal safety? And how about trying an objective stance – so you might want to ask the question, 'What is best for her?' in a moral sense."

"My problem with you, Charles, is that you are more thoughtful than myself, leaving me floundering in a mire of philosophical debate," Tom sits deeper into the chair.

"All that aside, let us approach the problems one at a time. Firstly, let us start with whether you are going to tell her, and how much you are going to tell her."

"I would like to tell her all."

"Including your addiction?"

"Must I?" he groans inwardly.

"Well, you can lie, I suppose, to someone you pretend to 'love'. Over the generations, there have been numerous examples of men lying to women they supposedly love. Methinks Romeo did lie to the fair Juliet, so you have a good early example."

"But I do love her."

"Really? I see little sign. Do you not think that St Paul had probably the best words to define love? He said, 'Love is patient and is kind; love doesn't envy. Love doesn't brag, is not proud, does not behave itself inappropriately, does not rejoice in unrighteousness, but rejoices with the truth; bears all things, believes all things, hopes all things, endures all things. Love never fails'." He pauses for a breath but carries straight on.

"So, let us examine your 'love' in the light of that worthy statement. And in particular the bit about 'rejoices with the truth', your case fails even at the first hurdle, methinks. Finally, and frankly after all these words, I need a drink. Your hosting skills are also failing, Tom." Tom is galvanised into action, disappears into the kitchen, and returns with two glasses and a bottle of southern French red.

"But surely I do love her. She is truly a wonderful woman."

"We are trying to discuss the important concepts of truth and lies, and all you can do is tell me that she is wonderful. My mother is wonderful, but I have no hesitation of lying to her day and night. Explain to me why you will lie?"

"I will lie, I suppose, because I don't want her to think badly of me. There, I have said it."

"At last, honesty. Do not lie to her, Tom. She deserves to know the truth. If you are a man, you will tell her the truth face to face. If you are a bit pathetic, you will send her a letter telling her the truth. If you are a selfish bastard, you will lie to her. Which are you?"

Tom knows what he will do.

Chapter Fourteen

Disappearance to Africa, Late March 1854

Mme Amelie

She is in bad way. He sees the pallor of her face, the way her hands grip her skirt, the crossing and uncrossing of her ankles, the darkness of her eyes. She is retreating into herself in her pain. He knows that he must not move, must not try to touch her. He must allow her to experience and overcome her shock without interference from him.

He has told her everything – the opium, the debts, the threats against his life, the promises of torture. But he has decided that she will be safer from danger if she does not know where he is going. So, he has not talked of Livingstone, or of his voyage to Africa, but has said that he will be leaving the country and that he will not be back for a year or more. She has listened in utter and complete astonishment and in utter and complete silence. She has spoken not a word and still has not, even though he has completed everything that he needs to tell her. At last, he rises, goes to the kitchen, and returns with two cups of tea. She looks at the tea with disdain. At last, she speaks.

"You have led me on. You have not thought of my feelings, of my love for you – there, I have said it. How could you have failed to warn me? You have thought only of yourself. I had thought… I had hoped…" Each time, followed by a pause.

"You had thought… You had hoped…" repeats Tom.

"I had thought that at last in my life, I had met an honourable man, who would treat me with kindness. Clearly, I was mistaken. Again."

Tom knows that he must not speak and must take whatever she says, must not try to defend himself.

"My life has been so hard. I was so demeaned in France. And now, I believed that God was going to bless me with warmth and love in my life. I have always tried to be honourable and please Him and hoped that I would be rewarded. I have not tried hard enough. He still believes that I need more punishment. And you are the instrument of his punishment."

He regards her with amazement. They have rarely discussed religion or God. She has not been to church during her stay in England to his knowledge. This sudden view of the world, couched in terms of a higher being, is a total surprise. He manages not to speak.

"Do not expect ever to see me again. I will certainly not await your return with bated breath." She stands and he can see the tears in her eyes. She dabs ineffectively at her eyes, which have started to swell, hurries to the door, and he hears her steps on the stairs and the front door closing behind her. He watches her walk away down the street from his window, and his own tears flow in abundance. He cries alone in the totality of his overwhelming self-pity. He cries for his loss of her beauty, for her pain, for his loneliness. Eventually, even though it is the middle of the day, he falls into a deep sleep.

He dreams of Africa. There are swamps and mountains. The swamps are full of snakes and rhinoceroses and are a translucent pink colour for some reason that he is unable to fathom. He is chased by a rhinoceros (also pink) and escapes up a tree, which is full of chattering baboons who tell him that he is unwelcome in their tree because his skin is too white. The sky changes colour and hailstones fall on the ground and are eaten by the snakes. In the distance, he sees a large cloud approaching. This turns out to be David Livingstone, who is wearing an enormous hat with a peacock feather in its brim. Dr Livingstone tells him to come down from the tree because he needs to travel on to convert a tribe, who suddenly all appear on the ground and start singing. He tries singing with them, but no words come from his mouth, as one of the young baboons has his hand over it and will not let go. Dr Livingstone has become a baboon and tells the young one to let go. Suddenly, he can sing but the words are all pink and he is not singing the same song. All around are animals, who are singing perfectly in tune with the tribe. The words appear to be 'Cherry Ripe', a song that he knows well but he just cannot get the tune right, and instead sings to the tune of 'Home, sweet Home'. Livingstone sends him to the corner of the lake, which appears at their feet and a passing leopard also sings 'Cherry Ripe' to him, but then turns into a red cheetah, who bounds away across a large prairie, which turns an azure colour as the sun sets. Amelie appears and tells him that she will have his ears boxed as he is a scoundrel. She kisses Livingstone and he wakes with tears falling down his cheeks. He is shivering and realising the cause, smokes a pipe as he watches the sun set over the roofs of Mayfair.

The following morning, he is awoken by his bell. It is Giorgiana, announcing that there are two men at the door with an enormous packing case for him, and indeed it is so. He gets them to put it in his Consulting Room and opens it. The case itself is around two feet by three feet by nearly three feet tall. It is full of bottles of medicines, salves, lotions. Dr Allen has also kindly included a number of pamphlets on the treatments of various tropical disorders. He empties the crate and scatters the contents over the floor of his room. He decides that he needs a professional eye and tells Giorgiana to send a messenger to summon the viscount. Surprisingly, his lordship appears rather quickly.

"I imagined that you might be a while. Did I catch you writing verse?"

"Certainly not. I am summoned. I am here. '*Veni, vidi, vinci*', as the great Caesar would have it."

"Quoting the great Caesar at this hour of the morning fails to endear you to me," Tom replies. "On the other hand, helping me solve the problem of the picture might recommend you to me for at least a week."

Charles grins, and studies the crate, sitting incongruously in the centre of the medical consulting room. Scattered around it, all over the floor, are its contents. He looks into the crate and sees a well-made wooden base, fashioned with strong planks of wood, and screwed into place on stanchions.

"It would be easy to construct a false base by making inserts a few inches in height and fixing them to the base at the sides of the crate. New planks could be inserted over them. Thus, one could make a cavity a few inches high. The canvas would have to be folded in half to fit in. We would have to do it with the utmost care, so as not to damage the adherence of the paint to the canvas. I believe that it could be done successfully, and if it is possible, then you will have a safe hiding place. We will also have to give the cavity a waterproof rendering, as the canvas will be damaged by the dampness of the tropics. I suspect that we could simply coat the walls of the cavity in tar and wrap the canvas in linen so that the tar did not adhere to, and in turn damage, the paintwork. How does that sound?" The viscount pauses for breath.

"Wonderful, wonderful." Tom is always amazed at the depths of his practical knowledge.

"I have visited Mme Deschambres to ascertain the exact measurements of the canvas. I assume from her grim look and refusal to speak more than a few words to me that you have told her all?"

"Nearly all – except that she does not know where I am going," Tom tells him.

"It would be safe to assume that she took the news harshly?" he asks.

"You could say that," he replies. He looks carefully at Tom.

"And you are still determined to leave?"

"Have I a choice?" and Tom shrugs his shoulders.

"Probably not," and he takes a rule from another inside pocket and applies it to the case. "It will fit with some ease, but we will need to fold it the once. I will get the Georgiana to summon a cab and will remove the case from you. I will have it back in two days, the Lord willing."

Tom looks at him. "'The Lord willing?" he queries.

"Just getting you in practice for a life of spreading the words of Christianity to the heathen," he smiles, departs with the crate and, true to his word, is back in two days.

"Watch," he commands, and they both look into the depths of the crate. It appears exactly as it had done before, but a little less deep. He

124

takes a screwdriver from his waistcoat pocket and unscrews the screws holding the planks in place at the floor of the crate. They lift with ease, revealing a black cavity, clearly coated with tar, and indeed the under surfaces of the upper boards are also black.

"I took the liberty of retrieving the canvas from Mme Deschambres." He produces a large roll wrapped in linen and on top with newspaper. "So now, let us with enormous care fold the canvas in half. We will need to make the fold extremely slowly." And with great care, they made the fold and only a minute quantity of the paint cracked. They triumphantly lower the canvas into the cavity, and he rapidly screws the top boards back into place.

Tom then repacks the medicines into the crate and soon has filled the case to the top.

"I will have to leave some things out; maybe the pamphlets can stay. I will try to memorise their contents before I leave."

"I will leave you now. I am minded that it was my money that paid for the picture, so I need to discuss with you whether you agree that officially the painting is mine. But of course, I would want to share a part of the proceedings, should I ever wish to sell it."

"Absolutely," Tom agrees.

He holds his hand out to Tom and gives him a warm shake.

"I wish you well with the jungle and the great doctor. Send me a letter or two, if you are able. I will be sad not to see you for so long a period," and to Tom's utter incredulity, a tear appears in both his eyes. *My dear, dear friend really will miss me. I will value those tears over the months to come.* Tom gives him a warm embrace. And then he is gone.

The next few days are a marvel of activity. The Reverend Farquhar confirms that his references are in order and arranges for the packing case to be taken from Wimpole Street to the ship in the Bristol Docks. Tom himself brings a trunk designed for the tropics and packed within it the clothing that he hopes will be suitable. But the reality is that he has no idea what that should be. He says farewell to no one as he knows that it is important that he should apparently 'disappear'. He arranges a seat in a train, leaving early morning from Paddington in a first-class carriage to Bristol.

On the day of his departure, early in the morning at around 8.30, he asks Georgiana to get a hansom to take his trunk to Marylebone station, and await him there. He looks out of the edge of the window, keeping himself mostly hidden behind the curtain, and sees the usual two men across the street, pretending to be fascinated by the railings of a house on the other side of the street. They watch the departure of the trunk with some apparent unease but, after a hurried conversation, decide not to follow it, as they had anticipated. Charles and Tom had discussed the strategy for the deception of his watchers, and they had agreed that it was most unlikely that they would be interested in his trunk.

Charles has arranged for another hansom driver of his acquaintance to arrive at my house at nine o'clock. Tom tells the cabbie in a loud voice to take him to St Pancras station.

As he is boarding the cab, he watches them out of the corner of his eye as they indulge in urgent conversation. One of them darts off, presumably to tell the boss of the development of events and his likely destination, while the other desperately tries to hail a passing hansom. Charles has already briefed his hansom driver that he is being followed by vandals, and he sets off at a cracking pace. Being unsuccessful in hailing another cab, my other watcher starts to run after our cab. We had however anticipated this turn of events, and as he approaches the junction of new Cavendish Street, my burly friend is awaiting him. A sudden movement of a foot is all that is needed to send their watcher sprawling into the road, and a passing Growler only just misses beheading him. Charles disappears into the crowd and by the time the man has collected his senses, they are long gone.

When they are out of earshot and approaching the Marylebone Road, Tom tells his driver to turn left towards Marylebone station, where they collect his trunk and drive back to Paddington station. They drive onto the platform, where the train has already taken up steam, and Tom barely has time for the porter to help him and his trunk aboard the carriage before he feels the wheels turning and they are gliding out of the station. Tom sinks back into his seat and looks around. The carriage is not full, most of the seats being occupied by single men, some of whom look like travelling salesmen, with their small cases containing their wares. There is just the one family, away in the far corner. To his great relief, no one appears at all interested in him nor does anyone appear to want conversation. Tom opens the day's Times. The headlines are full of stories of Russian advances and the general weakness of their supposed allies, the Ottomans. The first leader is on the need for the British and the French to send large forces to prevent Nicholas' troops from overwhelming the Turks. He feels a great surge of relief that he will be leaving all this conflict for the peaceful world of Africa. He looks out of the carriage window at the bleak winter countryside, as the first drops of rain spatter the glass. Already, he can feel the nourishing warmth of the African sun and believes that he has made a great and bold decision for his life.

They stopped at Reading Station and the only passenger to enter his carriage is a young woman. He thinks with much regret of his leaving behind of his dearest Amelie, and wonders whether he will ever see her again. At midday, they arrive at Swindon station, where he buys a surprisingly tasty meat pie from a stall on the platform, and eventually they arrive at Bristol in the late afternoon. A porter helps him to a hansom, which transports him and his trunk to the docks.

The Aurora is as large and as handsome a vessel as he could have hoped for and the captain a bluff Bristolian with a west-country burr in his speech. His medicine chest is carried on board by two muscled sailors and is well-stored in the hold, surrounded by crates full of vast numbers of beads, toys, and clothing, apparently to be used to barter with the Africans. He is given a cabin, small but well furnished, with a narrow bed, a basin for washing and shaving, a chest for his clothes, and most surprisingly, a writing table. The captain tells him that the previous occupant had been a writer (this said with a hint of scorn), who had insisted on the table, and that no one had bothered to take it away.

They set sail on the high tide the following morning and travelled down the Channel and past the island of Lundy with its vast colonies of strange-looking birds called puffins, the like of which he has never seen before. After that, they round the part of France, appropriately named Finisterre, and sail southwards. Slowly, the temperatures begin to climb until they reach the Bay of Biscay, where they encounter brisk winds and rough seas. He spends much time on his bunk, not being by any means a natural sailor. However, they have to suffer no real storms, and after many days, they pull into the wide mouth of the Tagus river. They stay but a few days in Lisbon, to exchange fine English cloth and wool for their excellent port wine and spices. Lisbon seems to him to be a fine modern city, full of delightfully friendly people, and he is sad not to spend longer.

They sail interminably southwards. Many fine books have been written on the pleasures of life on board ship. He fails to find it so. Frankly, when the weather is fine, the days pass in much tedium, and when the days are stormy, he is in his bunk, wishing that his life is ended. There is after all absolutely nothing to see for day after day, although occasionally the tedium is relieved by our vessel being accompanied by shoals of flying fish.

Once in a while, they see another ship in the distance. A week after leaving Lisbon, they pass within sight of the Canary Islands but do not land there. They approach the equator and the sun becomes a great primrose furnace. Sitting on deck in the breeze is the only way to keep cool as his cabin is a cauldron. As they approach the Cape Verde islands, they are approached by a British warship, the Pride of Wessex, a vessel of the West Africa squadron. We are boarded by two officers and twenty men, who search our holds with great thoroughness, opening all the packing cases, including his medicine chest. They neither see nor suspect the secret bottom to the case.

When they hear that Tom is joining the great Dr Livingstone, they are truly respectful. In general, their merry banter cheers them all up with their jests, mainly about not being able to find enough slaves on board. Frankly, though it is good to converse with other Englishmen, as although the officers of the ship are good hardworking men, nevertheless, after a few days, they have run out of mealtime conversation.

And so, for himself, the days pass slowly as they sail now relentlessly south eastwards. To his amazement, so good is the crew's steering that they arrive at the coast of Africa, exactly opposite Loanda. Navigation is a fine science and the captain goes to some lengths one breezeless day to attempt to explain some of it to Tom when they are on deck, but he quickly loses track of the scientific niceties. They agree in a comradely way that it is fine if Tom sticks to medicine and he directs the boat.

And so, after some forty-five days at sea, they sail past a vast sandbank through the entrance into the enormous natural harbour of Loanda Bay and dock alongside the quays, where his ears are assailed by a mixture of Portuguese and other unbeknown and presumably native African tongues. It is Friday May 20th, 1854.

Chapter Fifteen
Letter from Africa, December 1854

Sesheke
Central Africa
December 1854

My dear Charles,

It is of course disgraceful that I have failed to write to you until now. You probably have thought that I will have perished under 'a hot tropic sun', but it is not so, and I am alive and mercifully well, both physically and in my spirits.

I arrived in Loanda at the end of May and set about enquiring as to the whereabouts of Dr David Livingstone. At the start, I was met with blank stares and I was beginning to think that maybe the whole thing had been a terrible hoax. After three days of increasing desperation, I encountered a Portuguese man, who lived in the town and made his living out of trading between Portugal and some of the native tribes. He had heard rumours of a missionary, who was also an explorer, and was 'advancing on Loanda' (his words! He made it sound like an approaching army), with a horde of tribesmen from the south. The next day, this was confirmed by another Portuguese resident, who said that he was only a few miles away, but that 'the man is dying, and being carried here by his natives'.

He eventually arrived on May 31st, and indeed he was as close to death as any man could possibly be. According to the trader who accompanied him, a South African named Oswell, he had had recurrent bouts of 'fever', which had progressively weakened him over the course of his journey from the Zambesi. I introduced myself to his retinue, the only word for his large party of devoted natives, and they appeared delighted that there was an English doctor to assist. When I examined him, he was in a pitiful state. He was barely conscious most of the time, just occasionally opening his eyes and looking around in confusion. He was so wasted that I could barely find a semblance of musculature on his upper limbs. His fever fluctuated and was accompanied by rigors and bouts of flooding perspiration.

I had, of course, brought quinine with me, but I had also brought in my case, on the advice of Dr Allen, a new tincture devised by a German physician Dr Carl Warburg. Dr Allen had heard that this new medicine was more effective than quinine by itself. I had questioned Allen as to its contents, and he was remarkably unable to tell me. Apparently, Dr Warburg was the only one who knew, and he was keeping the formula secret, 'so that he could profit mightily from it', as Allen put it.

I was somewhat nervous about using an untried medicine on a new patient in a foreign country, but Dr Livingstone was so ill that I felt that desperate remedies were called for. To my delight, after two days, he awoke and asked for food. He tried to get out of his bed and regrettably fell immediately to the floor, so weak was he.

By the third day, he was fully alert and began asking many questions, including, naturally, who on earth I was. When I explained, he was absolutely delighted. 'The Lord has answered my prayer'. I nearly replied that it was the Reverend Farquhar, who had responded but managed to control my effervescent wit. A tiny bird warned me not to be clever with a man who had been so unwell, and in any case, he was a Scot, and you and I know that they in general have little humour in their race (In fact, he has proved to me since, that, in his case, anyway, this is quite untrue. He is able to tell the most delightful tales and stories of his adventures with both wit and perception). He also marvelled at the bed – we had managed to procure for him a proper European-style bed with a mattress. Apparently, *he had not slept in a bed for over a year, being accustomed to sleeping on the ground, occasionally with grasses under him.*

It took him three long months to recover sufficiently for us to consider setting off back into the bush. It was a tedious time for me. Loanda (or St Paul de Loanda to give it its correct title) is a city which has seen better days, if we are to be kind. A better description would be to say that it is an advanced state of decay. There are two cathedrals, both in poor repair. There are three forts, maintained in a reasonable state by the Portuguese. Even the harbour is in a poor condition, and has become so silted up that most ships with a deep keel have to dock at the entrance on the island of Loanda and then goods are transferred to the main town along a narrow roadstead. In a south-westerly gale (and they occur commonly), the waves dash over the island and deposit large quantities of sand in the harbour.

There are few Europeans here and only a handful of English, as the Portuguese authorities insist that no other nationalities may conduct business, so my social life was poor. Eventually, on September 20th, we left the city behind, and at last I got to experience the great land of Africa. By the 28th September, we had escaped the swampy mosquito-ridden lowland marshes and climbed towards the interior of the country, passing great drifts of mica and sandstone. Cotton and coffee grew along the roadside and the markets were full of native women spinning the cotton with a spindle and distaff in the old style. The countryside was beautiful with a profusion of flowers everywhere.

After walking the road through the large local town of Kalungwembo, we took to our canoes and navigated down the Lucalla river to Massangano, where, to my astonishment, there are the ruins of an enormous iron foundry, built by a man named the Marquis of Pombal. The work at the foundry apparently was never a great success, due to the regular dying of all the European labourers, whom he had imported to instruct the natives, overwhelmed by some unpleasant tropical disease.

And talking of natives, mostly they are charming and delightful, and I am learning smatterings of a number of languages. The matter that really troubled me is that, away from the coast, slavery is still rampant. It is performed not only by white men, but also aided and abetted by some of the local chieftains. David Livingstone is determined that it should be abolished.

And speaking of the doctor, he is the most excellent of men – warm, kind-hearted and treats all men (and women) with the same courteous behaviour. Black and white are no different in his eyes, and in this respect, he is much different from the Portuguese and the few Boers, who have made their way northwards from the Southern colonies. His native bearers and workmen truly adore him and will do anything to aid his progress. He has converted most to Christianity, and everywhere we go, he holds services. He also strongly believes that speaking the word of Christ is valueless without improving the lot of the common native so to that end we have a number of traders attached to our retinue to show the natives how to buy and sell with profit. Everywhere he goes, he also educates, and he has roped me into teaching about health, disease, and European medicine, even though my knowledge of local diseases is rather minimal! So, altogether a fine man, and I feel a great privilege to be amongst his team.

This land of Africa is very fine. Sometimes its natural beauty overwhelms me. In the last few weeks, everywhere the rains have brought out not only amazing shades of the colour green, but also there are marvellous flowering shrubs and trees. Although the flora is fine, the fauna is just incredible. The largest, lions, elephants, rhinoceroses, and hippopotamuses are majestic. The smallest creatures however are prolific – and sometimes more dangerous than the big ones. I received a bite from a spider last week. The creature was no longer than the terminal digit of my thumb, yet I experienced a fiery pain that incapacitated me for an hour. The natives and David just laughed! And the ants are vicious creatures. Some are white and some black, yet all are much larger than our British species. The black ones create slaves of the white and get them to haul and push bits of nourishment into their nests. They also intermittently without any apparent warning, have orgies of eating the white ants; often just biting off a leg or head.

Two days ago, the men found an elephant, apparently feeding and alone, close to where we were passing. Normally, the men keep well away from these great creatures, who mainly travel in herds and are capable of killing many men, even though the men like to eat the meat of the elephant. But having found this animal by itself, they immediately took out their spears and, creeping through the bush, surrounded it on all sides but one. At a signal, they all ran forwards and launched their spears at close range. The animal looked, to all appearances, like a porcupine, with some fifty spears sticking from its hide. Needless to say, it became incensed and ran furiously away, towards the side that was empty of men. This side was a small cliff of some twenty feet drop and the elephant went over. It was still alive at the bottom but gravely injured, and David was persuaded to kill it with his gun. Even though he used two 2 oz bullets, the animal was still alive, and was only finished off by a third shot to the head. The men mocked David's gun, suggesting that he melt down his buckles and metallic coat buttons to form heavier bullets, and that evening he did exactly that to my surprise – the man has a never-ending range of talents and skills.

The weather now is warm but not unbearable and certainly better now that the rains have started, October and November having been unbearable in the middle of the day. Temperatures are now around eighty degrees and the cooling showers at midday are luxurious.

We have travelled far and are making rapid progress on the rain swollen Leeambye river, which soon will become the mighty Zambesi. The natives tell me that we are going to reach 'a place of great falling water' soon and are excited about it.

My medicine case is intact, and I had a look inside the compartment three nights ago. All looks well in there.

I will send this with one of our natives, who is accompanying some ivory to Loanda. He has instructions to place it in the hands of an English ship's captain. I trust that it will reach you, and please show it to my darling Amelie, even though she may not wish to recall me.

Yours affectionately,
Tom

Chapter Sixteen
Africa, January 1855

Tom

He finished his letter to Charles last week, and in some ways, wishes that he had delayed posting it until today. Nothing could have prepared him for the utter amazement of 'a place of great falling water'. The natives here give the falls the name of *Mosi oa tunya* ('smoke sounds there'), and indeed you hear the noise from afar. They arrive by boat and stop about a mile above the falls, and transfer to smaller canoes for safety. At the end, they stop at the bank and walk towards the edge. The five vast columns of vapour are visible from many miles away and darken as they rise until their summits mingle with the clouds, giving them indeed the appearance of smoke. At their bases, the waters churn and foam and the whole scene is remarkable for its beauty; the small islands dotted across the river just as it falls are covered in vegetation of all types and are a multitude of colour, with many of the trees in blossom at the time of their arrival. The enormous baobabs tower over everything, spreading their vast root-like branches heavenwards. Below them are feathery palm trees and intermingled around are trees that seem to him to appear like cedars of Lebanon, but which are not quite the same, and which the natives call *mohonono*.

Carefully, they walk out onto a strip of land and creep on their bellies to the edge. At that point, a stream of about a thousand yards in width leaps down a hundred feet and suddenly is compressed into a narrow space of some fifty feet. The seething and roaring are caused by this fall and compression, which turns the water into a seething cauldron and several of their party cannot remain from their fear and giddiness.

As one of his principles, David does not believe in giving European names to places in Africa, but has made an exception here, believing that he is the very first European to see the vision, and naming them the 'Falls of Victoria'.

After some hours of pleasurable relaxation, they set off, their departure speeded by two hippopotami, who have come to the waterside to drink. These animals are so enormous and so aggressive in nature that they have no desire to disturb them from their drink.

As they travel eastwards, they take a road to the north of the river but following its course, and they started to rise into a modest chain of hills bounding the Zambesi Valley. They are passing through the most beautiful countryside at this time, having crossed the Kafue river. The hills are covered in flowers with small villages of the *Batonga* peoples nestling into the hillsides. They cultivate manioc and vegetables around each village, leaving the intervening hillsides mostly unscathed. Clumps of baobabs and other trees are home to birds, quite unknown to me in England and of unimaginable, beauteous colours.

As they began the climb into the hills, he has started to feel unwell, and has begun to perspire freely. In the afternoon, he suffers a full rigor with the shaking overwhelming him for half an hour. He can do nothing but lie down as the oxen pulls the carriage along with himself prostrate inside. He doses himself with Dr Wharton's tincture, but to no avail. After two days, he begins to vomit, and the vomit turns bright red with blood. On the fourth day, he loses consciousness for the whole day, but wakes on the fifth morning, feeling a little better. He has lost much weight and his limbs feel like jelly. Despite his temporary recovery by the following day, he is again extremely ill and catches a little conversation, hearing the voice of David talking to Oswell,

"This is not malaria, as there has been no response to the quinine. I fear something more serious."

Despite the mental confusion caused by his illness, he realises that he might be about to die. He is so amazed by the suddenness of it all. One day, he is crawling towards the edge of a great waterfall and then suddenly his life appears in danger from an unknown and unrecognised tropical illness. Amid a vast sadness that he might never see England, Charles or Amelie again, he suddenly remembers the painting, which he has temporarily forgotten for the last weeks in the excitement of the travelling and the sight of the falls. He has no idea what he should do. Clearly, if his crate of medicines is examined, it is possible that someone might realise that there is a false compartment. Alternatively, when empty, it might simply be burnt or abandoned in the bush. In his confused and ill state, he is unable to contemplate what might be required but he knows that some action is necessary. But what could that action be? In the heat and humidity of the African bush, his picture will disintegrate rapidly. And there is no safe way for him to get it back to Charles in England. He lets the problem sit in his mind as he drifts in and out of sleep, but no easy solution occurs to him.

And then suddenly, a possible solution – towards the evening of his eighth day of illness, he realises that they had passed a side road and David had pointed out that it was the road to a village called Caanga, where he said that there was an abandoned mica mine. Thinking about it, he realises that the inside of a mine and particularly a mine of mica, will be a cool and dry place with the mica absorbing humidity from the air, and maybe therefore a wonderful place to preserve his picture. But would he have the strength to walk down the road?

By good fortune, they have made the camp for the night just a few yards on, and he is able to rise painfully to his feet and sip some soup. After a while, he hears nothing but the regular breathing and snoring of the men in their sleep. He is aided by a full moon, bathing the ground in a strong glare and can see well without the need of a torch. He rises, slowly emptying his crate of medicines and removing the screws from its base. He extracts the canvas, which has been kept apparently in perfect condition. He walks slowly back to the side road and wanders down, having to stop and rest regularly. The entrance to the mine is simple to find, lying at the side of the road mercifully within a few yards of the main road – he would have not had enough energy for a walk of any length. There are no signs of the village, which must be further on down the road. Great sheets of mica lay abandoned all around the entrance, which have partly caved in and is reduced to around three feet in height. He enters on his hands and knees in some trepidation as to what he might find inside, fearing the presence of some vicious wild animal but there are no sounds from within. He can only see a few yards from the entrance but high up on the right side, he can just make out a small ledge, and realises that this will be a good place for the canvas. It will not be readily visible from a casual glance, yet not totally lost to a searcher. Tom places the canvas carefully up on the ledge, still wrapped in its linen protection, and leaves the mine entrance.

He walks slowly back to camp, feeling exhausted and hardly able to drag his legs along. Eventually, just as day was breaking, he manages to wrap myself, shivering and feverish into his rug and falls into a long deep sleep. He wakes to find David besides him, looking anxious. He knows from his face that his end is nigh. Tom asks him for a pen and paper and writes a last letter to Charles, asking David to post it to England, should he die. And having written, he lay back and allows sleep to take him away from the pain of his body.

Chapter Seventeen
London, May 2007

Darius' day has started unremarkably. He has staggered from his bed and attacks the orange juice. He has approached the cafetiere with inordinate care, his relationship with the whole business of coffee making being that of a priest worshipping at the high altar of caffeine. For him, the concept of a coffee-less life is simply impossible. As he slowly becomes a sentient being and glances through the glass of the window of his kitchen, he notices the threat of rain hanging over his suburban existence. He dresses and takes a little more trouble than usual, as he remembers the departmental secretary's words as he had left wrought the previous day.

"There's a young lady coming to see you tomorrow morning at 10 o'clock. She would not tell me what it was about."

"Who is she?" he had asked.

"No idea. I had rather assumed that she knew you. Her name is Judy St John James."

"Unless early-onset dementia is attacking me, that name rings not a bell. What does she look like?"

"Rather pretty," and with that no further words are spoken as the Head of Department arrives. He leaves smartly so that he cannot quiz him on the progress of his thesis. He will have only two choices – be honest and tell him of his lamentable lack of progress – or lie. To be frank, he is not really interested in the subject. He has chosen it for him. The thought now of 'Finding the real Medicis in Botticellis paintings' fills him with early morning gloom.

Rather surprisingly, the previous month, a journalist from the art pages of The Guardian had heard of the title of his thesis and visited him, asking what were to him a number of rather inane questions. Subsequently, he had indeed written a small article in the Arts pages of the Guardian about myself and my work. In fact, his article had made rather a play on my mentioning that there might be a 'missing Botticelli', a speculation made many years earlier by Howard Horne, and mostly forgotten over the subsequent generations of art historians. He had assumed that Darius' work, which mainly focussed on the Medicis, was what he was interested in. It appears that that was not so, and he has felt that the sensationalist element of mystery would be more of interest to the band of true socialists who continue to read the paper.

To show some respect to the impending arrival of Miss pretty Judy St John James, he dons a clean pair of jeans, boat shoes, and a check shirt that is unusually both clean and ironed, topped off by a casual linen jacket. He travels into the Strand to await her somewhat mysterious visit. Frankly, my office at the Courtauld is not a place where I would normally entertain. It is true that there is a desk of a reasonable size. Otherwise, everything about the office spells mediocrity. He is not really a home-proud individual but the lack of any wall-covering picture in a site where many of the walls are covered in Impressionist art worth millions, does cause me some sadness. There are two chairs; both remind me of my school days.

She is punctual. In the world of art, that strikes me as unusual. Fortunately for my self-esteem, it appears that my brain is also still working as I have definitely never met her before. It is true that she is pretty in a rather conventional way, with her mid-brown shoulder-length hair and neat figure. She is dressed informally in a rather fine tawny-hued sweater and light cotton trousers. We engage in a few pleasantries and then she comes to the point.

"Mr Bukhari, I am here because I read an article about your work in the Guardian last week," and there he was thinking that it is his looks or personality.

"Aha," he mutters as noncommittedly as he can.

"It appeared from the article that you have an interest in the times of Botticelli and the Medicis."

"Indeed," is his somewhat crisp response.

"I need your help with the uncovering of a mystery from the time of Queen Victoria." Inwardly, he groans – she is clearly a sensation-seeker. It turns out that this assumption is the first of many mistakes that he is to make that morning.

"Miss James, I am as you rightly said, an expert in late 15th century Florentine renaissance paintings. I know nothing of the Victorian times, except that there were people who were named later as pre-Raphaelites. I do have a colleague who specialises in that era. Perhaps you would wish his advice." Needless to say, he says those words with a heavy heart. What normal man would wish to give up the opportunity to sit opposite a pretty girl?

"Oh, no. you are the right person." His heart lifts to the Gods of the atheists in a small litany of non-religious praise.

"Please allow me to tell you the story and to show you some documents." He manages to remain silent and allows her story to emerge.

"My beloved grandmother died last year, and since my parents are not really concerned with matters of heredity, they asked me at her funeral to go through the contents of her apartment. My grandmother Elsie was aged 87 at her death and my favourite person in the whole world. She was sharp as a button, even to the end, although she could hardly move from the rheumatoid arthritis that deformed her joints. She had lived in a large flat in Clarewood Court in Crawford Street for many years with a lady who was her maid and general help and, for a while, my Nanny when I was little. As you will know, Crawford Street is in Marylebone, close to the station. The block of flats was built in Victorian times and had been in my family's possession from the beginning. In fact, I now live there myself as it is handy for the city, where I work. The original occupant was named Charles St John James, Viscount Dearly, and after his untimely death, lived in by generations of us St John James."

He decides to interrupt the flow at that moment by interjecting: "Untimely…"

But the lady is not for turning, as our recently ousted and much blessed Prime Minister Margaret would have said.

"I will come to that shortly," Miss James tells him, in fact with a gesture not unlike the aforementioned great leaderene (as the magnificent but somewhat trying Norman St John Stevas named her). He is left feeling six inches high and determined to try to keep his silence.

"My grandmother had many crates of papers, as she was a great hoarder It has taken me some nine months of intermittent work to go through them all. I say intermittent as, at around the time of my grandmother's death, I acquired a job at Rothschild's in the city of London, and I have had only limited time to go through the papers as they work you hard these days in banking."

He nods as sympathetically as he can, while trying to contain his envy at the undoubtedly vast salary that the poor lass has to force herself to spend.

"Despite her hoarding, she had managed to sort the papers into historically ordered crates, and I had left the crate labelled 'Mid-Victorian' to the end. It was full of letters and other paraphernalia, and it was late one Sunday afternoon when I came across a bundle labelled 'Charles, Viscount Dearly 1820–1855'. I was struck of course immediately by the shortness of his life, and assumed that his truncated existence was a result of infectious disease or even more likely death at sword point at the Siege of Sevastopol. Isn't that what you would have thought, Mr Bukhari?"

He is suddenly aware that he has been asked a question and is in the hideous position of not having been listening properly. He had heard 'Sevastopol', and all he can say was a rather lame, "Crimean War."

A crushing Thatcherite look wings his way.

"Well, we would have been wrong, Mr Bukhari. Inordinately wrong. Viscount Charles Dearly was murdered." And from that point onwards, she has my full attention.

"And you know that because…" and he lets the words hang.

"Perhaps you would like to read this." And she leans down and lifts onto her lap a large bag, which he had managed not to notice when she had arrived. From it she produces an enormous envelope, which, from the way it bulges, apparently contains many documents. She riffles through the papers and hands one to me. It is a copy of a page of The Times, dated 14th January 1855, and is in good condition, apart from a slight browning of the edges and a small tear in the upper left corner.

Viscount Murdered

The man discovered by police yesterday floating in the Thames has been discovered to be Viscount Charles Dearly, first son of Lord St James. The body was identified by the parents. Inspector Berenson of Scotland Yard told reporters that the body had been badly mutilated and had clearly been in the water for a while. There were also signs that the viscount had been tortured prior to death, although the Inspector would give no details. The police are treating the case as one of murder. Apparently, a gangland killing is suspected, although there were no indications that Viscount Dearly had had any previous dealings with any disreputable persons. The case remains a mystery.

He carefully returns the fragile page to her, not quite knowing what to say, nor indeed where all this is going and what relevance it might have to himself.

"You may wonder what this has to do with you and me, Mr Bukhari." He gives what he hopes is a wry intelligent grin, but which probably looks simply foolish.

"The case was apparently never solved, but it must have been partly because Charles Dearly's parents failed for some reason to help the police by handing over to them this notebook," and she produces from her bag of magic paperwork, a tawny-coloured leatherbound book, which she passes to him. He opens it and can see at once that it is a diary. The inscription on the opening flyleaf is

The Diary of myself, Charles St John James, starting in the Year of Our Lord 1853

"Now turn to Page 103, Mr Bukhari. It's headed 'Friday April 12th, 1853', and starts, 'Persuaded Tom to come with me'." And she sits back and grins in a slightly self-satisfied way. Despite her demeanour, he reads and becomes immersed in the young men's trip to Italy, the discovery of the paintings in the shop in the Rome, and the subsequent trips to the National Gallery. And of course, he enjoys the story of his friend Tom's romance with the lovely Madame Deschambres.

And at that point there are two pages stuck together in the diary. He looks up at Miss James.

"Just leave those pages and read on," she instructs him. He does as he is told but wonders somewhat.

But of course, when he comes to the story of Madame Deschambres' identification of the Botticelli, and maybe the missing Botticelli, he is riveted to his seat. A Botticelli, really, can it be? And he pauses and stares to heaven. She says not a word, so on he reads. He reads of the attacks on Tom by the gang members, determined to steal the paintings and the plan hatched by Tom to disappear to join Livingstone in Africa. He reads of their cunning plan to conceal the canvas in a false bottomed crate, and his journey to Bristol. And then the diary changes tack and speaks of many other matters. After a few pages, it comes to;

'December 28th, 1854. Received a marvellous letter from Tom in central Africa. He is having a great time and I rejoice for him'.

And it then returns to less interesting matters of the viscount's life. He looks up to see Miss James proffering some pieces of paper.

"You have arrived at the point where he receives the first letter. It is here."

"The first?" he queries.

"Oh yes. There is another."

He read the letter and is entranced with his descriptions of Africa and his travels – but realises that there is no mention of the painting. And then the last entry is dated January 2nd, 1855, and he reads: 'The New Year has come and with it bad things. Those evil men are still after Tom, and they seem convinced that I know where he is. They have threatened to come and get the information of his whereabouts from me by force, if need be. I shall remain faithful to his secret whatever happens. After all, what in these days is more important than honour and friendship?'

And the pages thereafter remain completely empty. And indeed, sad for their emptiness. And then he remembers that she has said that there is 'another'.

He looks up in expectation, but she is holding nothing.

"Mr Bukhari. Before I give you the last letter from Dr Thomas Fielding, I need to do two things. Firstly, it is possible that we are getting close to finding a treasure. We need to have a discussion about secrecy and the terms of what we may be about to be embarking upon."

"Indeed, Miss James, indeed. I assume that you have been thinking about this matter for a while and may have come to a strategy. For myself, I can hardly grasp the enormity of all of this. So perhaps you should speak first."

"In fact, Mr Bukhari, we have been talking a long while. It is lunchtime and I would like to eat. Do you have a tie?"

"A tie," he repeats inanely, while he desperately thinks of what to do.

"Yes, one of those thin things that go around a man's neck. We are going to a place that requires men to wear a tie." His mind spins. Needless to say, he has no tie with him. Where could he get a tie? The only other man that he knows to be in the building is his boss, whom he had seen entering at the same time as himself earlier in the morning. But can he ask…?

He looks at her. He can. Darius knocks on his door.

"Come," says Professor Sir James Marcus. He enters metaphorically on his knees.

"I wondered, sir…" he stammers. Sir Jameslooks at him incredulously.

"Yes, lad, spit it out."

"I wondered, Sir James, whether I could borrow your tie."

"My tie? My tie?" Across his eyes flash a public health advertisement that he has heard the day before for the prevention of strokes. Sir James' face has turned a nasty purple colour. There is a long pause.

And then the old man's face crinkles, and he says, "Of course, you may, my boy. I assume that it is to do with that pretty girl who has been sitting in your office all morning."

How could he possibly have known that? he wonders. He had looked at Darius and had sussed him immediately.

"My secretary, of course keeps me up to date with the important matters of art history going on in the department. And of course, a few other things." He carefully removes his tie from around his neck, folds it and passes it to Darius.

"Thank you so much, sir." And just as he is opening the door to leave, tie clutched in his hand, he throws out.

"Have a good lunch. Simpson's or Rules?"

"I have no idea, sir."

"Simpson's better, really. Especially if you are having an intimate talk. Tables far too close at Rules. Anyway, hope she's paying. Let me know when you bring the tie back. I will be slumming it in the canteen." And Sir James chuckles quietly as Darius creeps meekly out and hurries back to Miss James, slipping the tie around his neck as he goes. By a stroke of good luck, it matches rather well with his shirt and jacket, and he clearly comes out OK after her up-and-down look has surveyed him.

"We are off to Simpson's," she announces. "You will manage to make it on foot?"

He really thinks that is a somewhat unnecessary snipe in view of the extremely short distance between the Courtauld and the restaurant. But she softens it with, "The treat's on me. I know about your poverty-stricken academics." She is right, of course, and he finds himself breathing more easily.

They enter the revolving doors and are immediately surrounded by subservient lackeys. For a moment, he imagines that his eminence in culinary circles has at last been recognised, until he notices that all the attention is for her.

"Would Your Ladyship like a drink first or can I escort you to your table?"

'Her ladyship?' Has he heard correctly? It appears that there is a small matter here of which he has not been informed. He waits until they are seated in the large cuboid room, where the tablecloth is stunningly white, the glasses iridescent and the cutlery gleaming. He considers how to word the question.

"You seem well known here," he notes carefully. Clearly, his sad small phrase is pathetically circuitous.

"Indeed," is the reply. Pithy and unhelpful, you may think.

The head waiter, not as subservient as the others, he notices, approaches.

"The beef, madam?" he intones.

"Of course, George. And maybe my guest will join me too?" she turns enquiringly to him. What can he say?

"Thank you," are the words that emerge. His intended vegetarian stance will have to keep for one further week.

"And a bottle of the Crozes Hermitage, please George."

"Such a shame to eat fine roast beef without a Rhone wine, don't you think, Mr Bukhari?" What can he say?

"Yes, I like it here," she continues. "Are you a chess player?" she wonders in the same breath. Every sentence now appears to come with a mystery. He is starting to feel a tightness in his chest. What on earth has chess to do with anything?

"Very poor," he replies. "My father found my chess, like much of my life, disappointing."

"Really?" she replies, clearly a little surprised, "Simpson's is the home of English chess. But is he not proud that you are a lecturer at the Courtauld? Surely that would be a fine achievement for his son?"

"Regrettably not. He wanted me to be expert in mathematics or music, and preferably both. I failed at both." She laughs.

"Our parents, our parents." And she smiles quite graciously at him. The meat arrives, covered in the most beautiful silver server. When the chef raises the lid, he is confronted by the most enormous piece of beef that he has ever clapped his eyes upon. Two enormous slices are cut from it and placed on a white plate, followed by a vast Yorkshire pudding, roast potatoes, parsnips, and the lot is topped with a generous slug of rich brown gravy. He turns down the cabbage. Their glasses are charged, and she proposes a toast.

"To our adventure." He looks nonplussed.

"Oh yes, Mr Bukhari. I can't possibly go to the interior of Africa by myself."

"The interior of Africa? And WE are going there?" He trusts that his voice demonstrates serious alarm. He tries and fails to keep the loud alarm therein, however from diners at our neighbouring table, both of whom stop, with forks raised midway to their mouths, whilst they gaze at him in alarm.

"Oh yes, Mr Bukhari, for sure." The beef on his plate suddenly turns to Rhino flesh.

"And would you like to know why we are sitting in this particular room, Mr Bukhari?" He feels a desperate sinking feeling. This whole morning is becoming completely out of his control, as if he is on the high seas in a small boat and she is the great West Wind. He is being manipulated by a powerful good-looking woman and feels absolutely hopeless,

"Not really," he replies lamely.

"Oh, come now, be a good sport, Mr Bukhari," she mocks him with her nice eyes. He capitulates.

"Why are we in this room?" he asks, trying to be a 'good sport' and summons enthusiasm to my words. She does not reply but hands him back the diary and opens it at the point where the pages are stuck together. She deftly separates the pages, and suddenly he is reading Tom's account to Charles of the evening when he had brought Mrs Deschambres here to this very room on that night over one hundred and fifty years ago.

149

"So, not a coincidence then," he looks at her carefully.

"Indeed not, Mr Bukhari. And incidentally, may I call you Darius? You may call me Judy."

"Not Your Ladyship?"

"Oh no, I absolutely forbid it." She puts down her knife and fork, stretches her right hand over and lays it delicately on his left, mercifully the fork being inactive at that split second. He is, needless to say, charmed. He can't help but notice also that she is looking at him with some intensity.

She raises her glass, by now already only one third full of the Crozes Hermitage, and keeping her eyes on mine, says, "To our adventure."

They clink glasses, and in doing so, he acknowledges that there are forces at work in this room that are stronger than his.

At last, their plates are empty, and she reaches into the cavern of her bag and lays a letter on the table beside her.

"Darius, I am about to confide in you. I have chosen you for two reasons. Firstly, I read a brief article about you and your expertise on Botticelli in the Guardian. And secondly, within that article appeared a reference to a 'missing Botticelli', I had not been taking this diary and this letter that you are about to read seriously. I had not thought that this was anything more than a game played by two young mid-Victorian men. And then suddenly, it all appeared possible and I knew that I needed help. I fear that I know little of art and the world of art. I do, of course, know about you, however, Darius." And she grins.

He knows that another surprise is coming and tried to prepare himself for it – to no avail, as it transpired. He plunges into the icy lake of her superior knowledge.

"What do you know of me?" She grins, and suddenly for some inexplicable reason, he has a vision of Alice's enormous ginger cat.

"Darius, I had to be careful. I was about to entrust to you a vast and complex secret and possibly make you a rich man. I had to be certain that you had led a trustworthy life and that you were a person of high morality."

"And you discovered…?"

"That this was so. A private detective has been through your life with a toothcomb – your background, your lineage, your schooling, your academic life. Everything."

"And I am, OK?"

"Oh yes – more than OK. You appear as unblemished as a smooth pebble in a stream," she laughs. "And I loved the story of your parents' meeting – such pure romance. Your mother must have been in heaven."

"I think that both my parents were. They still love each other greatly."

"So, I am now going to show you two letters," and she passes him the first, apparently from the great Dr David Livingstone.

To: The Reverend Roderick Farquhar.
London Missionary Society
Chandos Street
London
January 12th, 1855
From: Shupanga, Mozambique

My dear Roderick,

I write with great sadness in my heart to tell you of the death of Dr Thomas Fielding. Tom died a week back of an Unknown fever (not malaria). He became ill rapidly over the course of a week and everything that I tried was to no avail.

He had been a marvellous colleague and indeed saved my life when he arrived at Loanda. His care and attention to myself at that time was meticulous. As I recovered, I appreciated the excellence of both his medicine and of his caring spirit. Everyone here on our travels had come really to love him over the weeks for the strength of his personality and the skills of his medical care.

Please give my heartfelt condolences to his parents, who had reared such a fine young Christian man. He is buried in a simple grave on the road near the joining of the Kafue river and the Zambesi.

May God preserve his soul.

David.

PS I attach a letter that Tom wrote and sealed with some care shortly before his death. You will see that it is addressed to Viscount Charles Dearly. Please forward it to himself. I have, of course, not opened it myself and expect that you will not wish to do so yourself.

He reads the letter and considers the matter. Unless the other letter throws light on their missing painting, it rather looks to him as if they had reached the end of a cul-de-sac. It turns out that this is not the end of the story, however.

"There was also this other letter in the bundle that I found," she tells him. "It was unopened, as were some of the other later letters to Charles. I can only assume that his parents did not feel interested in their contents. Either that or maybe they were so grief stricken that they could not bring themselves to address post-mortem matters. I cannot find any mention of him in the parents' letters after that time, so they clearly found the whole business extraordinarily painful, as he was clearly a much-beloved son."

"And there were no obituaries?" he asks.

"Just a brief one in the Times. It contained little of note, apart from referring to his poetry."

"And Tom's letter?" he asks.

For the final time, she delves into her bag.

Chapter Eighteen

The Proposition London, May 2007

Private and Confidential
The banks of the Kafue
January 3rd, 1855

Dear Charles,

I can barely raise the pen to write so this letter will be brief. My death is imminent, although David will not admit it to me.

Your canvas is inside the entrance to an abandoned mica mine high up on a ledge on the right. The mine is on a side road to the right as we were passing. The road – it's just a track, really – apparently leads to a village called Caanga.

Your friend,
Tom.

To look at a man's last words from down the ages is a sobering event. Darius suspects that they both feel Tom's agonal moments in their separate ways as he slipped from the globe, far away in Africa from his loved ones and his home. And we share a sadness for his parents, who raised him up, had seen him rise towards the peak of his profession, yet not achieve any definite pinnacle. Their son, dead from an infection, far, far away from them. She gently picks the letter up and returns it with some delicacy to her bag.

"I hope now that you have an idea of the proposition that I am about to put to you." Her mood is appropriately sober. He is silent and turns away from her in order to gather his thoughts and not to be confused by minor details, such as the warmth of her eyes and other distractions.

Thinking matters through, he feels that he needs to have a pre-emptive strategic approach to dealing with her rather well-signalled upcoming proposal. Maybe based in a similar way to the wondrous castle that he had seen the previous year at Carcassonne in southern France, with its outer defensive wall, then a gap and then an inner wall just as high and strong. He will reserve his second line of defences for later, just in case his first line is overrun. He carefully considers the matter in hand.

"It seems to me that before we venture off on some wild African painting- chase that we have much work to do. Firstly, I have no idea what we might be looking for. The description of Mrs Deschambres' excitement is not enough for me. I need to see some hard evidence. Secondly, I have not a clue as to where we might start searching. I have, of course, heard of Livingstone. I might be able to locate the Victoria Falls on a map if I was lucky, but as for knowing these other names – Kafue, Caanga and the others – I am lost. My knowledge of European geography is trivial. Africa is simply one vast forest to me." And he finishes there. He has plenty more personal objections but that will do for a start, I felt. For example, his enormous dislike of entering an aeroplane, let alone of getting his feet wet, are perhaps matters for later.

"Darius, the reason that I am talking to you is that I need your help. Your objections sound totally reasonable to me and I hope that we can work together to sort these matters out." Just as his resolve is hardening and he is steeling himself, she undermines his resistance with an utterly reasonable approach. What an annoying woman. His thoughts strangely become more positive.

"I would be foolish if I was not to admit that the possibility of finding a missing painting by Botticelli would be the pinnacle of my professional career, let alone what it would do to my personal feelings," he admits. He is having to be careful, as the second glass of the Cotes du Rhone is clouding both his judgement and probably his speech.

"I suspect that we should start with some sort of independent corroboration of what they picked up in that junk shop in Rome," he says, watching the red liquid shimmer on the inside of his glass.

She is shocked. "You cannot doubt…" and she trails off, seeing some determination on his face.

"I most certainly can. All we have here are a few lines written by two men with no background in art, let alone in the art of 15th century Florence."

"What should we do?" she asks. He rather likes the meeker version that he is seeing now.

"We start at the National Gallery. There should be records. Both Mme Deschambres and Mr Crampton should have at least made some notes of their meetings, and Mme Deschambres, who had the canvas in her hands for some hours, should have made a few pages of observations and conclusions. And these will be somewhere in the archives of the gallery. The challenge will be finding them." She nods.

"And then of course it will be interesting to see what the gallery did when the picture and Dr Fielding both disappeared. Nowadays, we could have put out an Interpol warrant, but in the 19th century, they were probably pretty powerless. But we shall see."

"So, we need to start at the National Gallery?" she observes. "Will we need help getting to the archives or can you do it?"

"Oh, I can easily get access there," he says boastfully. He has some wandering thoughts, questioning exactly how much access he can really get to the archives of the National Gallery, and whether the assistance of his boss may help to oil the wheels. He may have to tell him a part, or more than a part, of the story. But to do that can complicate matters.

And on that note, they part and he wanders back to his rooms, where he now sits motionless in the corner of his room, watching the vernal rain hissing against the glass and knowing that his life is to be changed in a way that he cannot have ever imagined, but changed it will be.

Chapter Nineteen
Inside the National Gallery, London

Darius

"It is not clear to me exactly how I can help you," the voice, sibilant, disinterested, with the arrogant tone of public school, Oxford, and art history in particular, courses unpleasantly down the telephone line. Darius would feel discouraged, had it not been that Sir Roger Court is known to be like this with everyone.

"I need access to notated records from September 1853 about the authentication of a Botticelli, brought to the gallery by Dr Thomas Fielding and Viscount Dearly, and inspected by Amelie Deschambres and Justin Crampton."

A long silence, then, "Well, we could provide them, I suppose. But why should we?"

What he wants to say is. 'Because I know where the painting is', but he has no intention of letting the miserable old sod have his curiosity aroused. Also, Sir Roger is known as a great gossip and the whole of London will know within a few hours.

"For my thesis, sir. I believe that you know that I am writing about Medici faces in early Florentine renaissance art, and I need to know what Mrs Deschambres had written about this particular Botticelli," he lies smoothly enough, he hopes.

Another silence, and: "Yes, I saw Simpson's article about you in the Grauniad. What an idiot that man is." A pause. "All right. Speak to my secretary. Come on Friday and we will have the notes ready for you."

"And I wish to bring my research assistant with me."

"Of course not. This is not Victoria station, you know. Anyway, who is he? Do I know him?" He knows he has him, the curious old goat.

"Lady Judith St John James." You can hear his interest crackling down the wires.

"Not the daughter of William?"

"I have no idea of the exact ancestry, Sir Roger."

"Well of course she is. He's on the Arts Funding committee with me. Splendid chap. Was at Harrow with me. Year below, of course."

"Of course," he mutters, easing the conversation along.

"Well, of course you must bring her. We will make a definite appointment now. Friday at 10am. and I will of course be there myself, as I would want to facilitate..." A short pause, "...your research." So much for his boast to Her Ladyship about his ease of gaining access to the gallery, when the mere mention of her name opens the door wide.

And the next Friday promptly at 10am, there they are. As his hand approaches the tall black door to the left of the main gallery steps to ring the bell, the door magically and majestically opens with a smooth and regular evenness. Not a human can be seen through the open doors, but when they pass through and approach a short flight of marble stairs, an apparently disembodied voice calls out, "Over here on your left."

And indeed, there is a glass sliding window, and behind, a large uniformed man with a peeked cap and a smile.

"Welcome to the gallery. Please pass me photo ID, and I will prepare temporary passes for you both. Sir Roger will be down – never known him come and greet anyone below the rank of viscount before – must be Her Ladyship here."

Darius thanks him viciously under his breath. Her Madamship sniggers, unbecomingly, he thinks. He is just about to tell her so when a simpering voice says, "Judith. How is my lovely goddaughter?"

So, not only daddy the year below at Harrow, but she is his goddaughter as well. Will his humiliation ever end? Apparently not for a while, as he initially ignores Darius while he escorts her. Darius follows meekly as they walk along the corridor and enter a pair of tall wooden double doors, chatting away about matters to which he is not privy. The doors have opened into an enormous room, set out as a library, and filled throughout its space with immensely tall racks, each rack interdigitated with wide mahogany tables clearly set out for reading with chairs along their length. They are ushered to the nearest table, on which is placed a large cushion. Darius looks at the clearly misplaced cushion, moves forward, and is about to place it on the seat for Judy to seat herself upon, when the cushion is grabbed roughly from him by his Harrowship.

"Bukhari, that is what you put our papers on when you read them, so that they are not damaged by the table. It is not for backsides." Darius' humiliation is complete.

They sit at the table. Sir Roger has eventually departed, leaving behind a research fellow, whose task appears to be to watch their every movement. They work their way through the documents, and at last he finds it, hidden amongst notes from *the Diaries of the Curators of the National Gallery*, volume two.

September 29th, 1853. Summoned to his office by Mr Crampton. On his desk scrolled out, is a painting in tempera on canvas. To my eye (and confirmed by Mr Crampton), it appears to have all the hallmarks of a painting by Sandro Botticelli. We briefly discussed whether it might be a Filipino Lippi, and indeed it is possible that some of the painting may also be his work, as sometimes they collaborated in the workshop. The painting is an Adoration of the Magi. Neither I nor Mr Crampton had seen it before, although it is of course known that Botticelli painted at least five other Adorations of the Magi, each however being known to be in existence this day.

Unfortunately, the two gentlemen, a Dr Fielding and a Viscount Dearly, who brought the painting with them, insisted on leaving after a few minutes so I was unable to spend enough time with the painting. Not only that, but there seems to be absolutely no provenance of the painting at all. They bought it in some Trastavere antique shop from the owner's assistant, who knew nothing. Most unsatisfactory. Signed: Amelie Deschambres

They look in wonder and delight.

"So, this might be it," she says.

"Looks like it," he replies. "The dates are correct, and everything fits." They become aware that they are being overheard by Sir Roger's research assistant and become silent. He returns to his searches, and on the next page came across:

September 30ᵗʰ, 1853. This morning Viscount Dearly returned the Botticelli, for we are convinced, despite the total lack of provenance, that that is what it is. I spent some hours with it, inspecting the lines of the robes, the brushstrokes on the skin, the physical appearance of the paint and the canvas, and am convinced that this is a genuine Botticelli. Like one other of his Adorations, it is peopled with Medicis, but differently arranged from that painting. AND it also appears to contain a self-portrait, like its famous cousin in Florence. I have spent some time ensuring that it is not a copy and am convinced that this is not so.

But there is something unusual about the paintwork, suggesting possibly that it is an overpainting. I could be mistaken about that and would be only able to confirm this by accessing the paint on a tiny corner. I would not wish to do that without the consent of Mr Crampton – and of course of the owner. Signed: Amelie Deschambres

And later:

October 2ⁿᵈ, 1853. Last evening, I went on invitation to Dr Fielding's house in Wimpole Street. There, he showed me also a painting of Pope Pius 7, Niccolo Chiaramonti, tempera on canvas. The painting is probably from the late 18ᵗʰ century and is poorly executed. Signed: Amelie Deschambres

And then:

October 15th, 1853. Dr Fielding has requested that the painting is returned to his rooms in Wimpole Street and I have arranged a porter, accompanied by one of our constables to do that this afternoon. Dr Fielding is not forthcoming about what he and the viscount want to do with the painting. I have reiterated that if they wish to give it to the gallery, we would be forever in his debt. Signed: Amelie Deschambres.

And then nothing more.

They are both elated by their finds. The research assistant makes copies of the pages and they wander out onto the square, having said goodbye to Sir Roger.

They sit on a bench in the square, watching groups of tourists marching behind women walking with raised umbrellas. There seem to be vast hordes of schoolchildren for some incomprehensible reason, but they try to ignore them, attempting to focus on the enormity of what they have discovered. It certainly appears there this is indeed a missing Botticelli, and that they are on the trail. The next hurdle appears to be the short letter from the dying hand of Tom Fielding. They must locate the cave. But all they have on the location is Caanga. They have made a cursory search, but the place does not appear to exist anywhere on maps.

"We need help with the name of that village." He is looking at the pigeons, in disgust at their pathetic unruly behaviour.

"Indeed," she replies and they both sit in thought.

"Well, it must be in the southern part of Zambia, because that is where Livingstone was in his travels. And we know from his diaries that he passed to the north of the Zambesi river and in the foothills not far from the river. And we are not far from the School of Oriental and African Studies. Supposing we went there?"

This seems to him to be an odd choice. Why on earth would they go there, as the obvious place was to go to the embassy? He does notice a twinkle in her eye but fails to think about it in depth. He is to be undone rather soon for his lack of thought.

"Good thinking," he says, "But if we are going somewhere, how about the Zambian embassy?"

"I suspect that they might wonder why we were inquiring," she replies. He can see the sense in that and allows himself to be persuaded. Clearly, they want as few people as possible knowing what they are up to. So, they stroll up Tottenham Court Road, cross into Malet Street, and enter the portico of the School of Oriental and African Studies. The porter looks up, and she says to him, "The director, please."

He looks at her and realises that he has missed a trick earlier. A drop of clear thinking at last prevails.

"Don't tell me – he's your uncle/cousin/brother."

"Actually, he's my father," and at that moment, a large handsome middle-aged man appears and gives her Judyship a big hug.

"Darling, how lovely to see you. What a delightful surprise. And I was just about to go to some dreadful staff meeting." He is a well-dressed man in an expensive-looking suit with silver grey hair and an enormous smile, apparently going from ear to ear.

"Daddy, this is Darius."

"Aha, good to meet you. Has my daughter been exhausting you?"

Mercifully before Darius is required to respond, she butts in, "Daddy we need help. We want to talk to someone about the Southern Province of Zambia."

"Good gracious me, you are a continual amazement to me, Judy. Of course, it's just how your mother would be. They are both very direct." This last addressed to him with an even larger grin.

"Well that would be Dr Heather Greenbanks," he continues. "She's my lecturer in Tonga and Shona. And maybe also Ndebele, but I forget exactly. Let's find her, shall we?"

And they take the lift to the third floor and turn left down a long and frankly dreary corridor, painted probably in the 1960s, when brown was a fashionable colour for walls. The paint is now peeling, and the sporadically spaced radiators are of the old, wide type, painted into a shiny silver colour with a metallic hue. He knocks at a door marked 'H Greenbanks' and opens it, without waiting for a reply.

He wraps his arms around the middle-aged woman who appears at the doorway.

"My daughter, Judy, and a co-conspirator, Darius Bukhari."

Darius looks at him. How does he know his surname? He gives me an unsubtle wink and leaves with a cheery wave and a, "Just help them, Heather, please."

"Come, come," she beckons, and they are ushered into a large well-lit room, with not only the usual desk and chairs, but also computers with headphones and other electronic paraphernalia.

"My language laboratory," she says, with a vague wave at the room. "Now tell me what I can do for you."

"We are looking for a place in the southern Province of Zambia," Judy explains and pauses. There is no response, so she continues, "Named Caanga."

"Now why would you want to know that?" Although he realises that they are getting some suspicious-looking glances, Judy, and he have, in fact, prepared their answer.

"We are writing a thesis on David Livingstone's travels and we know that he wandered near there in 1855, but we cannot find the place on any map," she speaks so sincerely that he would have been convinced, and so clearly is the Lecturer, who relaxes somewhat.

"How marvellous; he did of course travel through the southern region of what became eventually Northern Rhodesia and is now Zambia. He travelled north of the Zambesi, if I recollect accurately, from the falls all the way to the coast at the Indian Ocean. Of course, it will be a little different now," and she gives a cut-off laugh, more a cry of derision, if Darius is honest. Judy and he look at each other. They must be missing something, as obviously it will be different now, as a hundred and fifty years have passed. When they fail to respond to her little laugh, she explains for them, the ignorami, "I was referring to the river. In 1950, they built the dam at Kariba; the river is now a vast lake at that point."

She watches them carefully. She must have understood that they have not done their research and it seems as if she again becomes a touch suspicious of them.

"The language spoken there is Citonga and the peoples are the Batonga. I am an expert on the languages of that region, but not necessarily of the geography and so may not know the names of all the small villages although I do know many. In fact, I don't know of a place called Caanga. Maybe it was submerged by the formation of the lake. Many villages were indeed destroyed at that time."

Their faces clearly show their disappointment in a possibility that they have not allowed for. It seems on the cards that their incredibly valuable painting is rotting at the bottom of a vast lake.

"But I do know who would know the village, if indeed it still exists," and she pauses, clearly enjoying the return of excitement on their faces.

"Can we meet him?" Darius blurts out.

"She lives a long way away, I fear. In Southern Zambia at a small town called Monze. Her name is Edith Wharton, and she is one of Africa's greatest social anthropologists. If the place exists, she will know it. Just go to Monze and ask where she lives. Everyone knows her. She is however very old and in poor health. You will need to hurry, or you may find her underground."

"Edith has been a friend for many years and I truly love her for her wisdom and modesty. She spent so long studying the Tonga that she fell in love with their way of life, built herself a cabin there, and has lived amongst the people since she retired. And do not think that you can call her; she doesn't do telephones!" and she grins. Slightly maliciously, Darius feels.

"If you go there, do give her my undying love." She pauses. "Now, good luck with whatever your mission is really about," and she laughs, "and come and find me when you return."

And then she adds as an afterthought, "Just like Herod asked the three wise men to return to him after they had found the baby Jesus." And again, she laughs, slightly mockingly. Why does she say that? Does she know the real nature of their mission?

They stand to leave, noting the unsubtle hint, and as they are leaving, and having thanked her, she adds, "Don't forget to ask Edith about the poisoning at the time of the building of the dam," she remarks this sentence as casually as if she were chatting over a piece of coffee gossip with a girlfriend.

"What poisoning?" he asks.

"Oh, she will tell you, no doubt." And with that, she rises and shakes their hands. And just as they are closing the door, they hear, "Oh, and remember also to ask about the massacre."

They are sensitive enough to continue with the closure of the door. They tumble out of the building in a state of shock and adjourn to a small café to recover their poise.

"That was remarkably ghastly." He looks into Judy's eyes and she can only nod. "So many questions."

"Like she must have sussed us immediately, as we hadn't thought about the lake. How did we not think of that?"

"Quiet. We are two idiots." Darius can't help but agree.

"And then what was that about the poisonings? And as for the massacre…" her voice trails off.

"Do you wonder, Darius, as to whether we are getting into some situation that might bring down much trouble on our heads?" They sit, mulling all this over. Their mulling is frankly not helped by our choice of place to drink tea. Not only is it full of students from the nearby University College, who were behaving both badly and loudly. But also, the place seems to be the preferred local spot for backgammon-playing Mediterraneans, who play their game noisily. They manage the business of dice-throwing with a remarkable degree of physical violence. Both groups clearly regard us as unwelcome outsiders. Mutually but without speech, they agree to leave. They pay and walk into Regents Park.

The trees loom over them in their meanderings, shading them with their lush oaky canopy. Their wanderings take them past an old bridge over an overgrown waterway of some sort. Tall green spiky reeds rear up out of the water, creating a merger between clumps of wet and dry. A heron stands one-leggedly, still as a post, waiting for passing food. Two swans, still brown-feathered with childish feathers drift softly under the bridge, causing no disturbance of the glassy water-top.

They find a bench, looking down to the water and then beyond to the great Palladian Nash terraces arching pinkly forward; their gentle curve majestic, showing off beeches and sycamores in front. On the water, large ugly Canada geese drift aimlessly and noisily as they argue on their querulous journeys. A pair of Egyptian geese come around the bend, more serene, statelier, pretending that they have no knowledge of the Papyrus images of their forebears. They both watch them.

"Did you know…" Darius never gets there.

"Yes," she says. He looks. A tiny twinkle.

"How did…"

"You were going to tell me about ancient Egypt." Down, down he goes. *Silence better, methinks.*

Darius thinks of the plan and is appalled about the fact that it seems as if a long trip in an aeroplane is inevitable. Does he want to do this, or can he let her go alone? If she goes alone, why would he ever see the painting or her again? And how about all that money? Of course, he doesn't know her at all. Supposing she turns out to be an unpleasant person and be difficult, he will be committed to a long, foreign, and possibly dangerous trip with an unknown stranger. He reverts to his Greek mythology and thinks on that terrible choice that beset Ulysses. Will he be stuck between a modern-day Scylla and Charybdis? Between a whirlpool and a sea monster, as he crosses the Straits of Messina, or for Darius, the Mediterranean?

She too sits, watching the peaceful setting, letting her mind drift pleasantly through options and possibilities. She knows that she is excited about the impending adventure. She has had a privileged protected upbringing so that the dangers of foreign travel never cross her mind. Also, he has been chosen with care. He doesn't know that the private agency that she had used had also performed an in-depth assessment of his personality, as well as his suitability as an art historian. She understands from their report that he has qualities of steadfastness and even temperament. What she had not considered was that she might become attached to him. No one had told her that he has a sense of humour. Nor that he has a reassuring aura of charm and confidence. What will it be like spending time alone with him, miles away in Africa? She glances at him, sitting next to her with his mind clearly concentrating hard. Maybe he is thinking about the same matters as her. Maybe not.

They both start talking at once – and both stop in embarrassment.

"You go first." Always that courtesy of his.

"I think that we should consider the things that were said, and not said, by Heather Greenbanks. For example, why did she use that analogy about the Three Wise Men? Could it be chance? It seems rather a long shot to me."

"Yes." Darius' 'yes' emerges long, drawn out, and reflective. "Was that a coincidence or does she know what we are up to? But if she knows, then why would she let us know that she knows? Unless, of course, she has been put up to it by someone, to deter us." They consider that.

"But who else knows?" she wonders.

"Well, there is your father."

"How do you know what my father knows?" she looks startled.

"Well, he knew my surname when we were introduced, but you had failed to include my surname in your introduction. Maybe his daughter had talked to him, and he in turn realised what was up, and had prewarned Dr Greenbanks?"

"I suppose that's possible." She looks crestfallen. "Unless that ghastly man from the National Gallery phoned Daddy. They were at Harrow together, you know."

"Indeed, madame." She gives him a hard look, clearly noting the brevity of his comment, and presumably the 'madame'.

"So that's one mystery," she points out, "And what was that about 'poisonings'?"

"Not a clue." he responds, having little else to contribute and allowing his attention to be drawn by a squirrel, way above their heads, clearly contemplating a daring leap to a branch on a neighbouring oak. The squirrel leaps, misses, and to Darius' relief, catches a lower branch. She follows my eyes up.

"And stop looking at squirrels, these are serious problems." He is reprimanded.

"Yes, you are right," he humbles himself. Is that a tiny grin on her lips?

"And of course, the massacre." And once more, they both lapse into silence, idly watching the few passers-by.

"I can see no solution to all of this except to go to Africa, meet this Edith Wharton, and determine whether this 'Caanga' still exists and is not under fifty foot of water. And perhaps we had better go sooner – before the old lady passes on."

He is not one for commitment in general, as his failure to marry demonstrates. Nor is he one to make decisions rapidly, so it is a surprise to him to hear the words, 'I agree,' emanating from his mouth, but he makes a last try to prevent a long journey.

"By the way, are you sure that you are the rightful owner of the picture and that it is not shared with the descendants of Tom Fielding?"

"Quite sure. You note that in his final note, Tom refers to 'your picture'. Also, there is an earlier entry in Charles' diary, just after they have bought the picture in Rome that states that, since Charles has paid for it, Tom agrees that the painting belongs to Charles."

Darius' last attempt at procrastination has failed. He falls silent and she takes this as a sign of his defeat.

"I will buy the tickets, then," she tells him. "And of course, will pay all your expenses. Could you be ready to travel next week? Will your boss give you leave at this short notice?"

"I don't think that that will be a problem. I will, of course, have to ask, but the students can all be looked after by another of my lecturer colleagues, and my post-doc can look after herself."

And so, it is agreed, sitting there as they are, on a bench in a park on a sunny afternoon.

Chapter Twenty
Zambia, June 2007

Darius

One can say that Darius has led a sheltered life. Italy is as far south as he has ventured, so Darius has little idea as to what is awaiting him in the true tropics. Perhaps he imagines dark men with strong African accents. Perhaps he imagines azure blue skies. Certainly on a purely practical level, he has totally failed to imagine the power of the heat of an African sun in the middle of the day; the wall of instant enervation robbing one of the will to move, let alone walk at speed rapidly. They have to walk from the plane to the airport building; there appear to be none of the modern corridors on wheels snaking their snouts to meet the doors of the cabin. It seems like a mile, but in reality, it might have been a hundred yards. Later, he supposes that he will laugh it off in a haughty way as the experienced man of Africa, probably bearing a *Jomo Kenyatta* switch and a solar *topi*. He ducks inside and the moment the cool air conditioning of the indoors hits him, Darius feels a mighty surge of relief.

And then out of the blue, he has a ghastly premonition that this trip is a dreadful, appalling mistake. Never will he make days of this, let alone crawling around in the bush, looking for some non-existent canvas in a non-existent mine in a non-existent village. Meanwhile, Her Ladyship somehow has managed to remain cool and collected, and purports not to notice the signs of heatstroke that he knows he is readily exuding. In the Arrivals hall, an official in uniform gives him what he takes to be a radiant smile of welcome.

He speaks: "Welcome to Zambia." His English is perfect.

"Are you English?" Darius says.

He laughs at him – a touch maliciously, Darius notices.

"Oh no, but I read English at Oxford university so I can speak your language," and then there is an ominous pause as he ends the sentence with, "…bwana."

And Darius knows that he is in deep, deep trouble. He keeps smiling as he makes Darius unpack every single item in his suitcase and examines each meticulously. Then they resume a conversation.

"Why do you want to visit our country?" as he glances through his passport.

"I am a tourist."

"No, you aren't. You are a spy for the English government." Oh my, but this is not good at all.

"Do I look like a spy?" Darius askes.

He laughs, apparently friendlily, before, "I ask the questions, Mr Bukhari." Deeper and deeper, he is sinking. It could have been funny, if it isn't so terrifyingly full of possible catastrophe. Meanwhile, her esteemed Madamship is waving cheerfully from the other side of the barrier.

"Where are you visiting?"

"Monze."

"And who are you visiting in Monze?"

"A woman named Edith Wharton." He expects little reaction but to his surprise, the official's demeanour completely changes.

"Is this an old white woman?"

"Indeed," he replies.

"Welcome to Zambia, Mr Bukhari. Friends of Edith Wharton are friends of our nation." He pauses, and Darius looks at him, nonplussed, trying to imagine what has changed.

"I am a Mutonga, Mr Bukhari. I am from the Southern province. Mrs Wharton is the Ba-mama of our tribe. She has helped our people through countless crises. She has argued for us with the colonialists, who tried to enslave us. As I said, a friend of Edith Wharton is a friend of our nation. Goodbye and have a good trip." And he is out of the Customs hall in a state of complete delight and relief. Darius finds her drinking tea in the Arrivals area.

"You were detained?"

He tells her the story.

"Marvellous," is her only comment. "We had better go to Monze and look for the famous and very elderly Edith Wharton." And so, they do. They hire a car from one of the ubiquitous hire companies. It is a Peugeot 405 in a somewhat aged state, but with a functioning air conditioning system and solid suspension, apparently the only two important things in a car on African dirt roads. They take the metalled road towards the town of Livingstone out of Lusaka. And slowly, gradually, they lose some of the trappings of the modern Africa and merge imperceptibly towards the untouched Africa, if you like, the Africa of David Livingstone. But the merging only goes so far – the animals that he sees are not there, but the heat is unchanged; the single simple fields are much larger and full of more mono-agriculture; the Baobabs are still there, extending their thin spiny, rootlike branches towards the deep cerulean sky.

Kafue is a town designed by no architect. It must have happened without any plan or rationale, although it presumably exists because of the bridge over the river Kafue, a sleepy muddy swirl in the dry season, and apparently a roaring torrent between December and March. They stop for a drink and a sandwich, cross the bridge, and look down at the Kafue river, sleepily travelling slowly through banks of stone and scrub. African children, being no different to others, are playing, screaming, and splashing water upon each other. Women dressed formally and colourfully, sit by the banks watching, waiting. He sees no crocodiles, not even a Great Enormous one to gladden the heart of Roald Dahl.

And then it is there, so small that they nearly miss it, on a stone by the side of the road, with an arrow pointing to a dirt-potted track, 'To the memory of David Livingstone'. As they travel along the track, they find themselves rising up into shallow hillsides, with scrubby bushes dotted into the arid soil. After a short while, they come to another small track, crossing their track. A large sign tells them that he passed here in 1853, but if they expected more, they are to be disappointed. There is little else to mark his passing, so they sit and admire the admittedly fine views to the south, and Darius imagines him and his retinue travelling ever eastwards.

He is walking slowly now as it is evening, and they are looking for a place to camp. Tom Fielding is in the cart, being pulled along in his semi-conscious state by the oxen. A driver is sitting high on the cart, pretending to guide them, but in truth they need no guidance as the path is well-worn. They stop and make camp. The day's rains have ceased and a beautiful African sunset lights the sky, and rapidly vanishes as the sun does its fast tropical disappearing act. Tom is within 36 hours of death and knows it through the haze of his illness, which blurs his thoughts into a miasma of confusion. David Livingstone is agitated. He has come to rely on the friendship of his charming younger alter ego, and the prospect of loss fills his thoughts. He falls to his knees and prays desperately to his God for over an hour.

"Come on," she says, bringing Darius out of his dreams, "We must get to Monze before sunset." And she is right. They need a hotel bed so that they can spend the next day learning from Edith Wharton, and in particular, finding the mysterious, apparently non-existent, 'Caanga'.

Monze is dire, a town of dusty poverty. Essentially a one-mission town with the Catholics spread through one large rather gross building, labelled 'The Mission of Christ'. Next to it is the hospital, solidly constructed many years ago but now showing peeling sun-weary plaster, spreading south from the main road. Around them are shacks and small two storey buildings, one of which announces itself as the 'Monze Hotel'. They look at each other in some trepidation, but understand that it appears as if they have little choice, unless they throw themselves on the mercies of the Catholics. They approach the door, which is suddenly thrown open by a beaming colourful black woman of medium height and roly-poly dimensions.

"Welcome, welcome, o weary travellers. You have come many miles to the friendliest hotel in Southern Africa, and I, Grace Mungangwa, am the proud owner."

They are charmed. She bobs a curtsey and extends her right hand, with the left nestling in the right elbow. They shake the proffered hand, admiring her brightly coloured wrap and headgear.

"Follow me," and they do – into a spotless entrance hall, covered with polished wood and seemingly not out of place in a small English hotel. On the wall straight ahead of him is a map of southern Africa that Darius instantly recognises, for it is the map of Livingstone's journeys. He feels an overwhelming sense of destiny.

"Now you must help me with various things." their proprietor has morphed into hotel receptionist mode.

"I need to see your passports, and then I must ask you a very serious question."

Her smiles have vanished, and a stony hard appearance disfigures her face. Darius wonders whether they are entrapped in an African version of a Hitchcock movie. In his terrorised fantasy, he can visualise the shower in that motel.

"Is it one room or two?" and her large frame wobbles in jelly-movements, while the laughter spreads back into her face. They both laugh – Darius from relief, and Judith from anxiety, he assumes.

"Two please," and Her Ladyship's face loses its tension.

"Shame, shame," mutters our hostess. "And you such a handsome couple. Is she not a beautiful woman?" She is looking cheekily into his eyes.

"I agree with you that she is a very beautiful woman, but we have not known each other for long."

"And that is a problem?" Darius is clearly in some trouble and knows that he must change this topic before he sinks. Added to his problem is that he cannot help noticing that now Her Ladyship is watching him carefully. The two women seem like they have devised a brief test for him and are both hanging on his response.

"Perhaps we could see the rooms?" he carefully manoeuvres away from the edge of his female-induced precipice. The rooms are surprisingly delightful, with a décor that he can only describe as an Africanised version of 1930s middle-England. Chintz and flowered wallpaper abound. Solid metal bedframes with crisp white sheets and blankets are neatly turned back. Each room has an armchair with antimacassars liberally applied to the back and arms. There is a shared bathroom with an enormous old tub at one side. Frankly, to a weary traveller, it is unexpectedly heaven-like. She leaves us to it, descending the stairs rather heavily.

"Well," he says, "it all seems rather acceptable. How about you?"

"Frankly, I can't wait to soak for an hour in that bath, and then fall into a deep sleep."

And indeed, an hour later, sleep overwhelms them both.

Chapter Twenty-One
Finding Caanga, June 2007

Judith awakens, and for a moment, forgets. The curtains are unfamiliar. And then it floods over her like the rising African sun, and she is excited beyond measure. She tingles all over at the understanding that she is away from everything. Her life is unrestrained by London, her title, her duties. She looks out of the window and observes the dreary ordinariness of an African street with no tarmac and no recent rain. She sees its dryness and feels dust on her hands, between her toes, and rising through her sandals. She is still in her bed but the sensation of the layer on her skin makes her long for soothing raindrops spilling onto her neck.

She recalls that he is next door and listens for sounds of him but hears nothing. She understands that he has gradually insinuated himself into her mind with his insistent charm and his constancy. Judith has not met a man like this in a long, long while. The charm and intelligence seem totally natural.

She has also of course noticed his eyes; an unusual yellow/green/light brown mix. Sometimes she has watched his face from the side and let the view of the lashes sink into her. And then when he walks, his body has a coordination of apparently effortless strength.

She understands of course that he has become both her mentor and her mental lover. Nothing remotely physical has occurred, although there had been constant brief unavoidable touchings on the aeroplane, as they moved in their seats or moved past each other. Maybe on reflection, they had not all been totally unavoidable. Her hands slip a little lower under the bedclothes, but at that very moment, there is a small sound from next door. She lays totally still, listening. Definitely movement next door. She is out of bed in a flash, slips out of her door after a furtive glance to ensure that the coast is clear, and into the bathroom. She washes at lightning speed and returns safely to her room. She is downstairs before him but not before Grace, who has produced some respectable-smelling coffee. She asks whether madame would like bacon and eggs.

"Bacon and eggs?" her amazement seeps out.

"Ah, you imagined that we barbarians only eat mealie-meal and beans?" Her temporary loss of words is relieved by male sounds of stairs being descended, two at a time.

"Do you always come downstairs like that?" Judith cannot resist.

"At my school, being late for a meal meant there was less. So, yes, I always get a move on before mealtimes." She watches him being courteous to their hostess, while getting not only bacon and eggs but even toast and marmalade out of her.

When Grace returns with his food, "We are looking for someone called Edith Wharton," he asks, rather demurely, Judith feels. A large grin breaks across her round face.

"Of course, I know the great Ba-mama. She has been mother to us all for many years. We worship her. She is our friend and saviour. But now that she is very old, we all try to care for her in her last years. Now, what could you want with our mother?" We had of course also prepared an answer for this question.

"Darius is writing a thesis on David Livingstone and we want to ask her many questions about those times," she lies smoothly. A silence falls upon the room, broken by the chatter of happy-sounding children. Indeed, turning slightly in her breakfast chair, she can see them through the open door, walking past the hotel door on their way to school, dressed in their pristine uniforms. There seemed to be a radiant happiness on their faces, and she is charmed. Grace also glances at the children.

"We are so proud of our school," she beams. "It is run by the missionaries and they are such wonderfully gifted teachers. Our children lap up their every word, so that they may go to the big secondary school at Mazabuka. The teachers are very strict with the children, but the results are wonderful. They still wear their monks' habits even in this day and age," she tells them, seemingly in awe.

"How wonderful," Judith remarks cautiously.

"Of course, like all men, they have their weaknesses," she throws in. She suddenly feels a touch wary but cannot resist.

"Such as…" Judith encourages.

"Well, they play snooker and billiards." Even he laughs, presumably in relief that some sordid male practices are not being revealed.

"As bad as that," she ventures.

"Many years ago, they had the tables imported from Ireland where their order originates."

"They are Catholics, then?"

"No doubt of that," she has fallen into the spirit of the conversation.

"And then there is the beer. They brew that themselves." Somehow Africa is turning out to have features that she had not quite anticipated, but she laps it all up.

"Any more vices?" she asks, somewhat lasciviously, hoping to hear about the seduction of local girls, but she is to be disappointed.

"Oh no, none of that," Grace replies, understanding instantly the words missing from the question. "They are sworn to celibacy, the more's the pity," and Judith notes that a dreamy look has come into her eyes. At this point, he intervenes clearly to prevent the girls becoming distracted even more.

"And Edith Wharton?"

"Oh, yes," her mind quickly returns to the present.

"Leave the town on the Choma Road, and her house is the first on the left after the sign saying 'Goodbye from Monze. Come again soon'. It is a small white bungalow named Mauya. Give her my love, and I will give you a small basket of presents for my Ba-mama," and with that, she disappears into the back of the house.

They finish their breakfast, pack, and she emerges as they leave with a basket, the contents of which are covered in a clean white linen cloth.

They say their goodbyes, drive away, and after a short drive, find the house as she describes it with a large 'Mauya' sign in white letters on a piece of wood on a post at the entrance.

At first glance, there is nothing about the bungalow to excite one's interest. It is set at the end of a loose gravel path, ending in a single step to the green-painted front door. The surrounding garden is similarly nondescript. A few desultory plants here and there set into an unkempt area of grass. But the red of the jacaranda up the side of the wall and curling over the door catches the eye. There is no sign of life. All is still and peaceful, and Judith suspects that they both wonder whether they are too late. They have come a long way and it will just have been too bad if she has beaten us to it. He goes to knock at the door but realises that there is no knocker or bell. He has just raised his hand to beat on the wood when they notice at the same instant that the door is not fully closed. His hand falls to the side and they exchanged glances. I push gently at the door, which creaks a little as it opens.

"Well, don't stand there. Come in, whoever you are," a voice with a slight quaver, but still with some authority, and apparently North American. They do as they are told.

"Of course, I know who you are. Lady St John James and a young man." She cannot of course speak for him, but she thinks they are both a little taken aback. Not only does the speaker know her name, but at that moment, they are unable to see her – and presumably neither can she see them. They follow the sound and enter the room on the left, further down the corridor. She is sitting in an old tattered grey armchair with the sun streaming into the room through south-facing glazed doors. She is old; the word would be 'aged'. Her skin, clearly darkened by long exposure to a tropical sun, folds in deep brown creases over her deeper tissues, as waves ripple on a beach. There is little to her otherwise. What height she had once had, has been pushed downwards as gravity's inevitable forces work on an aged osteoporotic frame. Despite the warmth, she has a blue woollen shawl, wrapped around her shoulders, and under it, wears a grey thick-looking dress to her ankles. The shoes are black and flat and practical. But everything about her is overwhelmed by her smile. Definitely not the smile that one might expect of a little old lady as there is something decidedly wicked, even mischievous about it. But the eyes. What is it about her eyes? And then she realises that they are unfocussed. Perhaps she cannot see.

"Well, sit down, sit down." They sit on the only place to sit, a battered old brown sofa, with yet more antimacassars. Is this a Zambian cultural movement or is the similar explanation that they are a leftover from British times a more probable explanation?

"Alice," she calls. Alice appears silently and smilingly from a side door. "Alice, they need refreshment. Probably tea – they are English."

Alice looks at me enquiringly.

"Tea would be lovely." Could she say anything else? She turns to him. He can only nod, and to be honest, Judith notices that he is looking somewhat disordered. She realises that she had better start the conversation as he is temporarily indisposed in the art of verbiage. She has felt compelled to clear up the mystery of Edith's pre-knowledge of their existence, but she beats her to it.

"Heather wrote and warned me that you were on your way, and even gave a guess at your arrival date. She was actually spot on, so it gave me great pleasure to welcome you by name," and she chuckles. So presumably, that explains the mischievousness of the welcoming grin.

Alice reappears with a tray, holding three beautifully delicate porcelain fine-handled cups, a cream-coloured milk jug, and an enormous orange tea pot. She places it on the small table and vanishes.

"You will pour for me, dear. My eyes are not good enough these days," and again, the eyes just not quite focus on her.

"But now, tell me what an old woman can do for you two young things."

"We are looking for a village," Judith begins.

"Yes, yes. I know that. You are looking for Caanga, Heather told me." Just like that. She has their attention. She has their totally absolute complete attention. And she clearly enjoys her moment in the sun. Judith can bear it no longer.

"And you know where it is?"

"Of course." That omnipotent crushing heart-stopping crisis of tension.

"Heather told me that you were looking for Caanga, and for a moment, even I was uncertain. And then my old brain worked it out, and incidentally worked out why you couldn't find it on your internet-thing. But Heather really might have tried a touch harder, I thought. Lovely woman, but a bit of a scatty catty." Judith is rather shocked at these careless words about one of her daddy's lecturers, but she lets it pass due to the expectation of the coming moments.

"I expect that you are dying to know," she is milking it for all that it is worth. He can bear it no longer.

"Is it in the lake?" His patience is clearly exhausted. She laughs.

"Oh no, not at all. Miles away from the edge of the lake." They both relax into their seats. She can spin it out now for as long as she likes.

"It's not far from where Livingstone passed."

Yeeeeees, they both think. *She knows. She knows.*

Outside, an invisible Zambian bird sends up a heavenly three notes. She pictures its' multi-coloured hues.

"But some way from the marked trail."

Now how can that be? She wants to solve the conundrum but fails.

"The British colonialists tried to work out where Livingstone had wended his way from the writings of his diaries and set up a few markers at the roadside. You may have seen them on your way here." They nod. "But usually, they got it wrong. Sometimes, Livingstone himself was mistaken in his description of the trail. Sometimes they didn't read his words carefully enough. And anyway, they never bothered to ask any of the Batonga, who knew exactly where he had been – so the Batonga never bothered to tell them. And the Batonga let them put up their signs and laughed amongst themselves. So Caanga is a little way from the markers."

"And the reason that we could not find the village on the maps?" he asks, his impatience showing.

"Oh yes," she comes down to earth. "It's rather simple, really. The Batonga use language somewhat roughly. Absolutes for them are not as stationary as in the language of twenty-first century England. Even for you English, some place names have changed over the centuries. So, in the old days, the river is called Zambesi; with an *S*. Nowadays, we spell it with two of the letter *Z*."

"Same here for the Batonga. So, the village that was named 'Caanga' is now called 'Chanker'. It is on the edge and just below the foot of the escarpment. It is quite a large village, a centre for the valley. There is even a Health Centre, run by the Salvationists of Chikankata. To get to the village, you must take the road to Chikankata, a turning off to your right on the way back to Lusaka. You will see the sign. Then stop at the mission and they will show you the correct road to Chanker."

"Now, come and let us sit on the veranda and you can enjoy the view. For me it has gone, as my eyes are not so good, but I knew it so well that I can recall every detail," and they follow her outside and sit in rickety ancient wicker chairs. To say that the view is stunning will be to do it a misjustice. They are high up and have a view south forever. In the far distance, partly hidden in a blue-grey haze, the lake glistens in the mid-morning sunshine. Closer to, they see the fields and woodland, sloping downwards and then disappearing, presumably as the fall of the land down to the valley of the Zambesi become steeper. And closer to, in her garden, there is a tree that he fails to recognise. But then she sees the pears hanging from it. But it looks like no pear tree that she has ever seen. I ask her. She laughs.

"It's an avocado tree. See the fruit." She cannot believe it. Never in her life has she seen an avocado tree. And to her astonishment, it is dripping with avocados; there must have been many hundreds.

"Unfortunately," she continues and laughs, "I am allergic to them. Such irony. I have a tree laden with fruit that I cannot touch."

They sit comfortably in silence for a short while. The sun rises higher in the sky and burns down upon their fair pallid European skin. He has been quiet for such an unusually long period that his intervention is a touch unexpected. And when it comes, it is mind-blowing,

"Aha, latex-fruit syndrome." They both looked at him with incredulity.

"Explain yourself, Darius." He looks mildly embarrassed, as well he should.

"I only know about it because a colleague of mine has it. Are you allergic to birch pollen?" he asks Edith

"We have no birch trees here in Africa," she replies.

"Oh, yes, my mistake. Well, my colleague gets hay fever when the birch pollen is out in England and gets a skin rash if he wears gloves with latex in them. And if he eats avocados, disgusting things happen, which I will not relate, but I am sure that you could be able to imagine. He told me all about it – the syndrome is manifested by allergy to latex, birch trees, and avocados." A look of understanding spreads across her face.

"Well that would explain it," she says. "I went to the hospital once here in Monze and one of the brothers asked me to wear gloves, as they let me watch an operation in their surgical theatre. Afterwards, my hands were all red and itchy for days, and I had always wondered why, in a curious sort of fashion."

"Indeed," is all he can say. And then he relapses back into silence, leaving her both not quite sure how or indeed whether to follow up this allergy discussion, or to return to the conversation. She solves it for Judith.

"Is there a grove of trees in the distance, far away to the left?" And indeed, there is, in an area mostly brown with soil or some type of cultivation.

"That is the mission town of Chikankata. Go there, and find Paul De Vries, the doctor in charge. For myself, I have never heard of a mine, but Paul may know. If he doesn't know, get him to help you find Chief Charlie Chikankata. But of course, he himself may not remember – Charlie is even older than I am, if you can credit that." For the second time, she hears a little trace of a long-gone West Coast American accent. But she is smiling to herself and, clearly remembering moments from long ago. She does not want to disturb her reverie, so they sit peacefully for a while, letting their eyes feast on the views.

"It would not really be as Livingstone saw it; you know."

How could she have read my mind?

"He saw animals everywhere. More so of course here and the other less populous areas north of the *Mosi-oa–Tunya*. That's what the local people call the falls. Did you know that Livingstone refused to name any places in Africa? He would always use their native names, but he broke his rule at the great Zambesi falls. So overawed by them was he that he named them after his queen, apparently the only other thing that totally overawed him. But for himself, he continued to call them the *Mosi-oa-Tunya*, the smoke that thunders. What a man he was. He treated the animals and native people with great dignity, and the consequence was that he was truly loved by the people." She lapses into thought again. Judith seizes her opportunity.

"We bring much love from your friend, Heather Greenbanks." She pauses to respect her age and the smile on her face, as she doubtless is thinking of her memories of her time with our linguist.

"She told us to ask you of the poisonings at the time of the building of the dam."

And Darius chipped in with, "And the massacre."

Edith's smile vanishes and is replaced with a look of dreadful sorrow. She sits still, allowing the sun to warm her while she prepares the story for us.

"I was and still am, I suppose, an anthropologist – that is, I study us humans in relation to our age and culture. And as a social anthropologist, I studied the customs and organisation of a people, in our case of the Batonga people. We arrived…"

And Darius interrupts, "We?"

"Ah yes. Ted and me. We were both in the department of anthropology in the University of California at Berkeley when our Head of Department suggested that we might like a secondment to Africa. You Brits had suddenly woken up to the fact that you were planning to build a dam down here on the Zambesi. You were about to create a vast lake, and someone had noticed that there were people in the way. Somehow the message had got through to your people in Whitehall from their local colonial officials here in charge of the building of the dam that the local residents had no intention of moving. The civil servants in Whitehall at the Colonial Office made the Minister aware, and the Minister had a fit. He had apparently made a panicked phone call early one morning to his old friend, with whom he had been students at UCLA, and who was now the head of our department at UCLA, 'Expense was no problem', our Professor was told. 'Just solve our problem'. So, Ted and I, both young lecturers, with some experience of field work, were dispatched to spend six months and 'solve the problem'. We had a rush course in Citonga, the local language, said farewell to our families, and flew out here. Fortunately, neither of us was married."

"We arrived and bedded ourselves into the community as best we could. In the first few months, we watched while desperately improving our language coming. Building a dam and flooding vast areas naturally creates problems in any community. This community was totally ill-prepared for the flood to come."

"The community had clearly not changed in many ways over the years. They were half-naked and lived a simple agrarian life. Their houses were constructed of mud and wattle, with an occasional larger house of brick, topped off with corrugated iron. They grew corn pounded into their staple food of mealie-meal. Vegetables were grown in individual gardens, and some had livestock, mostly goats. The level of education was low, although the younger ones had been to the newly-provided primary school, and so could read a little, but in English, as there were few books in their native language. And of course, they could not comprehend that the water would create electricity for the copper mining at Ndola miles away," and she pauses, her eyes lost back in those times. Alice appears with a tray on which are perched three glasses of a suspiciously artificially pink-coloured liquid.

"Kool-Aid," she says, seeing their anxious faces. "It will not kill you."
Judith sips at it and enjoys the coldness and the slight tingle. But a tad
sweet for her taste.

"So, we spent the first months settling in and attempting to establish
trust. The atmosphere was frankly appalling. The people were highly
suspicious of the whole project of the construction of a dam. Many
believed that it was an attempt by the British to steal their traditional fertile
homelands in the valley. Some of the less well educated could not believe
that there was any connection between the construction work going on
miles away at Kariba with their having to leave their homes. They could
not conceive of the possibility that an enormous lake would be formed."
They are spellbound.

"Of course, the British, or in reality, the colonial administration of
Northern Rhodesia, had made provision for the uprooting of the people
and were ready to provide them with new areas in which to live, village
by village – an enormous task. Fifty thousand people lived in the area to
be inundated by the waters of the artificially-created lake."

"Fifty thousand," Darius repeats in a rather inane fashion. She smiles
at his wonder.

"Yes, and the planning had been meticulously done. Early on, we were
visited by an administrator with a map. Each village was allocated a new
area, mostly not too far from their current homes. A few, however, had to
be located at some distance, but more on that in a moment, as that was the
cause of the tragedy." They have nothing to offer but their complete
attention. Of course, they await the denouement of 'the tragedy' with
bated breath.

"Just as we were starting to make progress with the people, our initial
six-month period of stay was finished, and we returned to our friends and
families in California."

"But were you not anxious about what you had left behind?" he asks.
Judith looks at him, sitting there, basking in the sun, and reminded herself
that he has some good thoughts. She is talking again so Judith's reverie
has to end.

"Yes, you are absolutely right. In fact, we debated as to whether we should stay on, but both of us had some commitments at home. As soon as we were back, we discussed the situation with our boss and persuaded him that we should return early, so two months later we were back in the Gwembe."

"The Gwembe?" Judith asks.

"My apologies," she acknowledges. "That is the name that the Batonga give to the land that we now call the Zambesi valley."

"When we got back, most of the building of the dam was complete, but the river had not been blocked off yet. All the mechanisms were in place, and there clearly might only be days before the waters would start to rise. It became known to us that there were some young men who were organising resistance to any attempted move of the people. In particular, in one of the villages closest to the river, these young dissenters had convinced the villagers to resist. When the Rhodesian police arrived to organise an orderly evacuation, the villagers not only refused to leave, but threatened the police with spears. Essentially, there was a collective rebellion. The Chief of Police decided that if the police were seen to back down at the first village, there might be serious danger of loss of life later amongst the elderly and very young in many of the villages as the waters rose. He returned the following day with a large convoy of trucks containing armed police. The police surrounded the village, and advanced. Spears were thrown and they opened fire. Fourteen men were killed in a few minutes. Following that, there was no more resistance."

"Were the press involved?" Darius asks.

"It was not totally hushed up, but things were different in those days. This was a British colony. Journalists could not travel freely everywhere. They had to be licensed, and although they travelled freely to Kariba to be shown the wonders of the dam, few asked to go upriver. The Gwembe was an enclosed society, far from any decent roads. Remember also that there were but few Batonga who spoke English and even fewer journalists who spoke the language. The journalists were invited into the valley but not until the movement of the people was progressing in an orderly fashion. All that they saw was a peaceful transition."

Judith stares towards Lake Kariba and somehow sees everything in a different light. *I see the truckloads of police surrounding the village early in one morning; the slow coordinated incursion towards the village of ranks of police; the order being quietly given; the rifles raised. I could see two or three young men rubbing the sleep from their eyes, rushing for their spears, the launching of the spears; the halt, rifles raised, the command; the volleys ringing out; the men falling and dying in the arms of their mothers and wives. Death amongst the valley's peace.* For now, their veranda is silent, not a motion, not a word, as they picture the scene and mourn the dead in their hearts.

As the story has progressed, the African sun is losing a little of its heat as it falls inexorably towards its place of rest, accelerating as it goes. Alice emerges and places charcoaled wood on a pit that she has failed to notice in the ground to their side. By chance, she lights it just as the sun begins to be cut off on the horizon and the last glimmers of the lake are seen in the far distance. Judith is amazed by the speed of the sun's fall from the sky, and the rapidity of the ensuing darkness. From the corner of her eye, she sees a flicker as the charcoal lights, and Alice places a grill on the top of the flaming pit. A bat swoops over them, gliding effortlessly in a complex route dictated by the flying insects that it gathers up on its travel. From far away, she hears the noise of an animal calling, and then an even more distant response. All around the continual chirping of the crickets. On the far horizon, away over Zimbabwe, there are flickers of lightning as a tropical storm expends its energy, but here they are covered by a clear sky, bursting with a myriad pinheads of light, so many stars, so many stars. Judith, who is used to counting the stars visible from her London rooftop on the fingers of her hands, gasps in amazement at the vast heavenly tableau. Hearing her gasp, Edith glances and laughs at her.

"And every night, the same," she tells her.

"Such beauty," he says. "And the Batonga saw these same stars over the years from their homes by the Zambesi and believed that they and their followers would live there for ever with their lives a never-ending constancy under a Great Spirit, who would protect them. And then the police came, and their cultural story was ruined for ever."

"Exactly," she says. "Well put. That's precisely what they believed. They knew that the Great Spirit, who put the stars in the sky every night and brought the sun out to warm their crops, would protect them."

Suddenly, Judith wants to be close to her handsome poetic academic. He seems not only to have a fine brain and a fine body, but also a sensitivity.

"Did you hear of the Lusitu tragedy? No, well I am not surprised, really. Let me tell you that story as well."

"In retrospect, the timing of the projected move could not have been worse. The preceding years had been a period of inadequate harvests with the people living off 'famine roots', and relief maize brought in by the government. These famine roots grew on the banks of the great river Zambesi and were only eaten when the crops failed. With no crops to take when they moved, they looked for these roots around the location of their new village, and they found them, and arranged a feast to celebrate. Regrettably, the roots that they had found were not the same as the roots from their old fields."

"Eighty-seven men, women and children died of food poisoning at Lusitu. Ted and I got there quickly, as by chance we were in a village close by. The scene was ghastly. Bodies everywhere. Many other people were ill, sitting on the ground with a yellow colour in their eyes and vomit beside them. And of course, at first no one had any idea what had happened. It was only after the doctors came from the hospital at Lusaka, and after they had performed post-mortem examinations of the bodies did they discover that they had all died from liver failure from food poisoning. And then the story was slowly pieced together. I shall never forget the children, the children," and she weeps. They sit in an appalled silence and their minds can see the small dead bodies, lying on the ground. And overhead, the stars still look down, watching them.

He stretches his long legs, stands up, walks over, and kneels, before her putting his hands gently, so gently, on her hands.

"Judy and I know the honour you have done us in telling us these stories. We can feel your pain in our hearts, and we will treasure these moments for as long as we live. Thank you," and he returns to his seat. Judith's heart is in turmoil with the tragedy and the exuberance of the warm African night. In her turn, she wants to touch him, to thank him for his kindness both to her for his beautiful words, and to her for accompanying her to this tragic wondrous place. She wants to put her lips on his, to touch his cheek with her fingertips.

Alice gives them plates of steak and chicken and sweet potato cooked on the *Braii*, as they call it, and beer to drink. They are ravenously hungry and eat everything they are given, but she pushes the food around her plate. The sky has suddenly taken on its own expressiveness. A meteor shower arrives from the Eastern sky and they watch in awe. Amazingly, he picks out two separate satellites, passing overhead through the myriad of stationary stars. Judith cannot see the first and he comes and kneels beside her takes her hand and holds it pointed into the sky until she can see it. His hand is warm and large and enveloping.

By ten o'clock, they were all tired, but Judith is ecstatic. She can feel that they are very close in their quest. She can hear Botticelli's treasure calling to them from its hiding place. It knows that they are close. It wants to be found while it lies in its cold place in the ground. But she is anxious that it may have been ruined unless it has been placed with care. When they start, out Darius had told her that there was a risk of that.

"Mind you," he had said, "we know that hiding paintings down a mine is a good way to preserve them. In the second world war, the British government hid many of the treasures from the National Gallery down a disused Welsh coal mine, and they survived well. Goering hid many treasured paintings in mines in Silesia. He probably has the Amber Room hidden down a mine as well."

Judith had not heard of the Amber Room and he told her of the story of its creation in the early eighteenth century; its gift from Prussia to Peter the Great, tsar of all the Russians; its theft by the Nazis, and its subsequent disappearance.

She breaks her reverie.

"I hope that you will stay the night here with me. We have three bedrooms and Alice has already made up your rooms." He accepts on behalf of them and she takes them to the bedrooms.

She takes her to her room, points to a door, and whispers in her ear, "The rooms are intercommunicating, dear, but the key is on your side." And indeed, it is. She winks at Judith and wishes her good night. Judith undresses and slips quickly into bed. The sheets are cool and fresh and caress her breasts and thighs. She thinks of him, lying there alone in his bed and decides that now is the time. She goes to the door, unlocks it, and quietly pushes it open.

A voice says, "Too long I have awaited you."

Judith regrets to say that she sniggers, as she creeps to his bed and slips beneath his sheets. He is warmer and hairier than she had supposed him to be. He holds her hand and kisses her so gently on her lips. At that moment, her desire for him overwhelms her.

After, she sleeps like an angel, wrapped in his arms. When she awakes, a glimmer of sun is shining through the window. She beats a hasty retreat to her own room, dresses, and goes out to find Edith already seated at the table.

"I am so happy for you, my dear. He seems such a lovely man." *So, what exactly had been the point of 'her hasty retreat'*, she asks herself. But Judith laughs at Edith's omniscience and at her own embarrassment, whilst Alice, who has appeared as usual silently, starts bustling around, making them breakfast. He appears, looking remarkably well-groomed and showing little sign of their passionate night-time exercise. Another cloudless African day greets them. And after their breakfast, they say their goodbyes to this remarkable woman.

"Find Paul at Chikankata," she reminds them, and waves sadly as they pull out of sight. They travelled back through Monze and Kafue and find the sign to Chikankata. The road is now not tarmacked, and they have to drive slowly. Darius and she chat and once he reaches over and touches her knee. She puts his hand firmly and primly back on the steering wheel, glad though she is that his affection for her has apparently not vanished in the heat of the day. She looks out of the window and gradually sees fewer villages and more untended scrub and woodland. After a while, we arrive at the entrance to the mission with an enormous sign spelling CHIKANKATA, made of brickwork on an arch across the road. They drive under and immediately are surrounded with brick and tile-roofed bungalows with neatly tended gardens. They progress slowly down the road, which teems with African people, until they arrive at an office-type building with THE SALVATION ARMY MISSION above its door. They stop, parking alongside four or five other cars, and approach the doors. Before they can enter, they are stopped at the entrance porch by an enormously tall, slightly stooping middle-aged white woman in a white dress with SA on its lapels.

"Welcome to Chikankata," she booms. "You must be the Britishers." Needless to say, they are startled that they are expected but shrug it off as just one more of those things that happen in Africa. It is all beginning to seem like one of Agatha Christie's gossip-filled middle-England villages, where everyone knows everything about everyone. But the woman in front of us is too large and noisy to be Miss Marple.

"Maureen Sheldon," she says, rather unnecessarily as her name badge sits proudly over her left breast on her army uniform. "I am the laboratory technician here. I expect that you would like to see Paul, the boss?"

They agree that this is so, and she leads off at a brisk canter, while they have difficulty keeping up. Suddenly, ahead of us is a large, rather decrepit-looking building signed 'Outpatients'. The plaster had clearly been a gleaming white some years back but is now stained in a dirty white colour, with sores of yellowish/buff/orange. In places, the plaster has peeled down to the brickwork beneath. A colourful queue winds around the building, for the most part chattering cheerily away. She strides in past a battered sign, which reads barely discernibly, 'All military personnel must leave all weapons here'. They stop and read it in horror.

She notices that they are reading it, and says, "Oh, I must take that down. It gives such a bad impression, doesn't it? It's just a left over from the Southern Rhodesian war of independence. We had soldiers here all the time then."

Darius and Judith exchange glances, his with his eyebrows raised. Are they entering a time warp? But it will transpire that that is not at all the case.

The Outpatients is packed with people, all talking away in loud voices, while nurses in smart blue uniforms are attempting to weigh people, take their blood-pressures, and perform other nursing tasks. Every now and then a nurse will call a name and the fortunate recipient will exchange a big grin with her friends and rise to her feet, often holding the hand of a toddler, and with a small babe asleep in a large scarf on her back. Their leader strides through the pandemonium and raps on a door, entering before she can possibly receive any response. After a few seconds, a stooped old man leaves, and they are beckoned in.

He is short. Somehow, she had expected that he would be a large, bluff, big-shouldered man, but instead here is a small, slim being, with a full head of black hair, an outstretched hand of greeting and a broad grin.

"Welcome to you both. Paul du Vries. Please sit." And they do.

"You are looking for the mine at Chanker, or Caanga, as it was called at the times when Livingstone passed here? Of course, Edith called this morning," he adds, seeing the surprised look on their faces at his apparent prescience.

"And you know it?" she asks impatiently.

"Oh yes," he replies. "I once crashed the Land Rover just by it. I had never noticed it until that day. The villagers had for some obscure reason dug a ditch right across the track that we used to take our team on their monthly visit to provide health care in the valley. On this day, we had set off as normal, when suddenly, there was a great ditch in the road. I tried to stop but failed and the front wheels fell into the ditch. Mercifully no one was hurt, but the nurses and I were pretty shocked, and we sat by the side of the track until help arrived to pull the Land Rover out. As we sat there, I noticed, a few yards off, that the ground was covered in mica, a soft, plated mineral. And then I saw at that site, and in the middle of all the scattered mica, a large entrance to a cave, as I originally thought, on the side of a sloped area of ground. I sat, looking at this unusual sight and wondered exactly what all this was. Suddenly, I realised that this must be a long-abandoned mine. By the time that I had got it worked out, rescue had arrived, and I was needed to help get the Land Rover out, and the team back to base. Everyone was too shaken up to continue on down to the valley, I fear. To be honest, I did not think of the mine again until Edith called this morning."

It exists, it really does exist, but she cannot help feeling that something is terribly wrong. Surely Livingstone and his team had not travelled down here? She puts it to him, and he wants of course to know what Livingstone had to do with anything. She churns out the story that she had agreed about his thesis on Livingstone and his mention of a local mine that he had noticed near his route.

"Well I am sorry, but I am not an expert on Livingstone. I know that he passed near here because I have seen the signs put up by the government, and I agree with you that they seem a long way off, back on the main road to Lusaka. But I do know a man who will know all about him and his travels."

And he pauses, cruelly, she thinks, given the expectation that he must have noticed on our faces. *I wonder if everyone around here milks every moment for all its worth. Perhaps it's the heat and its effect on human nature.*

"By chance, he is one of my patients." Yet another enigmatic, meaning-filled pause. Yet another wicked grin.

I can't bear this, she thinks. Fortunately, at that moment, he stands up.

"Let's have a walk, shall we?" and then, "Tell Blenos and Amanda that I will be gone for a while," to the nurse.

And they all leave, followed by disconsolate glances from the waiting hordes of his assembled fan club. The advantage of being the boss, she assumes, is that instant unquestioned delegation is your absolute right.

They walk out, turn right down a small alley, and emerge in front of a large single-story building with an impressive portico-style entrance. They enter and walk down a long corridor. Immediately, it becomes obvious that this is an inpatient block, and they pass a women's ward and a children's ward, before they walk into what is clearly the men's ward. Paul strides down the long ward, with beds on either side. She is reminded of visiting her grandmother years ago when she was a little girl. She recalls the look of the ward and the smell of the flowers by her bedside – not that flowers are allowed nowadays in hospital wards. *Something about spreading infection*, she remembers.

They stop by the bed of a white-haired, skeletal old man, lying surrounded by many visitors. He smiles weakly at Paul, who speaks to him.

"*Muli kabotu.*"

"*Ndili kabotu, muli kabotu.*"

"Just a greeting," Paul mutters to us.

Paul then speaks to him and the visitors fluently in the native language. The visitors leave. And Paul introduces him to us.

"This is Chief Charlie Chikankata." And the man in the bed smiles wanly at them.

"Charlie, these friends have just arrived from England. They have come all this way to ask you a question." All this in English. There is an indignant reply in the native tongue. Paul is clearly amused.

"How could they have learnt to speak Citonga, Charlie, when they only arrived yesterday? Please speak to them." This is not promising, but then from the bed comes in perfect, if slightly stilted, English,

"Welcome to my lands, strangers from across the seas. Before you leave my country, promise me that you will learn to speak the language of my people's words." They are surprised at his sudden fluidity of the spoken English language, when they had assumed that there were no words there.

"Ask me any question that you wish, and I will try to answer, for Paul's sake."

He tells them. Darius asks their burning question, and he responds, "Oh yes, I know the mine. My grandfather told me that long ago, white men came and made a large hole in the ground in the hills above Caanga. They took away pretty sheets of glass from the earth, and then after a while, they left. We knew not where they went. This was a story that my grandfather had heard, handed down in our people's stories."

"And was Dr Livingstone here then?" Darius asks.

"I do not know, but he was certainly here with us. My ancestors say that he was a great white man, who brought us friendship and gifts. Oh, and maybe your God as well," and he laughs, until a grimace of pain silences him.

"And do you know which road he travelled on?" Darius asks again.

"Oh, but of course. He was as a god in our land. Every step was noted. The previous *Maguwa* ("the rather derogatory word for a white man," Paul whispered to them) just stole from us or sold our young men to the Arabs for slavery. Until the great doctor David came, we had known nothing but wickedness from the white man. When he came with his love and kindness, he opened our eyes. Everyone followed him, like your Jesus with his followers. So yes, we know where he placed every footstep. It is written in the history of my people."

"And did he travel through the places, marked near the road to Lusaka?" asks Darius. So, this is the crucial question. There is a collective holding of breaths. The chief looks at them both and smiles.

"Oh, no. A few years ago, when I was a young man, the white men came in their trucks with their instruments on legs, and placed markers to mark the path of the great Doctor David. But they placed the markers in all the wrong places. You see, when they came, they did not speak to me or the other chiefs. They just put up their marker stones, and a few signs – in their language of course – and left. In fact, the track that Livingstone travelled was more to the south, towards the river. In those days, the main track for our people was just below where you are now, in my lands," and he points towards the lake.

"Charlie," Paul asks. "Was it close to where the white men made a large hole and took the sheets of glass from the ground near our track down to Chanker?"

"Caanga, you mean," he corrects Paul. They are thrilled with anticipation. Everything is falling into place. She recalls Dr Fielding's note to his friend Viscount Dearly; *The canvas is inside the entrance to an abandoned mica mine, high up on a ledge within ten feet of the entrance, and on the right. The mine is on a side road to the right as we are passing. The road – it's just a track, really – apparently leads to a village called Caanga.*

It was all she could do to stop herself shouting 'Halleluiah' in Salvation Army style from the roof of the hospital building. And then the chief falls back on his pillow, clearly exhausted. They clearly need to leave, and Darius says farewell for them.

"Thank you, chief. We will let you rest now. *Twalumba.*" Both Charlie and Paul look at him in astonishment.

As they leave, she asks him, "What did you say?"

"I said 'Thank you' in Citonga." He looks irritatingly proud of himself. They walk slowly back towards their car.

"He's dying, of course. Cancer of the pancreas. No real treatment, except pain relief. You came just in time, as I doubt that he will last another week. Terribly sad – he has been a great headman for his people."

Paul walks slowly back to his outpatients and they follow. He pauses and turns to them.

"I must return now to help my colleagues. It has been good to see you. Have a great time at the mine." He shakes their hands, turns away and walks back towards the wonderfully crowded clinic and his work.

"Oh. One last thought. Do you have a torch?" he ventures, turning back to face them for a moment. They reassure him and he is gone.

Chapter Twenty-Two
The Mine, June 2007

Judith

They are a little quiet as they leave and take the road towards Caanga. She suspects that they are both somewhat shocked by all their new experiences in such a brief time. She thinks of the transience of a fine old man, who even in his dying hours values his culture so much that, thinking of his people, he could manage to berate us for not speaking his language.

The road slopes downhill and they have wonderful views over the valley to the lake, glistening at them. Suddenly, she sees it, scattered all over the ground. Broken, smashed mica pieces, the grey-pink coloured sheets glistening in the sunlight, everywhere. They pull into the side of the road and get out, staring at the glassy fragile sheets everywhere, littering the ground. Had these sheets been undisturbed for centuries? The place has an air of abandonment. One day long ago, the miners had left, leaving their debris and their workings. She sees them wandering off, starting their long walk back to their homes, maybe all the way as far as the British colony in the Cape.

She also understands that she is standing at the spot described by Tom Fielding. She can see him exhausted, sweating from his fever, hardly able to walk, but still carrying the picture. Had he wrapped it in anything? Would it have ever survived anywhere unwrapped, let alone in the heat of an African hillside?

He drags himself into the front of the mine and exhaustedly lifts the package up and places it safely on a rocky ledge. The sweat pours from

*him. He has the foetid smell of death about him. He leaves and just gets
back to his makeshift bed in Livingstone's ox-wagon. He writes the note
of a few words to his friend and lays down his head to allow some blessed
sleep to ease his mortal pain.*

She feels a pricking of tears in her eyes as she contemplates his lonely
death. Darius is watching her. He puts his arm around her shoulders, and
speaks gently to her, "He was a fine man, our Thomas Fielding."

She is comforted by the warmth of his words and his hug. They stand
for a while, then extract the torch and a spade from the car and walk
towards the small entrance, visible at the centre of the mass of crystal
debris, on the side of a small mound on the hillside. The entrance is almost
completely overgrown, only a couple of feet across, so they had to widen
it to allow themselves access. The work is easy, as the soil is loose and
crumbles as they dug the spade in. Soon, they have an entrance large
enough to climb through, and taking the torch, he bravely leads the way,
with herself being the camp follower. They are in a large room with a high
ceiling. He points the torch upwards and, way above them, something
moves. She clings to him, terrified. It moves again and then it becomes
obvious that the whole ceiling is moving. Bats, thousands of them. She
moves the torch slowly around and sees the ledge that Tom has described
in his letter. Although it may have seemed 'high up' to the exhausted
dying man, in reality, it is about five feet off the ground. And they can see
that there is something on it.

With enormous care, they lift down a large oiled cloth, wrapped
around some more material. They take the package outside into the fresh
air and the heaps of mica and carry it to a flat clean piece of ground. They
realise that this oiled cloth must have been the covering of the painting,
while the canvas was transported in the secret base of the crate full of
medicines that the doctor had brought to Africa.

Delicately, they unwrap the oil cloth, and then before them, wrapped
into a scroll is the canvas. Slowly, they unscroll it, and there, there is their
magical painting. And he had done a marvellous job. The paintwork is as

fresh as a daisy, with blues and reds preserved as if from yesterday. And even she can tell that it was indeed a painting of an *Adoration of the Magi*. She thinks that Darius is about to explode; he is so excited. He runs around in circles like a small boy, cheering and whooping. Then he comes over and kisses her passionately. After a few minutes, the calm descends and they both study the detail of the painting. He tells her that he sees faces that he recognises; both those of the *Magi* and in the followers of those principal players. He wonders whether he sees Sandro's face. The robes are truly stunning with the crimson and lapis blues sparkling in the sunshine. When they have calmed down a little, they realise that they need to ensure some degree of protection for the painting from the heat of the sun and any possible jerking movements on their part. So, they carefully rewrap the painting in the oil cloth and lay it gently in the boot of the car. They climb into the car and look at each other, have another enormous hug. He kisses her again with almost overwhelming passion. She hopes that he might suggest a celebratory tumble there and then on the roadside, but sadly she fears that most of his passion is reserved at that moment for the beauty of their finding.

They drive back to Lusaka and he books them in at the Best Western hotel in the centre of town. She is delighted that they are sharing the room, but a little bit cross with him for not asking her first. She manages to get over her irritation in about one microsecond. They take their picture, and the rest of the luggage up to their room and spread it out on the bed. The more they look, the more wonderful it so clearly is. He has no doubts of its authorship. When he tells me that he will have to submit it to 'tests' in London, she makes a strategic error by asking what the tests will involve. By the time that he has mentioned infrared reflectography and then cross-section analysis, she is lost and manages to change the subject eventually onto her need for food.

They eat at the hotel, not really wanting to be far from our treasure. She is playing delicately with my pork belly – surprisingly good – when he says, "I am just wondering about taking it through customs."

She looks up and realises that she had been so excited that she had not given it a moment's thought. Perhaps also she had not dared to think about it, as she had not wished to tempt fate until they discovered whether the painting really existed, let alone whether it was in good condition.

Chapter Twenty-Three
Lusaka, June 2007

Darius is lying here, watching her breathing quietly, her face towards him, clean-lined in its repose. There is something about this person that has captivated him, and he wonders on it. If he looks back, he is not really a romantic. He would have been the despair of Shelley and Keats. Nor has his life to date been full of commitment to others. His father used to tell him that he was selfish, and his father was of course right. His take on it might be that he was strong-willed. For example, he didn't allow himself to be brow-beaten into becoming a mathematician or a concert pianist or a city broker or all the other ideas that he had for his son. And when he looks at this woman lying here, almost perfect in her beautiful somnolence, he thinks of the thoughts that he knows that Sandro Botticelli had when he painted his *Adorations of the Magi*. He wonders if he would have been shocked at anyone who does not believe in Christ even handling his picture, let alone sleeping with an unmarried woman. And then he recalls, even in those days, that sin was not absent from society. That his great beautiful model Simonetta Vespucci slept with a man not her husband, a Medici, and that this did not stop Sandro adoring her himself. So not such a devout unforgiving Christian then.

She stirs and turns a little but stays asleep. He thinks on what it is about her that he finds has bound him close to her. Maybe it's that strength and determination that drives her on this journey. Does he admire strength in a woman? Yes, and he cannot bear the opposite, the subservience and passivity of some women that he has met through my life. His mother of course is strong. A fine artist of the piano, and strong enough to withstand his father's powerful antics over the years. But never could he find the right mixture of strengths that could induce concepts of permanence in a relationship. Has he found it here? He has no answer to that as yet, but he can feel the strength of his desire and attraction.

And her eyes are on him. So lost was he in his reverie that he did not notice.

"You were thinking," she accuses gently.

"Spot on," he laughs, his delights in boarding school English never having left him.

"Well, are you going to enlighten me?"

"Must I?"

"Absolutely."

'Can I resist that strength? Do I want to resist?' This seems to him a moment of importance. He looks at her and is lost.

"I was thinking about you. And your strength."

"Ah. And did you come to a conclusion?"

"No, but I was admiring." She looks at him closely, clearly debating within herself as to where they should go with this, decides that this is enough, and snuggles up to him. Afterwards she says something less than romantic.

"I could die for a coffee."

He laughs at their shared need and they get dressed, descend to the ground floor, and stroll into the large and almost empty dining room. He starts in on the coffee, and other delights of breakfast. He returned them to the last words from the previous night before they had sunk into sleep.

"We need to work on the travelling of our painting to London. We clearly have a first basic decision about truth and honesty." He has caught her attention and feels the force of her gaze on him. At that precise moment, he manages to drop a piece of the excellent marmalade, which spirals off the toast onto his shirt front. She laughs. He fails to see the humour, tense as he is about 'the decision of truth and honesty'. Bizarrely, an attentive waiter appears at his side and offers to wash his shirt.

"It will be ready and ironed in an hour, bwana. My sister has a dry-cleaning next to the hotel," he tells Darius. He looks for the smile, but he is deadly serious. He turns him down, graciously, he hopes, and he retreats.

She laughs.

"You were being very serious about truth and honesty," he is reminded.

"Well, we have to make a decision here. Will we declare the painting, or shall we try to smuggle it through customs?"

"So simply put. As subtle as only you could be," and she grins with her coffee cup poised in her delicate hand. "So, shall we weigh things up? For me, it looks like this. If we declare the painting, they might well confiscate it. But the upside would be that if we are honest, we will not be in prison. I don't fancy a Zambian prison, personally."

"I agree."

"But if we conceal it, we might get it home safely," she looks at him. "My preference would be on taking the chance." And her coffee cup does not flinch or tremble. His cool customer opposite. This is what he had been admiring earlier in that warm early-morning bed, and his thoughts return to her beautifully asleep. He wrenches them back.

"If, and I haven't agreed yet, we do that, then we will need to conceal or disguise the painting. Any solutions for that?" he asks a little forcefully. She notices, of course and he has her full attention.

"Not really," she says, and they are both lost in their own worlds while they contemplate the problem. Breakfast finished; they stroll out of the hotel into the bustling warm streets.

"Let's walk around and see if a solution presents itself." She slips her arm through his and he is instantly putty to her glass. They walk into the fresh morning African air, only moderately polluted by the fresh morning African commuter traffic. They wander around slightly aimlessly through what is frankly a somewhat uninteresting business area, and by chance emerge into an enormous bustling market. As far as the eye can see, there are stalls selling everything. They were excited by the colours, the smells, the shouts, and the crowds. Gone are the traffic sounds, vanished in the cries of men trying to make the customers believe that their cabbages are the best in Africa, and the woodworkers that their icons will bring success to any household fortunate enough to possess one.

But there are unusual and delightful moments and they move from stall to stall. He is vaguely wondering whether he might buy a small gift for his parents, when she stops very still and very serious.

"I, Judy St John James, am a genius." He looks at her to see whether she has been struck by a revelation or joined St Paul on a journey to Damascus, but notices little, except that she is staring at the stall that they are passing. It appears to be selling a number of rugs, most of which look simply unappetising to his eyes. He has clearly missed something, but it is not obvious what the 'something' is.

"Talk to me, genius, for I am your humble yet clearly blinded servant. I see little here that might attest to your genius, or your modesty," he adds, hoping for a flicker of a smile. He is not to be rewarded.

"Look with care, my blind servant. For your eyes must be opened to the understanding in front of us." He sees only native rugs, pretty but underwhelming. She takes him aside to a quiet spot between stalls. Two young men are there, clearly smoking a noxious substance. The men beat a rapid retreat, and they are left to the peace of the small space.

"The painting. Don't you see that maybe these rugs might be a solution to the hiding of the painting? We could buy a big one, wrap it up, and conceal the painting inside." Although she is delighted with her solution, he is not certain.

"All they would need to do would be to unwrap it," he points out. The smile vanishes. "But I think that you have had an idea. Maybe we could try to throw some more onion skins of confusion around it." He stops, trying hard to focus on procedure at British customs. Supposing they made it more complex. How thorough will customs officials be?

"I have a new suggestion. Let's take your idea and try to run with it. Would you be bringing this rug as a present for a friend?"

"Could be," she says.

"How about then if we bought four rugs, and the picture was in one of them? Perhaps they would not unwrap them all." They think about that scenario.

"Yes, that's an improvement." She is gracious. "Let's wander around a bit and see if we have any other inspirations." It is indeed a market for inspirations and the stalls are filled with crafts and knick-knacks. And then they come to a place where there are three or four artists, trying to persuade young people to have their portraits drawn. Two young girls, who look like students from Europe are being drawn. The likenesses are really rather good. And then he gets it. Another onion skin. They can do what the best do – hide their secrets in broad daylight.

"Have your portrait drawn," he suggests.

"You're joking," she replies.

"Oh, no I am not. And in fact, let's get a large portrait. And two more copies," he adds as an afterthought. She looks at him, appreciating that he is plotting but the proverbial penny fails to drop. "So, then each rug could have a picture inside it," he spells it out. "I am sure that you have three friends who would love a rug and portrait from darkest Africa, would they not?"

She thinks about it, and after a few seconds, turns to the nearest unemployed artist and asks him for a quote for a large picture of herself. After a little hustling, they come to a price, and she sits on his chair.

"Oh, and how much for two copies?" The artist looks at her in amazement. After he recovers his poise, they agreed another price.

"With delivery to the Best Western hotel by this afternoon. Fifty percent now and fifty percent on delivery?" she requires. His surprise is less this time. He clearly realises that he is dealing with a strange but powerful force. Darius could have told him that but keeps quiet. It takes him twenty minutes to finish the first drawing and they leave him to it to finish the copies.

While she is being drawn, he sits close by, soaking up the atmosphere of the market and warming himself in the bright sunshine. The local women, all around them, wear skirts of brightly dyed cloth and chatter to each other with their small children running around them.

By the time that he has finished the first drawing, the smells from the food stalls have made them both ravenously hungry. They eat their lunch, sitting at a small stall, wondering whether their scheme will work.

"So, let me see if I have got the plan right," she says, between mouthfuls of the kebab in spicy bread that they are devouring. "Along with the rest of our luggage, we are going to carry back four enormous rugs. Inside each rug, there will be a painting or drawing. And inside one of the rugs there will be a painting by Botticelli. The rugs and drawings are gifts for our friends as souvenirs and are intrinsically valueless for Her Majesty's customs. But we probably should be able to produce invoices. We anticipate that either the officers will not notice these vast packages, or they will glance cursorily at one or two. Is that correct?"

"If you put it like that, then I suppose that you are correct. Does it sound plausible?"

"Plausible, plausible," she repeats. "It sounds lunatic. Sadly, I don't have a better idea."

Eventually, they walk back to the stalls selling the rugs. They choose four of the largest but most ordinary and stagger back to the hotel with their purchases. They take one of the rugs, lay the painting on it, and carefully roll up the rug with painting inside and tie it with string. The painting is, of course, totally invisible.

Later that day, he delivers the portraits, and they wrap one in each rug. Finally, they number the rugs in ink at a corner from one to four, with the painting in rug number three, so that when they come to customs, they can keep tabs on which rug contained their painting.

He is reminded of a rhyme told to him as a young boy by his grandfather that came from a musical, starring Danny Kaye. In order to remember which drink was safe, and which contained poison, the great comedian had to remember:

The pellet with the poison's in the vessel with the pestle
The chalice from the palace has the brew that is true.

Their task is relatively simple; all they have to remember is that the painting is in rug number three.

They go out and book their flight home the next morning on British Airways and take their luggage in a taxi to the airport. The girl at the departures desk looks askance at their rugs, but apart from charging a vast sum for their secure place in the hold, waves them through. There does not appear to be any official concerned with stealing valuable cultural heritage, and they breathe a collective sigh of relief as the plane lumbers into the sky.

He hates flying, mainly due to his overwhelming fear that any plane he is on will fall catastrophically from the sky. Remarkably, flying with Judy is less terrifying. He finds that as they are taking off – the worst bit – she insists on chatting to him, and should he not maintain eye contact with her, she will pause, thus causing his eyes to drift back to her. By the time she stops, they are at some vast height and the captain is telling them that they could walk around, or whatever they say that you can do. Heathrow is but sixteen hours away, but as yet, they have no way of knowing what is in store for them.

Chapter Twenty-Four
London, June 2007

Darius

By the time that they skim over the houses of the noise-polluted citizens of West Isleworth and crunch onto the tarmac, Darius is not at his best. He has slept not a wink, as befits the frightened traveller, and Judy has dozed gently with her head on his shoulder for a while. Not wishing to wake her, he keeps as still as he can, but by the second hour, the pain in his left shoulder is close to unbearable. He shoulders on (so to speak), and then she mercifully shifts, and his upper arm slowly re-joins the remainder of his body.

They collect their cases and load them and the four rugs onto a trolley, which he pushes hopefully through the green Nothing-to-Declare channel. Needless to say, they are stopped by a customs officer, who appears as if by magic from one of those doors that normally remains anonymously closed. He looks like he is a young customs officer; a very young customs officer; short with thick black hair. Is it possible that he has left school? Darius' hopes rise. He feels that they might have a chance with a boy as young and hopefully as gullible as this.

"Please place all of your luggage here," indicating a long metal table, Not a smile; not a touch of humanity; not a 'Good afternoon' even. His hopes vanish. This is going to be a struggle.

"Please open your suitcases and stand away from them." They do as they are told, and he proceeds to make a very careful examination of the contents, neatly stacking shirts, sweaters, and other things in piles. He examines the linings with his fingers and needless to say, finds nothing anywhere to warrant interest. Darius can feel his tension rising. He notices a tiny bead of sweat on Judy's upper lip and prays that he doesn't see it.

He stands back from the table, "Please repack your cases." Not a wasted syllable there. Perhaps charm is not a requirement of officials of HM's Customs. They pack and close the cases and put them back on the trolley.

"Now place the carpets on the table one at a time and remove the wrapping." Judy points to number two, and he does as he is told. He looks at it and the revealed portrait.

"What is this?"

"They are all presents for my friends and family."

"Where did you buy these carpets?" He is inspecting the rug's stitching with care, as if he knows about these matters

"In a market in Lusaka in Zambia."

"Why were you in Zambia?"

"Visiting friends." He can tell that she is agitated by now. Her answers are crisply short. She is speaking in an uncharacteristic clipped voice.

"Do you have a receipt?" She produces it. He inspects it with interest.

"So how many of these Kwachas do I get for my pound?"

"About fifteen." He looks at the figure on the paper and Darius can see that division by fifteen is stressing him. To be frank, it had stressed him too.

"Not very expensive then," is his only comment.

"And I suppose that at this market, there was an artist standing around to make drawings of tourists," he speaks with derision in his voice, staring at the drawing of Judy.

"Indeed." Her words are nearly monosyllabic now. He gives a sigh, clearly getting bored.

"All right. Pack it up, please and put the next up here." He heaves number four onto the table and the same ritual occurs. He can hear his heart thumping, and he can see that a fine tremor has started to involve his fingers. He has just arrived at the end of inspecting number four, when an older man emerges from the depths of the rooms hidden from them non-officer types.

"Good afternoon, my name is James Briscott. I am one of Her Majesty's senior customs management officers," in a distinct North London accent. Darius diagnoses Kentish Town. An arm is extended and they each shake its hand.

"Well now, what are you up to, Pantelias?" So, the boy is of Greek origin.

"Sir, these people were pushing a trolley laden with carpets, so I stopped them to see what it was all about." He glances down.

"Hardly carpets, are they? More like rugs, if you ask me. And anyway, who are *these people, as you call them?* Do they have names?"

"I have not asked them yet, sir," their boy confesses. The man looks appalled.

"You don't even know the names of our suspected criminals?" And they get a smiling wink. "Didn't they teach you anything on your training course. It only finished a month ago, didn't it?" This to young Pantelias, who is beginning to look tense.

"Your passports please, sir and madam." They produce them, and he inspects them with some care, and then turns to the boy.

"Do you realise that you are about to apprehend a member of the aristocracy, Pantelias. What a feather in your cap this will be." To be fair, the boy looks mortified.

"Lady Judith St John James," he reads with a pause between each name. With every word, but especially after the first, the lad looks more and more terrified. He is beginning to feel just a twinge of sympathy for the poor boy.

"And where have they been?"

"Zambia, sir."

"How do you know that?"

"They told me."

"They told you. They told you," he repeats. "And perhaps they didn't tell you the whole truth and nothing but the truth. So, you haven't even inspected their boarding passes. What were you told at training? First the passports and then the boarding passes before you do anything."

"All right. Let's assume that they told you the truth. Now where is Zambia, son?"

"Africa, sir."

"Bonus points, lad. Where in Africa?"

"I don't know, sir." The boy looks desperately at him. He looks at the boy.

"Central southern Africa. So, what were you looking for, then? Drugs? Or didn't they tell you in those clearly useless training sessions, that the drugs are moved through West Africa, mainly Nigeria, not southern Africa. Big place Africa," he adds rather unnecessarily, Darius feels.

"Well, what about the pictures then, sir? There are pictures in these rugs," the boy in his desperation has scored a bulls-eye, but does not know that, of course.

Officer Briscott is suddenly alert.

"Pictures, what pictures?" Darius visualises a large men's prison in the Midlands.

He looks down and indeed sees pictures. He inspects one of the pictures with care. He looks at Judy with care, and frankly with more of an appraising male eye than Darius cares for. Then he looks at the picture again. Then he looks at the second picture. Once more, he takes a good look at Judy.

"But these are drawings of Her Ladyship, Pantelias. And really rather good too, if I may say so." She smiles wanly in acknowledgement. The smile is as tense as a ready bowstring but apparently that is only obvious to Darius.

"Well, they might have been smuggling some other sort of picture, some valuable painting," the boy says weakly, but regrettably accurately.

"Some valuable painting. Some valuable painting." He has this habit of repetition when he is trying to appear amazed at the boy's stupidity. "So, what's the thesis here, lad. Every day there are thousands of respectable middle-aged English folk smuggling Picassos into our blessed country from central Africa?"

Less of the middle-aged, Darius thinks.

"Thousands of Picassos out there, I suppose. Or maybe a Raphael or three."

Getting warmer, he thinks but manages to keep himself from speaking.

"Pantelias, for God's sake, let these weary people go home." And to them, "Apologies for delaying your homeward journey, folks. Welcome back to Blighty."

"And you and I," and he turns to the poor visibly shrunken man beside him, "are going to have a long training session."

And he disappears back into invisible custom-land spaces, followed by one dejected-looking trainee Customs Officer. They look at each other but manage not to speak, pack up the rugs, and pass through the exit doors to the usual collection of chauffeurs holding placards, and others standing around or leaning on the railings, looking eagerly for returning friends and relatives.

"A drink?" he asks.

"Strong," she replies. They sit, surrounded by rugs and cases, occupying a corner of a large bar/eatery/call-it-what-you-will in Terminal Four Arrivals Hall, as it is appallingly named. His father would have been disgusted at the abuse of the English language. Although it is only four o'clock in the afternoon, they both are drinking their double G and Ts at a rate that his aforementioned father would probably approve of.

"So close." Darius doesn't know whether he wants to laugh or just be very anxious. Maybe both at the same time will be appropriate. Normally, he thinks of himself as quite a calm person, but he needs to hold his glass with both hands, as he is still shaking rather a lot. She is pale around the mouth, with a heightening of those rosy English cheeks.

"*Thousands of Picassos out there, I suppose. Or maybe a Raphael or three,*" she copies his North London accent to a Tee.

"And what about that *Every day there are thousands of respectable middle-aged English folk smuggling Picassos into our blessed country from central Africa.*" They both manage a smile, but frankly if his looks as strained as hers, neither of them is really amused. He tells her that he isn't pleased with the *middle-aged* bit. That does produce a proper twinkle, and she looks fondly at him and reaches for his hand.

"Poor dear, and I do believe that he was looking at you at the time." His turn for a better smile. And slowly, and with the second gin, they regain their equilibrium, and for him, his hands stop shaking. They go slowly through almost every sentence in the customs hall and hold hands especially tightly at the moments of impending doom. They have taken an enormous risk and have been fortunate to escape with our freedom – and of course, their painting. His thoughts bring him back to the fact that they are sitting with an enormously valuable piece of art at their feet and no real plan for its continuing safety. His shares his thoughts with the member of the aristocracy sitting opposite.

"Well, the sooner we get the picture to my godfather the better."

His puzzled look clearly notifies her that his jetlagged and recently traumatised brain is hardly functioning.

"My godfather Roger. You remember Sir Roger Court, the Director of the National Gallery," she has to spell it out for the man sitting opposite her, that sad befuddled middle-aged man. It still rankles.

"Once it is in the gallery, it will be safe. I think that it would be madness to have it sitting around at one of our homes, don't you?" He agrees with alacrity.

"Supposing I ring him, and we put everything in a taxi." Clearly the sensible course of action. She pulls out her phone and dials.

He hears, "Sir Roger Court," followed by, "His goddaughter," followed by a longer pause, followed by, "Uncle Roger. It's Judy," and she explains that she needs to see him urgently and that she is unable to say why. And then her tone hardens.

"Well, I am sorry that you are just leaving but it certainly won't wait till tomorrow. We are just getting a taxi from Heathrow and will be with you in about an hour if the traffic is not too ghastly," and finally, "No." and the phone disappears into her bag.

"What was that last bit?" he asks.

"He wanted to know whether one of his assistants could deal with it," she laughs. "Did I sound rude?"

He considers. "Sharp," he says, "sharp would be my word."

She grins, "Sometimes he needs strong handling."

"Indeed," is all he can think of to say. He wonders whether he too will need 'strong handling' in the future.

Remarkably, the queue for taxis is short and they wind their way through the traffic with ease. Most of it, not surprisingly, seems to be going the other way out of London. The driver rather sportingly helps them in with their baggage into the gallery. Darius carries rug number three. Roger appears rapidly, looking unhappy and gives his goddaughter a quick peck on a proffered cheek.

"This had better be good, Judy. I am late for an important date."

"What's her name?" the goddaughter responds. No amusement on his brow. He just manages to acknowledge Darius' presence, as per usual. They go up to his office, looking down over Trafalgar Square and beyond to the Houses of Parliament way beyond. He plonks the rug rather unceremoniously on his desk.

"My interest in rugs, however fine, is limited," he grumps. Darius undoes the wrapping and lets her reveal the contents. He is absolutely still. Not a flicker of the lids, not a twitch of a finger.

Eventually, "My God. My God." He looks around and pulls his chair up behind himself and sits heavily.

"And the provenance, the provenance." And he feels that he is begging. He has turned his eyes to her, as if he is beseeching her to speak words of comfort to him in a state of anguish. And she is just about to speak, when he suddenly becomes a man of action, opens a door behind him, and shouts, "Julie. Here. Now."

Julie moves rather rapidly, Darius feels, and is in the room in about two milliseconds.

"First, the keys to the basement storage area. Second, security – at least two immediately. Third, no one in here at all, including you," and with a wave of the imperious hand, she is gone. He turns to Judy.

"Talk to me, just talk. You have the nerve to simply walk in here unannounced with a Botticelli *Adoration*. You might have killed me, you know. I had a triple bypass last year, remember."

"Sorry, Uncle Roger."

"And I am not your bloody uncle." She tells him the story and even the abbreviated version takes nearly an hour, and ends with, "We need your help."

"Indeed, you do, my girl," and he pauses in thought. And then the man of action, in his element, is back, "So, we need to move with great care. To start, we must ensure that precious few people know about this, so absolutely no talking to anyone. Then we need it in a place of absolute safety here in the gallery. And then I need to have my people working on it."

"What does *working on it* mean?" A reasonable question. Darius knows what is coming but to an outsider this is going to be meaningless unless he can be bothered to explain. He can't.

"We will need to have our Florentine renaissance experts attack it. They will bring in technicians to perform infrared reflectography, cross-section analysis, medium analysis, and also of course, close examination of the surface under a microscope. And we will need you to bring all of your written documents to me so that I can get outside experts to authenticate them." He pauses there. Frankly, he thinks that they are both so tired that although they might have many questions, those will all wait.

"Now, I suggest that we get security to take this away to our vaults. You should both go home, as even I can see that you are weary from your travels, and I shall go to my date. In fact, a drink with the Head of the Courtauld, if you must know, my dear," and he looks less than warmly at his goddaughter. And then suddenly, he manages to turn on the charm.

215

"But thank you both for bringing me this priceless object. I will give you a receipt and will be in touch soon." They leave his office, go back down the stairs, and get the receptionist to find them a black cab.

"Where to, guv?" the cabbie's not unreasonable and totally predictable question.

She turns to him, holds his hand, and says, "I don't want to say goodbye."

And he knows that he doesn't either.

"72, Clarewood court, Crawford street," she tells him.

So that's where she lives, he thinks wonderingly. He once had to visit the flats to deliver a parcel for a friend and remembered the great block of Edwardian flats, stretching the length of a complete block of Crawford Street and around the corner into Seymour Place. But he had never got inside and is interested to know what awaits.

"It's been owned by the family since the block was built," she tells Darius as they settle back into the comfortable black cab leather seats. "I have the use of it while I live here in London." The cabbie again proves helpful, dragging the cases and rugs inside the doors of the block, and the concierge helps them into the lift. And what a lift. It must have been the height of fashion at least fifty years ago with its double metal-grilled doors, both of which are manually operated. One has to fasten the hand-operated metal catch on both doors, and then quickly press the button before someone else pulls one to an unwanted floor. There are four identical uninteresting wooden doors opening from the landing where the lift arrives, and she unlocks that of 72. They enter and were greeted by a vaguely musty, not unpleasant smell.

"Welcome to my home," and she gives him such an irresistible, entrancing smile that he wants to fold her in his arms, but decorum holds him at bay. Frankly, the apartment, whilst being comfortable, can simply not be called anything but rather ordinary. It is true that the view from the south-facing drawing room is pleasant, looking over the rooftops to the classical Victorian architecture of Marylebone train station. The flat is light enough but the ceiling could have been a touch higher. The main bedroom also looks south but is a little dark, having been designed with not enough windows, given the lowness of the ceiling. The rest of the apartment consists of two rather small north-facing bedrooms, a bathroom, and an unremarkable kitchen, dotted as it is with units from another era. The back door of the kitchen opens onto a precipitous metal fire escape, which is equipped with insubstantial railings and descends alarmingly into the gloomy depths of the interior courtyard of the block. Clearly no sun ever penetrates here. He closes it rapidly to ensure that his vertigo does not overwhelm him.

She wraps her arms around his neck.

"Shall we go to bed?" Perhaps the finest words that a man could ever here from such a beautiful woman. They collapse into the comfortable silk sheets and soft pillows and are both asleep in a matter of milliseconds.

Chapter Twenty-Five
A Discovery, June 2007

Darius

Undoubtedly there are few greater pleasures in the world than to be woken by the smell of freshly made coffee. Darius props himself up on his elbow and surveys the messy piles of clothing on the floor and fails to be distressed by the unimaginative primrose paint on the wall below the dado rail. He has never quite been able to grasp the charm of the dado rail, but he supposes that it does enable walls to be demarcated by differing decoration and gives a room a feeling of increased height. The room is much enhanced by Judy arriving not only with a cafetiere, but also a tray with toast and, as she proudly announces, "My homemade marmalade." The coffee is delicious, and to his surprise, the marmalade has just the right level of piquancy, and exactly his personal taste in moderate sized chunks of orange skin. "Made from oranges brought over from Seville last January by my uncle." Darius has visions of Uncle Roger, laden down with bunches of oranges like a pompous version of an old onion-seller from his childhood on a bicycle. She looks at him suspiciously, correctly interpreting his look.

"Not him, idiot. Anyway, he told you that he was not a real uncle. One of daddy's brothers, named Peter. He's a professor of Archaeology at the Open University and spends large parts of the year with a collection of sycophantic students at a dig near Toledo. He always manages to remember to bring me oranges back when he goes in the Christmas break." And then anxiously, "Is it any good?"

He can only reply truthfully, "Absolutely delicious."

And then, toast crumbs and all, she snuggles back into bed and he lets her know more intimately exactly how wonderful her marmalade is, and indeed other bits of her. Mercifully, they have managed to slide the tray onto the floor before their lust got the better of them.

He had not noticed the telephone by the bed until it started to ring, and wonderingly watches as she lifts the receiver of a black piece of equipment, which might have been answered by Miss Lemon in an episode of *Poirot*, with David Suchet looking on.

"Good morning, Uncle Roger." He imagines the bluff uncle disclaimer from the other end.

"Yes, I do know what time it is," she is all lightness and charm, as she glances at her watch and jumps. "Oh, as late as that," she modifies her knowledge.

"Give us an hour then," she ends somewhat lamely. She looks abashed at what is clearly a capitulation.

"And there I was imagining that we were going to spend the day between the sheets." She hits him very gently with a pillow, before giving him quite a long sloppy kiss.

"He has discovered something and needs to tell us."

They arrive at the gallery just after 12:30pm and are escorted to his rooms. Sitting next to him is a man that Darius knows rather well. Despite that, they are formally introduced.

"This is Professor James Marcus, Professor of Renaissance Art from the Courtauld Institute. And these are my goddaughter, Judy and…" But his boss gets in rather quickly.

"You haven't brought the tie back yet." The three of them are somewhat distracted; Judy and Sir Roger by not understanding what on earth he is talking about: and Darius by the realisation that indeed he has forgotten to return his tie after the lunch at Simpson's. He is about to offer apologies, but he cuts in with.

"Delighted to meet your goddaughter," and he smiles at Judy. "I have news for you both. My friend Roger," he gestures to the godfather, "has done me the honour of showing me your painting. First, I must congratulate you on your find – for you and for us art historians, yours is the find of the century. Next, I would wish you to tell me the provenance of your find. He," and again the gesture, "has told me but I must hear your words."

She tells him.

"There have been whispers for many years," he says contemplatively. "Ever since Horne wrote that paper in 1900. So, it was all true. Personally, I thought that Horne had made up all the scraps on which he based his theory. I was wrong." They savour the unusual sight of a professor admitting to error.

"I have spent two hours in the vaults here with your painting and can tell you a number of things." And a pause while his eyes roam over them.

"Shall we have some tea sent up, Roger?"

Not another one spinning thing out, Darius thinks. *Is it simply the whole lot of us in the art world, or do we have bad luck?*

So, they have to sit back and make polite chat about their trip to Africa, while tea arrives, courtesy of Miss Lemon, or Julie, as Uncle Roger's equivalent is called. *Dresden china,* Darius remarks, feeling a tiny glow of honour.

Eventually, "The first thing is that your painting was almost certainly painted by Alessandro di Mariano di Vanni Filipepi, known to all by the familiar as Sandro Botticelli, although he might well have been assisted by his apprentice Filippino Lippi. Frankly, at initial inspection, and rather surprisingly, it might possibly have been completely painted by our Sandro by himself, a very rare event. I am not able at present to discern the brushstrokes of any other person. You see, usually the great masters had assistants who painted the backgrounds and the bodies and all the easy bits, while the master focussed on the eyes, the hands and sometimes, the flow of a robe."

He is now talking to Judy, as hopefully he presumably believes that, as he is his lecturer, he might know all this.

"Now, both I and Roger have examined your painting under the microscope to look at the brushstrokes and the paint. It is undoubtedly mediaeval, although we will need to do little bit of chemical magic to be 100% certain." Another pause. "And therefore genuine, despite the appalling lack of provenance."

"But the most fascinating thing is that I think that there is another painting underneath." And this time his pause is accompanied by a look of great self-satisfaction, as presumably well it might. They are both lost for words as this assertion sinks in.

Darius thinks through the implications while he continues, "I have seen flecks of completely different coloured paint at one of the corners. Although you will expect an undercoat of maybe white, or very pale green or blue to give subtlety to the hue, this is paint of a colour that you would not anticipate at all to be an undercoat."

"What does this mean?" she asks.

"Well, there are a number of alternative possibilities. First of all, the great man might have had a dabble at the edge of this picture of another painting. A bit unlikely, really, but we do have examples of this from down the centuries, don't we, Roger?" His godfather-liness nods.

"And then there might be a full painting underneath and he has overpainted it. We call this a *pentimento*. It's Italian, of course, and means literally a repentance. The artist has changed their mind, or 'repented', if you like. Until we have had infrared reflectography we will not know. And even then, we still might not know fully. We will be in the hands of the technicians. But I suspect that you could find yourself with a masterpiece under a masterpiece." And his face takes on a look of complete excitement.

"So, let me understand," she is showing some excitement herself. "There might be two complete paintings here."

"That is possible," he tells her gently.

"And then...?" she lets it hang there.

"Well if there should be another painting, you will have a choice."

Chapter Twenty-Six
London, July 2007

Darius

And indeed, a choice they have to make. The technician's work reveals that under their *Adoration of the Magi* is a complete other painting. They first see the results a few days later, sitting in the gallery with Uncle Roger and Darius' boss.

"To our astonishment," Sir James begins, "your painting has under it a painting that looks to be another *Birth of Venus*. Although it may be a copy of the famous *Botticelli* in the Uffizi, my view would be that this is much more likely to be the original. It is smaller, about half the size, and to me that is very suggestive that Botticelli painted this one first, and then made a larger version. It would be quite unnatural to make a smaller copy after the great painting. Of course, our reflectography does not allow us to see every piece of the detail, but you can see for yourselves the stunning similarity to the large picture." And he has brought with him a large print of the Uffizi painting for Judy to see. They all look in awe at the reflected view under their *Adoration* and at the print.

"We will need to think this all through with care."

"So, should we expose the painting underneath?" she asks.

"Very dangerous," he tells her. "In doing so, you will have to destroy the beautiful painting of the *Adoration*, and then you might have a damaged, or partly damaged painting underneath. In other words, you might be left with little of significance. But we must ask other colleagues for their views, of course."

"And that raises another problem." Roger is looking serious, hand clasped uncharacteristically anxiously before him. "Very soon, we will have to widen the knowledge of what you have brought to us. Frankly, it's a miracle that the news has not leaked out yet."

"And what does that mean?" Darius turns to Sir Roger.

"This is going to be, I am afraid, sensational news in the art world. And, I fear, in the world outside. There will have to be a statement." And then, a lengthy pause. "And I fear, a press conference." Everyone is immediately talking at once.

"Oh, no." says Judy.

"No other way." That is Marcus.

"Do we have to be there?" Darius' contribution. The two older men turn to look at him as if he has just returned from another world.

"Which planet have you been on?" Sir Roger enquires. He supposes that he is grateful that he has accurately sussed their facial expressions. He does not answer his question, which is he supposes rhetorical.

They all take a little while to calm down. Eventually, Roger tells them that he has already written a press release, which has been vetted by the gallery's public relations people. What's more, the man had the cheek to arrange a press conference for 11am the next day, and without any discussion with the rest of them. Judy is furious but realises that there is nothing she can do. He emphasises that it is much better to control the flow of information than have journalists creeping around the building and following them home etc. That of course is a powerful argument, so they reluctantly fall in line with his plans.

The following day's press conference is utter chaos. The journalists have been overstimulated by the carefully worded press release.

The National Gallery wishes to announce that a previously missing painting has been uncovered.

The painting is of *The Adoration of the Magi* and may be the Botticelli postulated by the late Mr Hubert Horne in 1900.

Underneath there appears to be a new and previously unknown painting of

The Birth of Venus.

A Press Conference has been arranged for tomorrow (Wednesday) at 11.00am.

Signed – Sir Roger Court – Director

The conference is packed with scrimmaging men of the press, and even though it is held in the largest room of the gallery, closed temporarily to the members of the general public, there is insufficient standing space. The cameramen, despite having a cordoned off area in the front, are packed as tight as the proverbial sardines, with news video men knocking into each other's equipment. Outside in Trafalgar square are assembled large news vans with multiple rotating aerials to transmit the words of the conference participants.

Sir Roger gives a summary of the findings and shows slides of the picture itself and of the underpainting of the *Birth of Venus*. And then he introduces them. They are thrown to the angry beasts of the jungle, known for their charming and gentlemanly behaviour. They tell them of some, but not all, of their discovery of the painting. And then it goes downhill with questions about their relationship. Judy marvellously manages to remain calm and not be angered about the personal and intimate questioning. Darius is seething but also stays outwardly relaxed, and eventually Sir Roger announces that the conference is over, and escorted us out, follows as they are by shouted demands for more information.

The gallery served them lunch in the privacy of the director's dining room, and they all slowly come back down to *terra firma*.

"Well that all went rather well, don't you think?" announces Sir Roger, and he laughs heartedly, despite the glowers from his goddaughter. His secretary comes in, still looking a bit like Poirot's Miss Lemon. At last, Darius realises that it is the old-fashioned curls over her ears that are the giveaway.

"The switchboard has been overwhelmed, Sir Roger," is her news. "From all around the world. The director of the Met in Manhattan has been rather persistent," she adds expectantly.

"Tell Simon that I will call him later," showing them how intimate he is with all the great and powerful men of art. "And how are you, young people after your slightly unsavoury ordeal?" he asks with apparently genuine concern. "Not much fun, eh?" Darius supposes that they have both calmed down by then.

"Such ghastly people," is how Judy puts it, and frankly he feels that her succinct reply is good. Darius doesn't want to dwell on it, partly because he is enjoying the lightness of the glass of crisp white Picpoul. Despite her anger, she has handled the gentlemen journalists with enormous aplomb as if born to it. He sits opposite and watches her similarly handling her godfather and his friend with infinite courtesy and apparent humour. He watches the little grimaces on her face and continuing mild tremor of her fingers and feels an enormous tenderness towards this strong young woman. She has worn a deep green knee-length velvet dress for the day, with a simple necklace and matching opal earrings. Her elegance shines through. If it had not been incredibly inappropriate, Darius would wrap her in a warm loving embrace, but even he cannot bear to upset the two older men.

"Of course, I think that we need to make a little trip now." Their eyes are instantly on him. "We need to go to Florence, to make a courtesy call on my old friend Umberto Ricci, the director of the Uffizi."

"He's been on the line," Miss Lemon-alike puts in her two pence.

"Well, call him back immediately and ask if we could visit tomorrow afternoon. Tell him that we will bring the painting." She rises from her corner behind him.

"And, Miss Franks," so she has a surname and it is not Lemon, "please make the arrangements. We need rooms and a flight."

"The Bernini Palace?"

"The Bernini Palace," comes the confirmation. And he turns to Judy.

"Slightly embarrassing question, my dear…"

"One room," she interrupts firmly, with just a slight grin in his direction.

"And the flight?" Miss Franks enquires.

"We will need the Cessna without doubt," and he smiles at Marcus, "Can't have the painting in the hold with the hoi-polloi's baggage, can we?" They laugh. "Ten o'clock in the morning suit us all?" Nods all round and she goes to the door.

"Oh, and Miss Franks." She pauses and does a nice little pirouette.

Aha, Darius thinks, *not quite like Miss Lemon and Poirot then.*

"Yes, Sir Roger?"

"We need to tell the customs people what we are doing. Tell them that we will bring it back Thursday. Please get all the necessary paperwork sorted. Ring the minister, if necessary."

"Of course, Sir Roger," as if this sort of thing happens on a daily basis. "and security?"

"Oh yes. Stupid of me to forget that. Thank you, Sheila."

So, it's Sheila now. Not at all, Poirot, and Miss Lemon then.

"The Met or private?"

"Oh, definitely the Met, heavy and prepared, I think."

Now Darius is totally lost. He knows what 'The Met' is but has no idea what the 'heavy and prepared' bit is about. He will eventually discover, but not until the following day. "And at the other end also please, Sheila."

Lunch ends with an excellent tarte tatin, the pastry as crispy and well caramelised as it should be, and they walk out into the drizzly rain of Trafalgar Square. She holds his arm tightly and he nuzzles her neck, as they walked slowly past the familiar landmarks towards Crawford Street. Somehow, London is appealing in its dull, damp familiar way. The streets are almost clear of pedestrians and they walk along, chatting while small drops of rain find their way down the backs of their necks. As they turn into Crawford Street, to their horror, they spy a mob armed with large cameras, besieging the entrance to Clarewood Court. He spins her around and they retreat into Baker Street.

"There's a back entrance in Seymour Place. We can escape them."

"You escape them. I need to go home, do a few tasks, and a tiny spot of shopping and will be back with you later," and he gives her a nice peck on the cheek and is off. He needs fresh clothing, so that he does not disgrace the dress-conscious Italians, and there is a very small thing that he needs to choose with some care.

Chapter Twenty-Seven
Florence, July 2007

Judith

He came back around nine o'clock, and Judith cooks him an omelette aux herbes with a green salad. He has dressed 'smart-Italian' and looks edible himself, so she takes him off to bed as dessert, and afterwards they sleep well. But before they sleep, a stunning event occurs. He lifts himself up onto his elbow and looks deeply into her eyes and tells her that he loves her with all of his heart. She has a great surge of longing and tells him that she too loves him. They fall asleep in each other's arms.

Roger said that they have to be ready to leave at nine o'clock sharp and indeed there is a gentle ring at that time. A large police officer is at the door.

"Miss and sir. Can we go now, please?" There is another even larger one in the entrance hall downstairs, and to her amazement outside is a large white van with flashing blue lights, flanked by white police cars also topped with flashing lights.

"Back car, please." They get into the rear seat of the back car, there being two officers in the front.

"Your colleagues are in the front car and the painting is in the van," the non-driver explains. "And we are armed so you will be quite safe,". She is suddenly terrified and clings to Darius' sporty Italian jacket. He appears totally unsurprised.

"Now I understand what 'heavy and prepared' meant," is all he says.

They go to Heathrow and the convoy drives through a small entrance and pulls them up by a small aircraft already on the tarmac with its engines running. The police emerge with their guns drawn, forming a cordon around them and a smart young woman officer escorts them onto the plane. They take off as soon as they and the painting are all aboard and have an uneventful journey to Amerigo Vespucci Airport. (*That Vespucci name again,* she thinks.)

"Such an advantage going in a private plane," is all Roger says after their morning pre-flight pleasantries. "One doesn't have to go to Pisa and sit in all that traffic."

At the airport, they are met by a van and two cars of rather handsome carabinieri and arrive at the Uffizi. A smiling portly man is on the steps.

"Roger," he says, and turning to the other, "And James. What a double pleasure."

Clearly the senior art world is a club for old friends. Darius and she are introduced.

"Umberto Ricci," and a small bow. "And a big Florentine welcome to the two young adventurers who have found for us this treasure. I watched the press conference in admiration. You handled those journalists like a professional, *Signorina*." This to herself. She notices the '*Signorina*' and regrets to say that she enjoyed the moment of Italian charm.

Surrounded by *carabinieri*, they enter with the painting, and ascend to a smallish room, with guards at the door preventing entrance to the general public. Their painting is set up on an easel beside another painting, clearly another *Adoration of the Magi*, and even to an untutored eye such as hers, by Botticelli. While the three connoisseurs discuss similarities and differences, Darius points out to her features of the Uffizi's painting. He shows her Botticelli staring rather arrogantly out from the picture.

"How do you know that that is Botticelli?" she asks. This causes a touch of embarrassment, and she is gently told that it is what everyone believes, but he is sweet enough to add that one could not be quite certain, especially as there do not appear to be any other portraits of the man. He is gently holding her elbow all the time, which causes her some difficulty with the asking of other intelligent questions. Other persons, mostly with the Medici surname are pointed out and she is directed to the brilliance of the general portrayal of the three distinct groups of followers-on of each wise man. Their three wise men have clearly finished an intense discussion, and Signor Ricci instructs his two assistants to bring the painting downstairs and they all, with their uniformed escort, process down the wide marble stairs.

They enter a room of great size, with two vast canvasses. One she recognises from its similarity to the underpainting of their *Adoration*, as the *Birth of Venus*. Darius whispers to her that the other is *La Primavera or Spring*, also by Botticelli. These glimmering enormous creations open up within her a great chasm of emotional intensity. They complement each other and yet are completely different. The sense of loveliness in the gorgeously naked female in the *Birth of Venus* is so powerful in its portrayal of utter, but slightly stimulating, beauty. She is so beauteous that Judith can feel her radiance coming from Sandro's fingers down the centuries to her personally. And the way everything focusses on her; the way that the other two figures lean in to frame her. And then she notices the little angel pressing her nubile body into the powerful god on the left (Zephyr, he tells her) and feels a terrible yearning to do the same to her god Darius, standing so close to her. It is at that point that she has some difficulty with her breathing but mercifully no one notices. And it is then that she notices the fingers of Venus' right hand spread in an unusual way across her right breast. She asks Darius about it. He looks at it for a long time and turns to their three seniors.

"Judy has just asked me why Venus' fingers of her right hand are spread as they are, and I was unable to answer. Could one of you explain it to her – and to me, come to think of it." There is such a long silence that she wonders what is going on. She expects her ignorant observation to be put in its place, but it appears that this is not to be so. Eventually, Sir James says slowly and with uncharacteristic hesitation, "Not only do I not know, but I am ashamed that I had not noticed before that indeed the spread of those fingers is indeed unnatural."

Another pause. This time, it is Umberto, "There are of course other anatomical peculiarities. For example, you will notice that her whole pose, resting on her right foot is not quite tenable, we call it contrapposto. Her abdomen is elongated, as is her neck and the whole body forms a lovely curve. All of these matters add beauty to the creation and undoubtedly were intended by the maestro." The others all nod. Even Darius is clearly familiar with all of these facts.

"But I have digressed. You have asked about the fingers of the right hand. And I too am ashamed to say that I had not considered the significance of them."

And, at that point, she has a sudden momentary vision of Sandro, standing before his canvas, drawing the fingers, and creating the magical bond from down the centuries between us. She sees him with the sun streaming into his studio, thinking about the concept of beauty and his creation. His brain is transformed with light that is both real and his creation. She sees that he is both in love with her, his Venus, and the whole wide-ranging meaning of beauty. He remembers the beauty of running in the Tuscan hills as a child, the colours of light as a teenager, and the glory of creation as an adult.

She must have gasped or made some noise. They are all looking at her. Perhaps she appears to have had a vision or a fit or an absence. She smiles and reassures them that all is well. Darius grips her closely, concerned and loving. She leans into him in her gratitude for his love and understanding.

And then another bizarre thing occurs. Darius speaks to everyone.

"May Judy and I have two minutes alone together?" They consider. She has no idea what is going on. She looks at Darius. He is inscrutable.

"I see no reason why not." It is Umberto. "But I must leave one person here, maybe one of my assistants, just for security."

"Of course."

Everyone leaves, and they are alone, surrounded by the enormity of creation. Suddenly, he falls to one knee. She is alarmed, imagining a fall.

He fishes into his pocket and produces a small box. Suddenly, she understands, and as he begins to speak, everything slows down in her perception, as people say it does when one has an accident.

"Judy, will you marry me?" he speaks the words with confidence and love, while gazing into her eyes.

"Of course, I will." He opens the little box, and there, shining at her, is a beautiful ring, with a diamond surrounded by two sapphires. He puts it on her finger. It fits perfectly. She is amazed.

She is about to ask, when he says, "I asked your father who didn't have a clue, but he asked your mother who told him 'size J', and he rang me yesterday. That's why I had to leave you yesterday. I have a friend…"

She silences him by putting her lips on his. After a long embrace, he goes to fetch the others, and they return. Roger immediately spots the ring on her finger, walks over to them and to Darius' amazement, having virtually ignored him so far, whispers in his ear, "Congratulations. I cannot think of a better man for our Judy." Talk about being knocked down with a feather. None of the others apparently have noticed and no one enquires why they had needed their privacy. They go to Umberto's office, where he opens a bottle of champagne.

"We have some detail to discuss. But first, I wish to congratulate the two young people for their tenacity and expertise in tracking down a lost jewel."

And then Roger asks the question that has maybe been on many lips.

"We need to continue for a few weeks to perform a few more investigations. But after that, we all need to consider what is going to happen to this painting."

"I think that Lady Judy must be considered the rightful owner of the painting, although I suppose that we will need to have the opinions of English lawyers, God help us." Marcus' views come out thoughtfully.

"What about the claims of this young man?" A nod in his direction.

"Maybe his claim is not so important." Umberto and Marcus look in horror at Roger, who grins benignly at them across the table.

"But surely he has a good claim." This is Marcus, seeming to become a touch irritated.

"Look at her left hand," is all Roger needs to say. He slowly places her hand on the table. There is silence as the sparkles enlighten the brains, and two and two are put together. And then pandemonium. Hugs from the elderly for her; handshakes for Darius. Umberto opens the door and demands another bottle of fizzy drink; this time it's Asti Spumante, befitting to the pride of his nation. They drink long and deeply to their future happiness.

"What I don't understand," Umberto begins, "was that, when we met, I did not notice any…" and his voice tails off and a slow enlightenment creeps over his face, "Of course. I am so stupid. Those two minutes together that you requested." And again, he clearly realises that more words are not needed.

"So, we may well not need to trouble the lawyers too much. Thank the Lord." Roger's wishes doubtless reflect all of their thoughts.

She decides that it is time that she expresses a few views of her own about what she still considers to be her painting.

"I have thought about the matter of where we should keep the painting." Four pairs of eyes are suddenly riveted on hers. Their owners are absolutely still and silent. Even the noisy Italian gallery outside seems to be holding its breath.

"I would want many people to see the painting. In any case, the security and insurance would, I imagine, be a nightmare if we kept it at our home. I would like it to hang in the National Gallery." Roger leaps to his feet in excitement and gives her an enormous bear-hug. She pushes him gently away.

"But there will be a few conditions." He suddenly shows signs of strain and slumps back into his chair, still giving her all of his attention.

"First, I need to be sure that my husband-to-be agrees." All eyes…

"Sounds pretty reasonable to me," he gives them the response that they clearly all desperately want.

"Next," even she can understand that she has them at her knees. It is not an uncomfortable sensation. "Next," she repeats, "I am aware that the painter was from Florence. I am also aware that there is another similar *Adoration of the Magi* here in the gallery. Finally, of course, the wonderful and enormous *Birth of Venus* is here." A slight pause. Maybe Umberto is going to have at least a stroke if he has to wait much longer, "so I would wish to acknowledge the claim of this gallery. It seems to me also that it would be wonderful to display our painting here alongside the other pictures, with maybe some views of the underpainting depicted with it. Maybe it could be close to the *Birth of Venus* itself so that art historians and others could compare?" she asks gently, and Umberto nods vigorously.

"I have thought carefully about how this *Judgement of Solomon* might be achieved, and I had wondered whether it would be possible for my painting to be here for three months of the year and live in London for the other nine months." They all look at each other.

"Sounds pretty reasonable to me," Roger manages to copy both Darius' words from a few minutes back, and his accent, to a *T*. She looks at him with surprise as she never thought that her Uncle Roger could possibly mimic anything, let alone have a sense of humour. Umberto is on his feet, giving her yet another enormous hug. These old men are rather adept at the business of bear-like hugs.

"I have not quite finished yet." Again, that power. She loves it. "There is the question of money." Looks of consternation, but Uncle Roger glides in, smooth as a knife through butter on a summer's day.

"Suppose that you were to donate the painting to the Nation… that is, um – the gallery, we would negotiate on your behalf with Her Majesty's Revenue. I am certain that they would treat the case with great sympathy and, what can I say, understanding. Perhaps we could persuade them that your generosity would ensure that there would be no inheritance tax for your family for now and in the future. And I am sure that the gallery would want to pay you a large sum each year for the privilege of hanging the painting. And doubtless, the Revenue would not wish to tax that large sum. Does that sound a good start?" she looks at Darius. He smiles agreement.

"So, gentlemen, how much would we get if we sold the painting on the open market?" She really didn't want them getting all their own way and thought that a touch of down-to-earth capitalism might enhance the future financial negotiation."

Roger keeps smiling, but she can sense the underlying anxiety, especially when Umberto bounces to his feet and comes in with an emotional, "Millions. No, hundreds of millions. This is the greatest find that we will ever experience in our lifetimes. It would create a sensation in the markets, particularly with the underpainting." Thus, probably ruining Roger's day. The others agree with his proposal that we might realise this vast sum.

The rest of the day passes and the five eat at a wonderful restaurant chosen by Umberto, on the banks of the Arno, looking out at the river. The restaurant has delightful copies of art works by Botticelli, Ghirlandaio, and Fillippino Lippi on its walls. Umberto tells them that the owners claim that Botticelli and Ghirlandaio had regularly eaten here.

"My countrymen will claim anything if they believe that it will make them money," he says. They all laugh in agreement.

A Finale

They apply to be married in Westminster Abbey, partly for the honour and partly to honour the great Livingstone, who had been buried there amongst much pomp and drama in 1874. Of course, Judy has the necessary residential qualifications. Judy's father and godfather also, Darius believes, applied a little pressure (or money, as they call it) which convinces the dean that it will be appropriate.

At Livingstone's dramatic funeral service in the abbey in 1874, Queen Victoria had sent a personal wreath, which was buried with his coffin. HM Stanley, the reporter who 'found' Livingstone in Central Africa, had been a coffin bearer and had to restrain one of Livingstone's faithful servants from throwing himself into the grave.

On their way back down the aisle, Judy, and Darius halt. By pre-arrangement, the organist stops playing the Trumpet Voluntary. They bow their heads in silence to give thanks for this man, driven by the beauty of his ideals, and his love of Africa and its people.

The End

Appendices

This book has a true and real basis in many times past, the times of renaissance Florence, of Victorian England, of the Africa of David Livingstone, and of modern London and Zambia. It is also of course stuffed full of my own fabrications.

I have read much around the historical subjects of the book, but this is a novel and not a textbook, and so it seemed to me that an index, or some of those irritating footnotes that interrupt the reader, would be inappropriate. Nevertheless, there are a few books and articles that I have read that have helped me, lightened my journey, and might prove of interest to a reader who wants to know more.

On the original concept of a missing Botticelli *Adoration of the Magi*

The whole idea for this book is based on Herbert Horne's brilliant observations set out in his paper of 1903, published in the very first edition of *The Burlington Magazine for Connoisseurs*, a sadly long-lost publication, and brought to my attention by Clio Perkins (see below).

A Lost 'Adoration of the Magi' by Sandro Botticelli. Author - Herbert P Horne. The Burlington Magazine for Connoisseurs, Vol. 1, No. 1 (Mar. 1903), pp. 63-69

Don't expect a simple read, as the arguments and references to various scraps of material are appallingly and complexly intertwined. And don't expect that I have held to the facts of Dr Horne's paper.

On the St James Bible and the Coming of the *Magi*.

Sandro Botticelli and all Florentines would have read most of the actual words on Page three of this book in the Vulgate version of the Bible. Pope Damasus I commissioned Saint Jerome to produce one standard Latin text of the Bible. Jerome completed the translation in AD 405, and his version was known as the *editio vulgate* because he used the common (or vulgar) language of early medieval times. The words of St John's Gospel were copied – mostly accurately – by various scholars and are similar to the beautiful verbiage used in the St James version of the English text. 1516 saw the appearance of the first printed versions of the Bible, translated into German from Greek by Desiderius Erasmus.

On Greek myths.

These are at the core of Sandro's discussions in Chapter Two. For a witty broad overview, read Stephen Fry's *Mythos*, a light look at how the world began, or plunge into Ovid's *Metamorphoses* if you will. But for the lover of the art of language, read *Cerce or The Song of Achilles by Madeline Miller.*

On Florence. the Renaissance, and art.

Georgio Vasari (1511–1574) singlehandedly invented the whole subject of Art History, and hundreds of Professors of Art History worldwide owe him their salaries and their academic departments. His defining book, entitled *The Lives of the Artists*, is really rather a good read, and includes plenty of personal anecdotes that keep the reader stuck in. Not only that, but he wrote such an erudite text that this ancient tome is still referenced hundreds of times each year in modern papers.

Over the centuries there have been many translations. Personally, I have used the one by Julia and Peter Bondanella and published by Oxford University Press. But reader, beware – in order to cram the story into less than 600 pages, this paperback edition uses a font and line-spacing designed only for the youngest and sharpest of eyes. The OUP should be ashamed of itself!

Appreciation of the works of Botticelli and fellow artists of the 15th century was muted by the later excitement of the art of the early 16th century or High Renaissance (Michelangelo, Raphael etc.). It was not until the late 19th century when the Pre-Raphaelite artists revived the general interest (and monetary value) in Botticelli and others.

On Sandro Botticelli (1445–1510)

Alessandro di Mariano di Vanni Filipepi was renamed Sandro Botticelli, 'Little barrel' in translation, probably by his older brother. Down the ages, the name has stuck, so I have used it here. A hyperactive child, he was removed from his school by his sensible parents and apprenticed to a great renaissance painter, Filippo Lippi. After his time with Lippi, Sandro was befriended by members of the all-powerful Medici family, the effective rulers of Florence.

Sandro lived all his life in Florence, bar a short period in Rome, when commissioned by the pope to help in the painting of frescos for the Sistine chapel. In his early years, he had a fine wit and turn of phrase and enjoyed the company of friends and other artists. I have attempted to portray that here in his discussions in Chapter Three with Domenico Ghirlandaio, who was also born and apprenticed in Florence. They knew each other and collaborated in 1492 on The *Coronation of the Virgin*, now in the Bass Museum, Miami.

Later, after the fall of the Medicis, Sandro fell under the influence of the radical monk Savanorola and sank into a poverty-stricken isolated old age. He never married.

On the '*Birth of Venus*'.

To my eyes, the *Birth of Venus*, painted by Sandro around 1483, and now hanging in the Uffizi gallery, Florence, is the most beautiful painting in the world. The name is however self-evidently quite inappropriate. A 'Birth' it most certainly is not – Venus is already a grown woman! The name possibly was not given to it by Sandro himself. He might have called it 'The appearance of the creation of Beauty' or some such title had he wanted it to have a title. The clearly inappropriate title, by which it is still known nowadays, was probably given to it by none other than the great Vasari.

The generally accepted view of art historians is that the model for the naked female in the painting is Simonetta Vespucci, a great beauty of her time and possibly the lover of Guiliano de Medici. Frankly, this seems unlikely to me. Firstly, Simonetta had been dead at least five years at the time that Sandro painted the *Birth of Venus*. Tragically, both she and Guiliano died young; Guiliano assassinated, and she of unclear causes, possibly poisoned by her jealous husband. I have read endlessly on the subject of Simonetta, much of its complete speculation, based on no facts at all (Welcome to Art History!). For a balanced view, read a thoughtful piece of work on the subject – A *PhD thesis by Judith Allan, entitled Simonetta Vespucci: Beauty, Politics, Literature and Art in Early Renaissance Florence.*

Secondly, this theory of the basis of a human origin does a great dishonour to both Sandro and his concept of Beauty. Somehow the world of art history has allowed Simonetta's physical beauty to obliterate any more intelligent explanation for a depiction of 'Beauty.' For this book, I have chosen to allow the beauty of Venus to originate from within Sandro's artistic thoughtful mind, and not as the copy of a mortal being.

There is no record of the physical whereabouts of the painting between its creation, and 1540, when it was seen by Vasari in Villa di Castello, Cosimo de Medici's magnificent country house outside Florence. So, in Chapter Four, I have devised a little scenario to explain its 'disappearance' and subsequent 'reappearance' at Castello. Domenico Ghirlandio didn't die until 1493, so he would have had at least ten years of the pleasure of the daily viewing, before it passed to the Medici family – but not to Lorenzo il Magnifico, as the great man had died in 1492.

The story behind the picture – essentially, what was going on in Sandro's mind, has been speculated over by wise art historians over the centuries. I have not felt compelled to adhere to every whim of these wise men. So, for instance, there is argument over exactly the name of the nubile wench wrapped around Zephyr. Many believe it to be Aura. Frankly, that seemed implausible to me, as you will have discovered in the text.

Should you want to read an excellent setting out of the philosophy and origins of Beauty in Sandro's times, then don't read the big tomes, read the first half of *Botticelli's Birth of Venus, Primavera, and the Classical Tradition: A Study in the Reception of Venus in Quattrocento Florence by Brittany Susan Hardy (A thesis presented in partial fulfilment of the requirements for the Honours Program January 18, 2017)*. She discusses the origins of the myths, the poetry, and the thinking in the Florence of the 15th century in a readable thoughtful manner.

Art historians tell me that every element of Sandro's paintings had meaning. I have not felt compelled to stick to that thesis for this story, as I wanted to portray the artist's persona and allow freedom of thought for the reader. For example, there is the question as to who greets Venus on the shore. I liked the neatness of it being Pomona, but lots of people will probably disagree. Similarly, I hope that you will forgive the discussion of orange trees and laurels.

I am not a professional art historian, so I have a brief message to those who are – *Please forgive the unsatisfactory interventions of this amateur, who has the nerve to invade your subject so rudely.*

On the *Adoration of the Magi*

Sandro warmed to this subject, previously hardly painted, and there are a number (maybe seven) extant paintings by him. The most famous is presently in the Uffizi Gallery in Florence and is dealt with in glowing terms by Vasari.

Is that really Sandro?

Is the person staring at the artist in *The Adoration of the Magi* in the Uffizi truly Sandro Botticelli? This is unresolved in my mind. If it really is Sandro, then why did not Vasari tell us in his book, written soon after Sandro's death? He gave names to all the famous Medicis in the painting, so why would he not name Sandro – especially as he wrote a whole chapter in his book on him, and Vasari was also quite clear that Sandro painted that particular *Adoration of the Magi*?

Finally, you will probably prefer not to read *Botticelli's* Uffizi *Adoration: A Study in Pictorial Content* by Rab Hatfield, published in 1928 by Princeton University Press. I did because I was writing this book.

On more stuff from the 15ᵗʰ century

Because I felt that I should, I also read the *Book of the Art* by Cennino Cennini, written in the earlier part of the 15ᵗʰ century. I was simply fascinated with this tome from very early on. This is another wonderfully written book, full of technical and practical advice for the budding artist, as fresh as when it was written over six hundred years ago, and not to be missed.

On the Romantic poets

Percy Bysshe Shelley (1793–1822). Most famous works – *Ozymandias, Adonais, To a Skylark*. Drowned in his boat – the Don Juan – off the coast of Italy; his body was identified by the fact that a book of Keats' poems was folded in his pocket. *The Courier*, a leading Tory newspaper of the time, carried a brief obituary that began: 'Shelley, the writer of some infidel poetry, has been drowned: now he knows whether there is a God or no'.

John Keats (1795–1821). Most famous poems – *Ode to a Nightingale, Ode on a Grecian Urn, To Autumn*. Died of tuberculosis in Rome in the arms of his best friend Thomas Severne.

Lord Byron (George Gordon Byron, 1788–1824). Most famous poems - *She Walks in Beauty, Don Juan, Childe Harold's Pilgrimage*. Adventurer, politician, lover of men and women. One of his lovers, Lady Caroline Lamb, summed him up in the famous phrase, 'mad, bad, and dangerous to know'. But to be fair to Byron, Her Ladyship's behaviour to him was equally appalling. Nowadays, any decent magistrate would have slapped a restraining order on her as a result of her disgraceful and intrusive stalking of His Lordship. He died tragically young of sepsis, at Missolonghi in Greece. The Greeks loved him so much that it is said that they insisted on keeping a part of him (they chose his heart), and buried that in Missolonghi, before sending the rest back to England for burial. Huge crowds viewed his body lying in state in London before he was buried in the church of St Mary Magdalene in Hucknall, Nottinghamshire.

On Medicines of the mid-nineteenth century

Dr Fielding's little exposition at the start of Chapter Seven on the discovery of the use of the bark of the willow tree is all totally accurate. It is a great story and can be read in full in the *Philosophical Transactions of the Royal Society of 1764.*

AND, should you be so minded, and but a few pages further on in this same edition of the *Philosophical Transactions* is another wonderful paper; not such an easy read, though. It is by another country priest, Thomas Bayes, who, in 17 pages of tightly packed pages of mathematical formulae, sets out the complete mathematical foundations of the modern study of probability!

On Slavery in the United Kingdom.
Slavery was officially abolished in 1833 by the Slavery Act. But it continued surreptitiously until the government decided that the act must be enforced and despatched a number of warships, known as the West Africa Fleet, to intercept the slavers. Although the fleet was formed initially of just two ships, by the mid-19th century, it had grown to 25 vessels and 2,000 personnel, and was by then an effective force.

On David Livingstone

I had more enjoyment reading David Livingstone's Missionary *Travels and Researches in South Africa* than anything that I have read in the last year (and I read voraciously). Not only is the quality of the writing of the first order but he is a marvellous observer of nature and people. His wisdom and kindliness stream across the pages. I am aware that there have been many criticisms by others of his leadership skills and indeed of his personality, but few will want to engage with them after reading his incredible travelling saga.

Note – Throughout I have used the spelling of Zambesi (with a *Z* and an *S*) for the great river of southern Africa, as it was spelled in Livingstone's day – and not with two *Z*s, as currently spelled.

Livingstone's journeys through Africa:

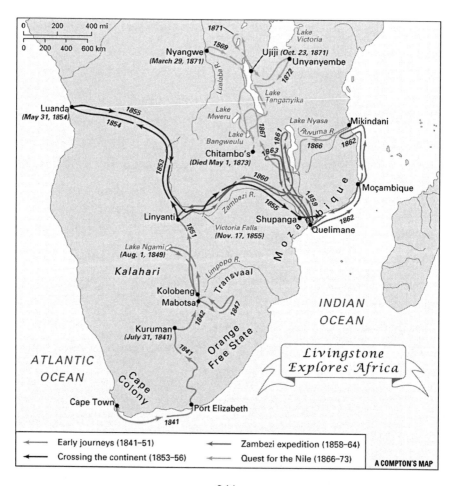

On the Kariba dam and the loss of life.

The massacre, followed by the Lusitu poisoning tragedy, are all as factually accurate as I could make them. Try the paper by *Gadd K et al, The Lusitu tragedy, Central African Journal of Medicine 8 495* (1962), and the books of *Scudder T The Ecology of the Gwembe Tonga, Manchester University Press (1968), and Coulson E, The social organisation of the Gwembe Tonga (1967)*. Also, the paper by Scudder in the proceedings of a symposium entitled *Man-made Lakes at the Royal Geographical Society, London Ed R H Lowe Pub Institute of Biology, London (1966)*.

My readings were supplemented by conversations with Dr Paul du Plessis from the Salvation Army hospital at Chikankata, and with the late Chief Charlie Chikankata of the Batonga people. Those conversations were greatly facilitated by the late Hazel Carter, Lecturer at the School of African Studies (SOAS) who helped me to learn to speak ciTonga and by the late Jean Fardon and the late Edith Shankster who taught me practical Tropical medicine at the Salvation Army's Chikankata Hospital.

On those others who have helped me

Occasionally, I read the closing words of a delightful book by a well-known author and scan with amazement the list of copywriters, editors, assistants, publishing people, and other professionals who have helped, and a tiny bit of me is rather jealous. But it's only a mere transient blip, as most of the time I am glad that I don't have vast hordes of earnest young people with degrees in English from great universities to tell me that my grammar is poor, my imagination weak in this chapter, and so on and so on.

For myself, I value my extended family including

- A wife, Judy, who encourages me, feeds me the best food in London and never chides or questions me if I don't write for days on end (and the lack of inspiration happens frequently – some days I write for eight hours; some days I don't feel in the mood).

- A son, Adam, a constant wonder, and inspiration to me.
- Another son, Charlie, who helps me so much by not only advertising my writing on Facebook and other mysterious media, but also inspiring me by raving about my writing. Does a writer need more?
- My wife's niece, Clio Perkins, a graduate art historian with (amazingly fortuitously for me) expertise on the Italian Renaissance. She was the person who sent me the Horne paper to read (see above), giving me the inspiration for this book. And then as if she hadn't done enough, she helped me with reading, criticising, and the editing of Chapters Two to Six. Clio, I am in your debt.
- A cousin, Tim Vicary, (a published writer and novelist – read his books; they are gripping) who gives me the feedback that I need.

So that's my personal dream team. This old man loves and is grateful to you all.

Robin Vicary, September 2020